To Mark, Susannah, Arabella and Joseph

An Equal Stillness

An Equal Stillness

FRANCESCA KAY

Weidenfeld & Nicolson

LONDON

First published in Great Britain in 2009 by Weidenfeld & Nicolson,
an imprint of The Orion Publishing Group Ltd
Orion House, 5 Upper Saint Martin's Lane
London WC2H 9EA

An Hachette Livre UK Company

1 3 5 7 9 10 8 6 4 2

A CIP catalogue record for this book is
available from the British Library.

ISBN (Hardback) 978 0 297 85549 1
ISBN (Export Trade Paperback) 978 0 297 85550 7

Typeset at The Spartan Press Ltd,
Lymington, Hants

Printed in Great Britain by Clays Ltd,
St Ives plc

Extract from *High Windows*, by Philip Larkin reproduced courtesy
of Faber & Faber.

The Orion Publishing Group's policy is to use papers that
are natural, renewable and recyclable products and made
from wood grown in sustainable forests. The logging and
manufacturing processes are expected to conform to the
environmental regulations of the country of origin.

www.orionbooks.co.uk

And immediately

Rather than words comes the thought of high windows:
The sun-comprehending glass,
And beyond it, the deep blue air, that shows
Nothing, and is nowhere, and is endless.

– Philip Larkin

Write the life, they urged me, even at her graveside; no one but you should do it. Who better? You with your command of words, and besides, you were the closest.

At the graveside. I remember. The varnished wood that would not have pleased her, the stiff fan of lilies and white roses. Kaspar in his velvet-collared overcoat; Patrick relying on a stick to shore him up. There were few others in the churchyard on that January morning, looking down into a surprisingly deep hole. Roddy and Louella MacNamara, Margaret Metcalf, Elizabeth Foy, my brother and my sisters with their children. The sun was shining but a stern wind scythed into us off the encircling moors. Later in the year there would be a service at St Martin-in-the-Fields to which those who did not mourn but would remember her could come. This handful of people by the fresh-dug grave were the ones who felt they had to make the journey up to Litton Kirkdale, the ones bound up in Jennet Mallow's life rather than her art.

And here's the thing. Life or art? A catalogue raisonné of Mallow's work will be ready for publication within the year, there are already several monographs and catalogues in print. These list and detail Mallow's paintings; what more need anyone know? Her life, like most lives, was in public uneventful but in private, like everybody else's life, marked by the most significant events – birth and love and loss and death. Unlike everybody else, however, Mallow was an artist, and her art was the yield of lived experience. Her upbringing, her family, her friends, her influences, the places where she lived and the way she lived in them, all formed the ground from which her painting grew. If her painting is important – and the consensus is that she was one of the most important artists of the last century – then so is her experience, and that is what justifies this biography.

Or, rather, what justifies it to me, and those who kept insisting that I write it. God alone knows what Mallow herself would have thought. She was a very private person, reticent to an extreme, and she always held that an artist's history, except in the widest sense of social context, was irrelevant to her work. She refused all blandishments to write about herself, and although she did keep notebooks, letters and occasional journals, they were not for broadcast. On the other hand, even when she must have known that she was dying, she did not destroy them.

No, I cannot be sure this book would have her imprimatur. But I do know that it would have been written by someone in the end, and that she would rather it were by me than by a stranger. A biographer who had never met her could not expect to understand the particular pressures on the life she lived as well as one who shared it. Which is not to say I cannot be objective. Mallow's part in that tragic death for which she was condemned can be explained but not excused, and I have had no recourse to whitewash. More than an outsider might, I saw her many failings. But I also saw her strengths, and the steadfastness with which she followed her vision.

If I could, I would not have written Mallow's life, I would have painted the woman herself. It was Virginia Woolf who said, 'Not in our time will anyone write a life as Sickert paints it.' Leaving Sickert aside, but considering great portraits – Giovanni Bellini's *Doge Loredan*, El Greco's *Fray Hortensio Félix Paravicino*, Mallow's *David Heaton* – one knows this to be true. Painters convey the souls of the long dead across the bridge of years to a hundred thousand watchers who knew nothing of them. But as I could never have painted Jennet Mallow I have tried my best with words, and to do her justice I have sometimes taken liberties with them. I am a poet by training and a poet, like a painter, has access to allusion. It will be clear to the reader that I have imagined Mallow's thoughts and feelings when I could not have known them. In my defence I can only plead that I had no choice, if the picture I would make of Jennet Mallow were to be rich, intense and full of colour, not an outline sketch. And when I invented what she might have thought, I did it, unlike a stranger, with honesty and love.

Jennet Selina Mallow was born on 11 November 1924 at the rectory of Litton Kirkdale in the upper valley of the river Aire. It was not the home her mother had envisaged when she married Richard Mallow. Then, in 1917, he was a good-looking man in uniform, a regular army officer, grave with the dignity conferred on him by experience of war. Stiff cloth and high leather boots as gleaming as a horse's eye, and a fresh scar on his forehead. The scent of lime in his already greying hair. Lorna was eighteen, and in exile from the place that she called home – the Blue Mountains of Jamaica, where her father had grown coffee until he died, when she was just thirteen, in an accident at sea. Lorna's brother, Harold Rhys, was in his last year of school in Dorset at the time of their father's death and Lorna, with her mother, went to stay there, temporarily she believed, to convalesce from grief. But only two years later Harold was killed at Ypres, and his death robbed Lorna of her homecoming and the plantation of its heir. Lorna's mother, doubly bereaved, had no desire to go back to Jamaica, but preferred to stay in Sherborne, where her sister lived. Lorna, still a child, could not be expected to manage the plantation on her own and there were no other children. So the house and lands were sold at no profit, and Lorna, fatherless and brotherless, adrift and mourning, met Richard Mallow at a Christmas party and decided that as a door marked exit he would do.

They were married when Richard was next on leave, and Lorna was a soldier's bride at a time when other brides, and mothers, sisters, daughters too, prayed their men would live. Lorna did not expect Richard to survive. The other men in her life had not. She placed a photograph of him on the table by her bed in her mother's house in Sherborne, and she waited there for widowhood. She supposed that when it came, she would be independent and could at last go back to the Blue Mountains.

But the war came to an end and then Richard was home and inexplicably set against staying in the army. His father had been a major-general and Richard was predicted to enjoy the same success. Instead he made his mind up to become a priest. In 1923 he was ordained. Lorna, still perplexed by Richard's immortality, and by then the mother of a child, Barbara, consoled herself with thoughts of clerical preferment. A life at Lambeth Palace, golden-headed sons and vases full of crimson roses: that might be one way out of provincial dullnesses and boredom, even at the cost of exile from Jamaica. Or Richard might be made the bishop of Kingston. But Richard himself had no such dreams. He asked only for the humble living at Litton Kirkdale, and in an unwise moment of candour he told Lorna that he hoped to die there.

Litton Kirkdale. This parish of squat houses, a church almost indistinguishable from the stones around, the little congregations, shepherds, shopkeepers, the round-faced children with their impenetrable dialect, and the vast surrounding space, the overarching sky. But a place too of extraordinary light and radiance, an ancient house whose grey stone walls echoed the walls that rose up across the dales above it, where the water of the river which ran

6

through the rectory garden mirrored the pale-dove light of early morning and the lilac gentleness of evening too. Quietness and open spaces; some comfort there for Richard's soul. Lorna said she hated it for the cold and rain, but something in it must have caught her, even against her will, for when her second child was born she named her after a waterfall which spangled from the limestone cliffs a mile or so away. A name that Lorna also knew from gravestones in the village churchyard, the name of the fairy queen who lived in a cave behind the waterfall where, on summer days, Lorna Mallow recaptured sometimes the scent of green and water on warm rock which was for her the scent of childhood.

Rock. The colours of it, life of it, its textures and its temperature. Warm when it has sunshine stored, ice-cold in the winter. Jennet Mallow thought of rock the first winter that she spent in London, when she was twenty-one. London seemed to her a stony city. Beautiful in the vertical white lines of the houses by Hyde Park, the flat grey ribbons of the streets and the stark plane trees. But that winter it was very cold and the streets were scarred with spaces where the bombs had flattened houses; black gaps in otherwise white jaws. The faint flame of the gas fire in the hostel where she lived made no impression on the chill and damp. Her knuckles red and chapped and swollen. She remembered a winter she had spent as a young child, recovering from diphtheria. The acute boredom of hours alone in her bedroom. But then the consolation of a fire that for once in a parsimonious house was left to burn all day. Peggy came with a scuttle full of coal and little twigs of kindling and swept the tired ashes up and laid the fire and lit it. And the minute that she left the room and closed the door behind her, Jennet darted out of bed, nipped the half-burnt sticks out of the fire with small brass tongs, and dropped them on the red-tiled hearth to cool. Then she drew with them on the white-washed wall behind her bed, behind its tall mahogany head-board, where there was just space enough for her to stand.

Dark grey lines and shading on the clean white wall: trees and birds and mountains. She could not see her drawings whole, it was too cramped there, squashed behind the wood; but she could feel them, and she knew they lived. In the night she dreamed of them, or pictured them, if sleep, as it so often did, eluded her. Lying in the utter dark, when there was no moon and the fire had long since died, she saw her drawings move. A great cat stretching out its claws, a skein of geese, a forest of pine bowed by the wind, a swiftly running river.

The flip side of the hearthrug was a mop to wipe her fingers on, and to clean the wall with, but when Peggy found the mess and the soot marks on her sheets and nightdress, she was angry. I'll tell your mother on you, she said. You wicked child. Her mother was angry too, but a few days later she bought Jennet a box of coloured pencils, a block of paper and a board to rest the paper on. Jennet did not draw in secret after that, but always she remembered the magic of those hidden lines in the cave behind her bed, and walking in the wintry city she saw them once again: stark uprights dark against the skimmed-milk whiteness of the sky, the black silhouettes of birds.

The black silhouettes of birds. It was a bird that Jennet Mallow was drawing when she met David Heaton in the life room at the Kensington School of Art in January 1947. A dead bird, a taxidermic relic of the past. She did not know what kind of bird it was, a goldfinch perhaps; its age-faded feathers gave it an indeterminate and melancholic look. It was not the bird she wished to draw. In her mind were eagles, condors, wild birds with fantastic spans of wing, soaring over boundless plains, startling shy animals, bending the long grass beneath them with a downrush of cold air as they swept past. Later she would paint these birds, but now on the classroom wall was a print of Ruskin's kingfisher, perfectly observed, and in front of Jennet was this sad dead thing on a wax-coated twig, and every one of Henry Coldstream's students must first prove to him that they could draw. Jennet banished her great birds of prey and drew as carefully as she could the tilted head, the little beak, the angle of the tail. And she could indeed draw well: it was on the strength of her almost untutored draughtsmanship that she won a scholarship to Kensington in 1945.

At the school which Jennet went to in Harrogate, girls who were considered bright were not allowed to study art. Clever girls did maths and Latin, dim ones drawing and needlework. They were taught by women who in the main had had to fight for their own education against Victorian prejudice and consequently saw their pupils as wave upon wave of new recruits to a constantly engaged Amazonian front line. But even as a child Jennet, although evidently clever, was not malleable enough to fit her teachers' expectations. She did extremely well without apparent effort. She drew obsessively, filling the margins of her exercise books and every spare scrap of paper with faces, eyes, fish, spirals, the black silhouettes of birds. She could run as fast as a deer pursued, but she would not play team games. She noticed things that other children might not notice: the beauty of an apple seed, the colours particular to bus tickets, the hunched shape made by an old woman scrubbing at her doorstep. But she kept her observations to herself; she was quiet, reserved and watchful and, like a small wild creature only tame by hearsay, she made the fainthearted nervous.

In her final year at school, having by then proved her academic credentials by passing her School Certificate with distinction and being offered a scholarship to Somerville College, Oxford, Jennet was finally given permission to join an art class at a nearby academy. It was in many ways a disappointment. In lesson after lesson students painted autumn leaves in watercolour or drew careful arrangements of wild flowers. But at least there were colours, and pencils, enough to take the edge off Jennet's hunger. As she was not being groomed to pass particular tests, the class teacher, Miss Dundas, left her to her own devices, and for a while Jennet had some time and space to do what she had always wanted.

Many years after she retired, Miss Dundas gave an interview to the *Yorkshire Post* in which she spoke of Jennet's brilliance. A most outstanding scholar, she said, with a precocious gift for form and colour. I was proud to be her mentor. She did not tell about the time when, leafing through Jennet's unattended sketchbook, she came across a series of nude drawings. Bold breasts so unabashed, unconcealed triangles of hair. Drawn from what? Miss Dundas had asked herself. Memory or observation? If not Jennet's body, whose? Miss Dundas had a shameful vision of Jennet studying the naked body of a classmate or, worse perhaps, standing in front of a full-length mirror, one hand curved under her own breast. It was an image she could not shake out of her head.

Richard Mallow had not wished to send his younger child to school. With Barbara, the elder girl, the decision had been simple. She was a querulous little thing, slow to read and write, like her mother in temperament, but unlike her in looks. Where Lorna was fine-boned and pale, Barbara was chunky, and her skin was oddly splodgy, pink leaking into whiteness, like strawberries in cheesecloth being squeezed for jam. Easily bored and unresourceful, Barbara needed company, and Richard thought she would enjoy a boarding school. But Jennet was so different, so lithe and bright and darting that to shut her in an institution would be like locking up a firefly or a swift.

Richard Mallow had never been a sociable man, and was even less one when he returned from war. He was not a natural pastor. His parishioners put up with him but they did not seek his company. From time to time he dreamed of preaching from the pulpit in a shroud. Once he had believed that Lorna, so innocent, so fair in spite of her own sorrows, would be his lit flame in the dark. He remembered how she had looked up at him at the party where they met, her mouth so soft and pretty. But after years of marriage that mouth was thin with disappointment and besides, if he closed his eyes to kiss it, he saw the mouths of dying men. Mud and blood and waste and pity; an eyeball pinioned on barbed wire. All flesh is grass, he told himself, and wished that it were true. In so many people flesh was all too livid; he wrote about its horrors in his secret poems.

In his nightmares Jennet was his solace. His sweet, dancing, dark-eyed daughter, as fresh as the sap of new grass stems, as pure as clear, cold water. He did not want to let her go. He did not want her freshness tainted, he did not want her to grow up and play lacrosse at school. Persuading himself that she had been left fragile by diphtheria, he insisted that she stay at home, where he taught her himself, in his study, in the afternoons. Strange things she learned for a little girl: geometry, the Greek of the New Testament, French from the works of Racine.

It was Lorna who in the end sent Jennet away. Coming down from her bedroom one morning she heard children's chattering voices and looked to see who else was there. But it was only Jennet, on her own, sitting where she always sat, on the wide windowsill at the first turning of the staircase, her face pressed tight against a black lead strip between two panes, talking to herself. What will God play with when the sun goes down? she asked. Well you're a foolish girl, and that's a foolish question. She turned her head when her mother called her name, and Lorna saw the child's dark brows beginning to take on her father's frown. Is there any end to the loneliness of children? Lorna's heart constricted and she applied to Barbara's school in Harrogate without consulting Richard. When a place was offered for Jennet she accepted, and faced Richard with the fact.

Loneliness. Further up the Kirkdale valley from the village, an underground spring wells up to fill a deep, round pool, half hidden in a limestone cleft by a thicket of ash and rowan. Jennet, who from an early age used to go out exploring on her own, discovered it and swam there by herself whenever she could. The water was so icy that it knocked the breath out of her and froze away all feeling, so that she could imagine she had fallen into a different world, where there was nothing but the rush of water and the wind. That private communion with water, the first shock of it, and its baptism of her bare skin, left a print on Jennet's soul, and all her life she would remember it with longing.

It was not loneliness but the constant press of other people, and the timetables, the unrelenting bells, which Jennet found oppressive when she went to school. But in five years of it she made a lasting friendship with a girl called Margaret Metcalf, read a great deal of poetry, wrote some of her own, and acquired an education that supplemented in more conventional ways the one she'd had from Richard. And it was while Jennet was at school that another terrible war began, which made Lorna mourn her brother anew and thank God she had no sons.

Barbara Mallow, who was seventeen in 1939, went to Doncaster to become a nurse, and from there to St Thomas' in London. Jennet's idea had been to join the WRAF as soon as she was old enough, but Richard was so adamantly set against it that she was forced to change her mind. In Richard the new war had stirred half-buried memories, and as the world slid heedlessly towards conflict he watched it from his fastness with increasing disbelief; how could the same men who had undergone such calvaries only two decades ago now send their sons to suffer? Richard Mallow was a general's son; his father's hand had been among the hands that signed his friends' death warrants. All those Abrahams whetting their blades for Isaacs. Until the eleventh hour Richard Mallow prayed that God would stay the knives. When he saw there would be no reprieve, his always contingent faith was broken. But he was over fifty then, and felt himself to be completely powerless; Litton Kirkdale was his only haven. He knew he could not share his doubts with the people of his parish, seeking hope and cheer and help with knitting woollen socks for soldiers. Instead, as camouflage, he put on a cloak of fierce belligerence, and for the next six years he thundered out impassioned sermons on the righteousness of war to the newly widowed, and families made fatherless. Sermons about just war and just causes, about the Archangel Michael with his flaming sword, the massacre of innocents, the slaughtering of lambs. Young men dying on the cold dark earth, known only unto God. But nothing on that earth would have persuaded Richard Mallow to consign his beloved daughter, his Armistice child, to the burning pyres.

And so, in October 1943, Jennet Mallow took up her place at Oxford to read Greats. If it had not been then, she might have been happy there, but in those bleak war years, when all that was important was happening beyond this place of pale, hungry girls, bereft of men except the elderly, the unfit and young boys, Jennet was dissatisfied and restless. Later she would describe what she remembered of that time as a series of geometric shapes in drab earth colours. Gothic triangles of brick in burnt sienna, the liver-shaded slab of wall around her college dark against a flat grey sky, circles of thick white china on which were slapped brown squares of minced pork offal and two grey-tinged potatoes. Cold cubicles with brown-stained baths a quarter full of tepid water. Long dark tables and long corridors, linoleum-floored and studded by rows of doors. Whey-faced girls in tweed on bicycles, wavering lines and turning spokes, riding through incessant rain to other corridors and other quiet rooms in which precise and mannered voices talked of poetry as if it were reducible to parts of speech and form.

After a year of it, Jennet had had enough. She needed to do something useful. Reading Greek and Latin felt like self-indulgence then. And she was very homesick for infinities of sky, for wind fresh off the moors. Oxford in the winter was a dungeon to her, a dank place where no light came in and real life was forgotten. Then a letter came from Margaret Metcalf which suggested an escape. Margaret was working as a land girl in South Cornwall, and she wrote about the need for fresh recruits. Jennet volunteered, gave up her place at Somerville, and was quickly assigned to a farm about five miles from Truro.

No wind from the moors there, but the salt breath of the estuary and the sweet-rot scent of cows. Kind Mr Lawe's prize herd of Friesians, black and white in satisfying patterns, the heft and weight of them swaying from their hips, balanced on their dainty legs, their skittish, frisking tails. It was Jennet's job to milk them and to clean their sheds: hard work, and the animals were a bit intimidating at the start, with their mutinously lowered heads and refractory heels. An unremitting schedule too: wet winter mornings and her fingers chilblained on zinc buckets, the slurry and the slide of mud across the farmyard, the well-trampled fields. Milking in the dark by gaslight, carting heavy churns and loads of hay. But there were real pleasures, once she'd learned them: the female closeness of the milking, the white expression yielding to her fingers, the solidness of a cow's flank, their warm, rich smell and their generosity; the sheer presence of those patient cattle giving freely of their bulk, their heat, their comfort on the coldest mornings, and in the evenings, when she penned them in, a share in their unquestioned safety.

There was the magic of the landscape too, new to her who had never travelled, never been much further west than Sherborne, where she had spent dull holidays with her great-aunt and grandmother. On this south-western coast the fields were green and gentle and violets blossomed in December, but the cliffs were steep. For the first time Jennet saw how the horizon curves, the line of light that marks off sky and sea. She had seen other shorelines before, but it was from this rocky one that she first witnessed the vastness of surrounding seas, as if she were a gull.

Jennet had her Sundays free, and walked for miles, alone, or with Margaret, scrambling up cliff paths and headlands, absorbing the colours of the water and the earth. She tried to hold them in her mind with words at first, for they made her think of poetry, but there were no words exact enough for her, or still unused. Waves unfurling like bales of shot grey silk unspooled, the sky ribbed with clouds like mackerel bones? No, everybody who stares out to sea and then tries to describe it dips first into the same old pool of words, which was too stale for Jennet. Since early childhood she had felt in secret a discoverer's conviction: that she would find

15

something new. So in place of words she turned to paint. In Cornwall, that sense she had always had of a mysterious, pre-verbal power returned. Her resources were very limited; paper was rationed, she had only a student's box of water-colours, a few tubes of oils and rudimentary skills. Knowing this, she did not aim for finish, but for apprentice work. On her own she began to learn the basis of her craft.

Ultramarine blue deep, Byzantine blue, cobalt cerulean. Jennet Mallow might not have had the colours or the skills then, but she knew she could acquire them. Christening the sea and sky with their precise richnesses of colour – tur-quoise, azure, sapphire – was like learning a new language, one she found she loved. Until that time of physical exhaus-tion and solitary thought in Cornwall, Jennet had not known what she really wanted. She had not dared to think of art as a way of living. But now, here, suddenly, it struck her as the only way; the only way that she could say out loud what she knew was worth the saying.

In the year that Jennet spent at New Kea Farm she put to-gether a selection of drawings and in July 1945 she sent it to the Kensington School of Art. It was the only art school she had heard of. In August she was invited to attend an entrance examination. A bearded man enquired why she drew so many cows. She was given a great sheet of blank white paper – frighteningly blank, more space than she had ever had before – and told to make a study of an elderly lady posing as Aphrodite. Next to Jennet a silent man with a crooked back drew nothing but the model's knee in the dead centre of his sheet. A letter came the following week to tell her she had won a scholarship. Saying goodbye to Mr Lawe and to the cows, she went back home for a few weeks to Litton Kirkdale.

*

Back home, where Richard Mallow dreamed of mushroom clouds and walking skeletons and woke up crying in the night. When he talked, spit collected in the corners of his mouth. Lorna looked thin and liverish. That summer of the war's end was a blazing hot one; the grass was parched and the river through Litton Kirkdale narrowed to a greenish rill. Jennet had changed too: burnt brown from outdoor days, not only slight but newly sinewed, as strong and supple as a stem of willow. A gypsy girl, Lorna complained. She and Richard had accepted the art-school plan with surprisingly little protest, their stores of parental disappointment already drained, perhaps, by Jennet's leaving Oxford. Richard, in any case, was too lost in the labyrinths of depression to care much about the course of anybody else's life. Lorna, although she would not have said so, might even have been pleased. She would have liked to paint, she thought. Her life lacked passion, that was what was wrong with it; if there were more colour in it she might not find herself so often sleepless, with her own hand pressed between her legs. Village fêtes and Sunday Schools, long Yorkshire winters and an unambitious failure of a husband – if Lorna could have exchanged all these for an hour of pure pleasure, she would not have hesitated. But women of her age, and generations of women before them, shackled by their children, with no money of their own, did not have the amplitude of choice. She was a little envious of Jennet. But it did occur to her that with both daughters gone to London, she might be freer of Litton Kirkdale. Kensington? A perfectly acceptable address.

Lorna thought back to that box of coloured pencils she had bought for Jennet when the child was ill. How gratifying to have been the source of inspiration. She wondered if memories of colour could be carried in the blood. A startle of green hummingbird's wing, the yellow allamanda.

The startle of a wing. Jennet was defining each herl of the dead bird's feathers with a sharpened 4H pencil when somebody behind her said, Well, there's a waste of time.

David Heaton in his army greatcoat, his beaky, bony, narrow face, black hair wing-like, looking down at her and laughing.

Why are you wasting time like this? he asked. This is a life class. That bird is dead.

Really? I hadn't noticed, Jennet said.

Come to the Black Prince with me. You'll learn far more.

David Heaton's mocking mouth. His hand held out. Forget your silly bird, he said.

Why pencil in the filaments of a feather? Because description is revelation of a sort, and for Jennet Mallow, after a year of art school, it was the only way she could come anywhere near the truth. She had hoped that revelation would come fast. In the past year she had learned much about the craft of painting. Oil paints and their application, distemper, gouache, palette knives and primers, solvent, varnish, resins. The words of poems in their own right, the names of different brushes. Sable round, sable bright and sable filbert. Badger fan, long-handled hog, Raphael petit gris pure pointed squirrel. Jennet revelled in the delights of these, and in the feel of paints, the ooze of them, the scents of linseed oil and turpentine, breathing them in deeply like a closet alchemist when no one was watching, reading and re-reading the incantatory instructions and the recipes. *You will need gum*

Arabic, distilled water, honey, glycerine, ox gall and pigments.
Ox gall. Magic.

But the magic wasn't instantly effective. Jennet looked at her painted bowls of apples and her dancers, her accurate pencil drawings, and saw that there was something missing. Something essential and impossible to name. That talent she had always had to catch a likeness, to make something realistic with a line, was reinforced by knowledge now, and practice, and her tutors were well pleased; but Jennet knew that it was not enough.

Therefore, the fine lines of a feather. Jennet understood she must be humble, even if humility came hard. She must first learn how to see a swan before she fumbled for analogy. The bird must be a bird in the beginning, its own bird-being: not metaphor nor archetype, but intrinsically its own self, unremarkable, miraculous and real.

The dreaming power of the draughtsman in his cave. The potency in clay-dipped fingers, in the stone he holds. The lines he leaves long afterwards still stir and flicker in the blackness, waiting for new eyes to let them live. Eyes glinting wide and green in the utter dark. Hunters bring their torches to the lines, and the horns of bulls, and blood. Ox gall. Honey. And in return the painted lines reel in the wanted animals, lasso them, bones and meat and blood. In the dark the hungry lines are singing: concept made fact; wish magicked into art.

Jennet could attain that power, the votive power of the initiate; she knew it. Dreams could flow out of her mind into her fingers and take lasting shape on canvas. She could be the one who paints the eyes onto an idol's face and turns it from stone to flesh.

All through the days and days of childhood Jennet Selina Mallow, sitting on her windowsill on the first landing of the staircase of the rectory at Litton Kirkdale, had looked out across the thin fields laced with loose-stone walls and wondered if there would be ways to say them. She had seen the beauty in an apple seed and she wanted to proclaim it. But it was very hard to do. That much she learned at art school, where, surrounded by encouragement and praise, she felt a fraud; a movie actress making apparent progress at an easel while between takes a finer hand fills in the picture.

Bird. The name that David Heaton gave her.

What sort of name is Jennet? I thought a jennet was a mule.

One of the other men laughs. No. A little Berber horse.

Ah, that's good. Dark eyes like a little Arab. But Bird is better. Look at her ruffled feathers. That's what I shall call her. Bird. Wild bird, blackbird, lovely bird, calling bird . . . except she's rather quiet.

There is so much smoke in the Black Prince it is as if the fog which tonight squats over London has its source inside the pub. The walls and ceiling are stained yellow and there are scars on the paintwork of the windows from the battens that used to hold the blackout blinds. These have not been needed for a year and more; tonight the light seeps through unchecked except by grease on steamed-up windows into the winter darkness, and every time the door is opened, smoke swirls out to meet the fog. Two regiments of wraiths in combat.

The damp wool of David's khaki coat steams faintly and absorbs the smells of beer and frying, cigarettes, before exuding them again in continuous exchange. David keeps the coat done up and through it his thigh is pressed tightly against Jennet's. There are other people there: three men, one of whom Jennet knows from classes, a woman who has hair so sleek and gold it seems to glow. She is slim and holds herself as upright as a lighted candle, her hair aflame and her eyes on David, always. She plays with a silver cigarette case, flicking it shut and open as she listens to him talk. The lines of her mouth are very clear and perfect, painted red. She lifts her cigarette to them as if kissing it.

Jennet watches the dancing movements David's fingers make, accompanying his words. There are a lot of words; he talks quickly, loudly, words tumble from him like water over boulders in a tarn. When he laughs the others laugh too. When his hair falls across his forehead he thrusts it back abruptly. His nails are bitten and very dirty. Jennet has never crowded into a pub like this before or sat thigh to thigh with strangers, but she would not have them know it.

David Heaton and his friends in the Black Prince, drinking pints and pints of beer, while Jennet watches his fingers fly and feels the hot pressure of his body. Well, Bird, he teases, what's brought you to this perch? There is no need for answer. The others are making more than enough noise, and the blonde, whose name is Corinne, touches David constantly, fluttering her hand against his cheek, against his arm, resting it on his khaki-covered shoulder. She borrows somebody's tweed cap and puts it first on David's head and then her own, dowsing the glitter of her hair. So, does it suit me? she asks David, and Jennet sees it does.

The gin in Jennet's glass is tinged with blue, and oily, distracting in the way it catches light when she swirls and tilts it. There is talk of music, names that Jennet doesn't know, Thelonius, Dizzy Gillespie. I should have been a trumpet blower, David says. Or a miner. I would have made some money then, maybe. In fact he has already made some money with his paintings, and he teaches two days a week at Stockwell. David Heaton isn't starving. What can I do to make you sing? he says to Jennet. More beer, its yeasty, sour smell; and sound and smoke spiral around Jennet until her head swims and she has to lean on David.

At closing time they leave the pub together, stepping out of warm fug into icy cold and fog so thick they can barely breathe or see. The halo of a streetlamp like a yellow thumb-print smudged against the sky. David takes Jennet's hand and keeps it and they walk like that, stumbling, feeling for the way, to the house where Corinne lives, because she has offered soup. A tall, thin house off Portman Square, it belongs to Corinne's husband but she lives in it alone, for reasons no one has explained to Jennet.

Corinne unlocks a black front door on to bare floorboards and blank walls; the house seems almost empty. She leads them downstairs to a basement kitchen where their beer-breath clouds on the unheated air and Jennet stands against a disused range, watching the way that Corinne moves, as sure and proud and as self-conscious as a dancer. She finds three tins of Crosse and Blackwell's soup: one cream of mush-room, two of oxtail; she empties them together into a chipped enamel saucepan which she sets on a gas ring. When it comes, the soup is glutinous, mole-brown and lumpy, but they drink it anyway, from teacups, and after-wards they eat pilchards and cream crackers from more tins.

I should go home, Jennet says. It is very late. She thinks about the hostel room in Maida Vale, the ineffectual gas fire.

Don't go, Bird, David says. Corinne has lots of beds. I'll show you.

Up uncarpeted flights of stairs, past barely furnished rooms glimpsed through half-closed doors. On the third floor David pushes wide a door into a room where there is a bed, a mattress covered in striped ticking and a small pile of unfolded blankets. There is no light except the dim light from the landing; wires hang from the ceiling but there is no bulb. When David shuts the door behind them the room is very dark. Jennet can hear the sound of voices from below, Corinne's sharp and angry laugh.

22

Bird, says David softly. Bird. You mustn't catch cold in here. It's so very cold. He pulls her gently to him, his hands around her waist, his face bent down to hers. 'The north wind shall blow, and we shall have snow, and what will poor Robin do then?' Jennet whispers, but David isn't listening, he is kissing her instead. Something shifts and lurches inside Jennet, as if in urgent need of space, as if an interior music has suddenly changed key. David's hand slides in her clothes, beneath her layers of shirt and jumper, underwear, his cold fingers on her breast. He moves her with him to the bed and they crumple on to it together, mouth to mouth, his free hand fumbling at his clothes, the snap of buttons, her lisle stocking torn, and then the blind snub thrust of him and a small pain that is also an answer or an invitation. But David doesn't take the invitation up, he just jerks once, twice, abruptly and he cries out as if it were she who hurt him. Then he is still, heavy, a dead weight on top of her, and after a minute he says: Sorry. But it's because you're lovely. And at once he is asleep and she has to edge away from him, under the fence of his outflung arm, to go in anxious search of light and water. In the dark she cannot find the handle of the door, her only guide is the thin seam of light below it, and she has to feel her way inch by inch before she can escape.

There is a lavatory across the landing and a bathroom next to it, with a working lightbulb and a mirror, but no towels or paper to wipe away the wetness and the blood. For a long time Jennet stands in front of the bathroom mirror, searching her eyes for signs of womanhood, maturity, but there is nothing new there, only her white face in the harsh glare – the eyes dark and the lips smudged, the hair bedraggled – as if it were a portrait left out in the rain.

Later, in the dawn, lying wakeful on the narrow strip of bed left unoccupied by David, she watched the bedroom door, which she had left an inch ajar for the comfort of the light, open very slowly, and a shape slink in, as careful as a thief. Jennet shut her eyes then, so she would not have to see Corinne brooding in the greyness over David, staring at them both while David slept.

Mirrors. Windows and glass. Jennet Mallow's early paintings, and her last. She painted that self-portrait staring into a mirror later on in 1947, and it is still the image of her that is best known. Those guarded eyes, the defiant, upthrust chin and the tangled, matted hair. Iconic, gypsy girl. In the same year she painted an extraordinary picture – a rectangle of unearthly bluish-white, peculiarly lucent, an iceberg white, through which is faintly visible the stylised outline of a glass. It was unlike anything she had done before and unlike the work of her fellow students. With it she won that year's Whistler Prize.

As soon as it was light enough Jennet slipped off the bed where David still slept noisily and sidled down the stairs, hoping to leave the house unseen. The brass bolt on the front door screeched. Out on the pavement she looked up and thought she saw a curtain stir, but no face appeared at the window. The fog had gone, to be replaced with sleet, sharp as remorse on her stubble-scratched skin. The slick, wet streets of London were deserted but for one or two delivery men and early office workers. A milkman with a horse and cart. Jennet, in yesterday's clothes, lonely as a stray cat, shivered in the cold, not sure if she should be feeling happiness or shame.

Hardly anyone was up yet at the hostel. Willing the warden not to peer out of her room, as she almost always did at the merest clink of keys, Jennet let herself in quietly and, in defiance of the bath list (strictly limited to two a week), ran an inch of lukewarm water to splash away the stickiness and the unfamiliar smell. She touched her mouth, her breasts and the place between her legs, which somehow now was less her own, less private. In that ancient, rust-stained bathtub, Jennet Mallow considered whether she was in love with David and decided yes, after last night she must be, yes, she had to be in love.

The breasts of the model in the life class are triangular dangling flaps of skin, and all over her the skin is parting from its trellis. Jennet can see the structure of her ribcage; loose scallops of flesh hang off her thin arm-bones, her belly falls in terraced wrinkles. A grey tuffet of pubic hair too sparse now to conceal her cleft; red patches on her shins and knees and elbows, as if she were used to going on all fours instead of standing. Her buttocks too are red-patched, flat, and from the back, lacking the definition of a waist, she looks less like a woman than a scrawny child.

Jennet draws the poignant space between the woman's thighs and wonders if lovers ever put their hands there, if children leased her womb. There is something lonely in the set of the old woman, in the way her shoulders droop, the smell of damp on her, which makes it seem unlikely that she is kissed, caressed or touched. How long before I look like her? Jennet asks herself, and for the millionth time her mind returns to David. It has been three weeks now and she has not heard from him. His friend Dermot, the one she'd met already, is in and out of the same classes and always says hello to her, but she cannot ask him about David. If Dermot, if the others, had not known that she spent the night with David, it would be so easy. She could engineer his name into a conversation, ask about his teaching, discuss the style at

Stockwell, anything. But that Dermot knows, and worse that Dermot might know the details, is humiliation enough, without her having to admit that she has not heard from David. And that she is longing to.

Instead, as usual, she says nothing. When Jennet started at the art school there were not many students, but now the classes are filling fast with ex-servicemen and women. Older than Jennet for the most part, taller and much louder, they crowd in to the painting rooms, and talk and laugh and jostle. What had once had the air of a scriptorium – quiet, intense, devout, motes of dancing dust held on a single beam – was now more like a busy pub, noisy, cheerful, smoky. These new arrivals had shouldered untold tensions, seen in life what others with more luck see only in their dreams. The walking skeletons of Belsen. One of the men swung himself around on crutches; another's face was scarred and burnt. Dermot, like David Heaton, had been a prisoner of war. Released into postponed adolescence after years of forced maturity, they were shaken bottles of champagne uncorked, profligate and fizzing. Squashed up between them in class-rooms filled to bursting, Jennet kept her head down and got on in silence with her drawing.

Different kinds of silence in the rectory at Litton Kirkdale. The silences of empty rooms, the silence in Richard Mallow's study as he worked there. His was a heavy, blanketing si-lence, the sound of noise shut out; as a small child Jennet used to think of it as the sound of anger. All those words in her father's heavy books: damnation, torment, glory; like flies silenced behind thick glass, furious and ineffectually buzzing. If those books were ever opened, Jennet thought, the repressed words would fly straight out, stinging crossly, spiky, inky wings and legs.

Another kind of silence surrounded Jennet's mother, and it had an edge to it, a high-pitched whine inaudible to adults. Lorna Mallow was a taut string plucked, vibrating soundlessly but with a soundlessness quite close to screaming. When she was a child, Jennet did not understand the reason why.

All these silences, hanging like cobwebs in the house. Jennet touched them with her fingertips, tasted them with the curl of her tongue, drew them round herself at night, as dusty as old lace curtains, familiar, not unfriendly. Like any veil or curtain they were easy to break through. Just opening a door or window tore holes in them by letting in the sounds outside. The sound of the wind off the fells, the creak of branches and, in due season, the mellifluous thrush, the wood pigeon's persistent call.

Margaret Metcalf, Jennet's friend from school and Cornwall, had also moved to London after being a land girl, and was working as an assistant radio producer at the BBC. She was living with, but not married to, a physicist, Richard Benjamin, who had come to England as a refugee from Germany in the 1930s. Both Margaret and Richard were committed members of the Communist Party, and in the spirit of friendship, Jennet sometimes went with them to public meetings. These, held in a room above a pub in Highgate, were mainly about recruitment drives and sales of the *Daily Worker*, but occasionally there were visiting speakers. The testimonies of two of these especially stayed in Jennet's mind. One had been an airman in Bomber Command; out of his aeroplane flew some of the four and a half thousand tons of high explosive that fell on Dresden on St Valentine's Eve in 1945. Twenty-five thousand people, give or take; blasted, suffocated, seared alive. The other was an Italian

Jew who had only just survived at Birkenau. She talked about the flames rising from the chimney, children's teeth like little pearls. Four-year-olds, their mothers gone, pleading to be allowed to stay. Nine women slept on each bare plank that served as a bunk. Eleven pounds of phenol for injections; carbolic acid, enough to stop a thousand hearts.

These two were not, of course, the first to speak about the atrocities of war. Jennet, like everybody else, had already read other eyewitness accounts. But these speakers at the Party meetings, the one with a comfortably familiar Yorkshire accent, the other with her halting English, were less than an arm's length away, drinking the same weak cups of tea, sharing the same smoke-filled air. The Italian woman showed them her tattoo; Jennet could have touched it, as Thomas touched the wounds of Christ. With her own eyes, dark and almond-shaped and beautiful, that woman had been made to see what should never have been allowed to happen, whether unseen or not.

What should we have done? Jennet implored Richard Benjamin, who was also a survivor, his parents and a brother having died among the millions in the camps. And what should we do now?

Use the skills we have, he told her sternly. Put every ounce of energy into making sure that nothing like this will ever happen anywhere, to anyone, again. Work night and day for peace. Look to the socialist union. The Soviet Union is our hope.

If she had been more confident, she might have questioned Benjamin's conclusion, but she was not, then. She did ask herself what use there was, or ever could be, in her drawings of nudes and birds. What was this lonely impulse towards painting? Necessity or self-indulgence? Her father still woke wet with sweat from nightmares of his war. There were thousands of men like him, and women, children, who knew that they were lucky to be alive, but whose lives had been irreparably damaged. How much would they give, these survivors, for a painting, and how much less, those who did not live? There never was a picture worth a life. Bread and fire and water, these were the essentials, not line or form or colour. Jennet knew her sister Barbara did more good with her germicides and vaccinations than she could ever do with a paintbrush. But still. The truth of clouds, the truth of water. Not simple questions. She had to find out for herself just how much truth, and how much pain, could be expressed in colour and light.

Overhearing other people's talk in classrooms. The sound of David Heaton's name – *David Heaton* – leaps from its background like a high relief, like notes struck clear against a mumble. David Heaton's exhibition at the Redleaf Gallery, marvellous pictures – do you really know him, Dermot? – private view, unusual to be given a one-man show so early, spoken of as the finest talent of our generation. Straining to listen, Jennet learns the opening was yesterday; she should be safe this afternoon.

But Corinne is in the Redleaf Gallery, leaning on a desk just inside the entrance. She was invisible from the street. By the time Jennet sees her, she herself is seen, and it is too late to retreat. They greet each other with a mutual coolness. Have you come to look at David's pictures? Corinne unnecessarily enquires. She offers Jennet a printed sheet of prices. There are two other people in the gallery – a middle-aged woman and a man in a blue suit – and Jennet joins them in a clockwise progress round the paintings. David's paintings. Oils mainly: phosphorescent colours slashed on to the canvases, unearthly greens and browns and blues. Great streaks of paint thickly applied; in some it looks as if he'd flung his brush away and instead used his fingers, dragging them claw-like through the paint. Landscapes: twisted stumps on blasted heaths, moonlight deathly cold on a ploughed field, a hill with three trees on it like three gibbets. A tangle of forest with writhing boughs, an ochre plain covered with a thousand bent, black crosses. Lazarus rising from the dead: an indistinct figure seen from the back; in the centre of the painting a splintered coffin lid propped up at one end of a grave towards which a man in khaki uniform is crawling. David has painted this man in careful detail. It is obvious his flesh is decomposing; it has the bluish sheen of well-hung meat, and his teeth show through a hole or wound in his right cheek.

There are some charcoal drawings too: etiolated figures with outstretched limbs, and a series of ruined towers rising out of rubble; six of them, under each of which is written a single word. *Where. Dead. Men. Lost. Their. Bones.*

Jennet looks at these drawings for a long time, and wonders a little, if they were separated, what a buyer would make of the one word *Their*. Someone has already bought the drawing called *Bones*, and the *Lazarus* painting, and there are red spots under several of the landscapes. She is absorbed in her study of David's lines, the vicious thick ones, the finer ones more faltering, tailing away, when he says, Well, what do you make of them? Jennet spins round, appalled to be caught by David in the act, the intimate act, of looking at his pictures, heart-lurchingly glad to see him in the flesh again. His blue-black hair, his bony hands, the high bridge of his nose.

They're extraordinary, she whispers. I don't know what to say.

Good, he says. Good. He comes closer to her, looks down at her gravely, like a doctor, lays one finger lightly on her lips, traces their outline softly, his fingertip as soft on them as the

30

softest sable brush. Her lips part, and she shivers. All the time his eyes stare into hers. Infinite darkness in which something stirs. I should paint you, Bird, he says. Because you are so lovely. Come home with me this evening, let me paint you. Come back and save my life.

Behind them Corinne is closing metal drawers, one by one, slamming them shut with a sound like the retort in the barrel of a gun, jangling a clutch of keys. I'm locking up now, darling, she shrills at David. No one else will come now, and I am getting bored.

All right, he answers, still looking down at Jennet. Bird and I were leaving anyway, weren't we, Bird? He takes her hand and leads her out of the gallery past Corinne, whom he kisses as he passes, lightly, on the mouth.

There were pleasures to be learned then, and in the following nights, and in the mornings too. The sweetness and the shelter of an encircling arm, the way a woman's head fits the space beside her lover's collarbone. A finger placed precisely on the point at which sensation furls, then concentrates and catches, intense as two flints striking. A tongue tip on a nipple and a man's mouth kissing; her drowning, deep accession to his kisses. His mouth, his tongue a live wire rooting for connection, hers a responding contact, two bodies linked, one into the other, two for a time made one. And, afterwards, after the thrill of his capitulation, which thrills her because it is within her power, her gift, then his docility, his grateful drifting into peace. The wild thing, hard and fierce in pursuit and inflammation, soothed by what she can give.

When David is asleep, or half asleep, Jennet explores the relativity of their bodies; the answering curve her back makes curled against him, the sling of his thighs underneath her, the weight of his arm on her ribcage, his hand resting on her breast. So beautiful, the long lines of a man's forearm, the hollows of his neck and shoulders, the narrowing slight slope where his hipbones meet his groin. And the dark hair tapering down his stomach, an arrow to its destination; the ripple of rib and sinew when she laces her hands across him, the twin scooped concaves on each side of his spine. His semen on her hands, and its scent of grass.

Jennet's fingers were not strangers to the nub and folds of her own flesh. Solace in secret; she knows that, she has already learned her body can find pleasure. She knows that she could expect more of the act of love with David than the first ignition, ardent but unquenched, and the pleasure of its giving. But David, sober, is quick and purposeful; single-mindedly intense. As soon as he achieves his aim he pulls away from her, collects his own apartness around himself again.

Jennet did not mind that then. She did not even mind that David's sheets, unlaundered, stank of wild cats. In those first few weeks with him she was on fire with happiness, and every time he entered her, her womb contracted as if to draw him in closer, with such delicious, aching tenderness it almost made her cry. Making love with David, discovering David's body, falling in love with David, reminded her of things that were inevitable, and perfect: stones stroked smooth by water, the intricate cores of seashells, the murmur of blood flowing through the chambers of a heart.

Shall we be married, Bird? he asked, but she knew it was the firelight speaking, glowing through an amber glass, and she did not dare to answer, or to hope. David was quicksilver, secret; he disappeared for days on end and she had no more means to pin him down than she had of harnessing the wind. He always kept a distance. Sometimes, late at night, after the Soho pubs and drinking rooms had closed, after the last revellers had gone, he would soften and say sweet things to her, tell her that he liked having her in his bed. But even in the early days Jennet shared that bed with ghosts, and with bottle after bottle of cheap whisky. Often David fell asleep while still inside her, grinding slowly to a halt like a spinning top unwound. Even wide awake, he seemed strangely far away. So she knew that when he talked of marriage it was in the same spirit that he talked of moving to America, or buying a boat, or forswearing art in favour of the silence of Mount Athos. David spun elaborate fantasies in skeins of glittering gold. Jennet did not expect to marry him. She imagined she would live alone forever, in a corner of a vast white studio, spending nights with David as he chose.

Meanwhile David painted Jennet: Jennet asleep, Jennet reading, Jennet at a window, and Jennet as Mary Magdalene, a woman with the dead Christ at her feet. He made dozens of drawings of Jennet nude. These early drawings were not especially explicit; Jennet's features were only roughly sketched, so that she was emblematic rather than identified. The later ones were different. But they were years away, and for the moment Jennet was content to play the role of David's muse. It bit into her time, though, as David would insist she sit for him at every stage of painting. He said that way the finished pictures were more lifelike. In fact, he did not care to be too much on his own.

Given David Heaton's exacting standards, it is strange that in several of the paintings Jennet looks half dead. His study of Jennet sleeping, for example, shows a woman of bluish pallor, lying back against a crumpled sheet, her mouth slightly open, her tangled hair outspread. She is so pale it seems as if she has been drained of blood: the cotton twisted under her might be the fabric of a shroud.

At this point in her life, Jennet's is a commonplace story. It could be yours, perhaps, or your mother's or your daughter's. Afterwards it's useless to apportion blame or wonder how a clever woman could ever be so careless. David may not have known that Jennet was a virgin when she met him. Certainly he did not ask. For her part Jennet hid her innocence from him as if it were something shameful, and consequently neither she nor David found the words to ask the necessary questions.

Corinne will know what you should do, David said, when he found Jennet doubled up over the lavatory pan and finally she shared her worry. By then her breasts were swollen and she was retching on an empty stomach every day. It'll be all right, Bird. Corinne will know someone who can do it.

Oh dear, said Margaret Metcalf, and told tales of knitting needles and women dying alone in agony of sepsis. Why didn't you get a cap?

For want of anyone else, Jennet in the end turned to her sister. They had never been close, but they saw each other from time to time and Jennet hoped that, as a nurse, Barbara would have the answer. She badly wanted to avoid having to confide in Corinne. She was scared and lonely then, bewildered by David's confident assumptions, and her own conflicting feelings. In a book she owned of reproduced Italian paintings there was one she loved, a Mantegna of the Virgin and her sleeping baby. The child swaddled in tight bands as if in his grave-clothes. Now she found she could not look at it without the tears welling.

34

*

Barbara, plump and prissy in a teashop, a self-important pigeon puffing out her feathers, still in her nurse's starched, white headdress, although her shift was done. Well, you're no better than you ought to be, she says mysteriously to Jennet when she has heard what Jennet has to tell. But she will ask a friend, she says, or rather, an acquaintance; someone she knows who is similarly afflicted by loose morals. Instead, and against a promise sought and made, she writes immediately to the rectory at Litton Kirkdale. And three days later, there is Lorna Mallow, thin-lipped, frost-faced, waiting in the warden's office in the hostel. You little fool, she hisses. Now you will waste your life as I did mine.

Should Jennet have protested that she was not a child, nor subject to her parents? Years later she would wonder why she had allowed her mother to take charge in so peremptory a way, but even in the wondering was the whisper of betrayal, for would she then have wished her child unborn? Looking back to that cold grey room, the straight-backed chairs set side by side, Jennet remembered mainly that she was very tired. She used to dream of snowdrifts, clouds, white spaces in which she might subside and close her eyes. She felt hollowed out by sickness and too weak to argue when Lorna marched her to the Rector of the art school and made her tell him she was leaving.

The Rector, a sweet-faced man, a noted religious painter to whom conception was the work of angels, laced his white fingers together and looked sad. I have seldom known an artist of such promise, he told Jennet. I hope you will keep up your painting.

Jennet's trunk was packed, the same one she had had at boarding school. Her mother checked that the wardrobe was empty and nothing was left beneath the bed. Lorna and

Jennet folded blankets, holding two corners each, Lorna agitating her end crossly so that dust flew like transparent insects through the air. She aligned the folded blankets with the foot of the iron bedstead and straightened out the single pillow at its head. It was as if the occupant had died, thought Jennet, glancing back into the room before they left. A solitary bed unmade, which might have been a soldier's, or a lunatic's, or a nun's.

Sunlight on the effigy of a stone knight in the chancel and her father's voice invoking benediction on her head. The Reverend Richard Mallow had been less steely than his wife about their sinful daughter, but had also been persuaded that she must marry David. At once, said Lorna. As soon as possible. Then we can pretend the baby's premature. But she knew there'd be gossip in the village: that stuck-up Mrs Mallow and her daughter, how the mighty are so satisfactorily fallen. As a rector's wife Lorna was a failure, lacking the essential human touch, and things were hard enough for her before this disgrace descended on her household. Even so she would not be defeated, she would hold her head up high and get Jennet married properly, in a white gown and a veil, and never mind the sniggers.

So Jennet in her mother's dress cut down, a web of faintly yellowed lace, with David wavering between impatience and amusement: We can always get divorced, Bird, if we want. And David's parents, Malcolm and Heather, and his sisters, and Peggy, the rectory housekeeper, as witness. Malcolm Heaton turned out to be a manufacturer of safety pins in Wolverhampton, rather to Jennet's surprise. She had understood he did not need to work. Malcolm and Heather seemed a little disconcerted by their son.

Lorna had arranged it all: the removal of Jennet back to

Litton Kirkdale, Richard's journey down to London for an interview with David, the wedding and the breakfast, which they ate, the Heatons and the Mallows, in the dining room of the rectory, insulated from the summer sun. Pork pie and cold ham and beetroot; fruitcake; smears of colour clashing on their plates. The honeymoon was a week in Westmoreland, after which Jennet was ordered home until David could find her somewhere suitable to live.

Privately, unadmitted to her mother, Jennet was grateful for this edict. In her condition there was something comforting about returning to her childhood. She would have liked to be with David, and she missed him, but at the same time she was glad of her old bed and clean cotton sheets. For the few months of that summer and autumn she was cocooned in idleness and rest, and she grew stronger, rounder, her belly cupping close its charge like the calyx of a rosebud round its petals. Towards September Jennet felt the baby stir and shift, the gentlest movements first, like ripples, which soon become more purposeful, until she could see the outlines of small elbows, feet, seeking egress through her skin.

The long, warm days and the steady ripening of her child gave Jennet an ease she had not found before – a peaceful, happy languor. There was nothing that she had to do, and although she mourned the wealth of paint and canvas she had left behind in Kensington, she made the most of what she had, and painted. The stone-mullioned window on the first landing of the staircase in the rectory, with the sunlight slanting through. The reflection of a misted window in a bathtub full of water with a pinprick of gold light in it and a thin sheen on the surface of rainbow coloured oil. Landscapes of long fields divided by their ancient walls into vertical strips of form. The softness of the greens and the subtle greys of stone.

That summer, the summer of 1947, was the time when Jennet first began to sense the awakening of her true vision as an artist, together with the quickening of her child. Something, some atavistic power over shape and colour, crept into the spaces she had left for it. She began also to experiment with new techniques, searching for the right medium to express the sheerness of light on water or on glass, the shades of mist, and so came to the craft of tempera: colour dispersed in emulsion. It required egg yolk; only the yolk and not the sac, and to separate the two, she would let the egg yolk trickle through her fingers, a warm globe of pure yellow with the potential of a new life sacrificed, in this case, for the alchemy of colour.

David's flat was shared with other men and suited him; he did not want to move. But Lorna Mallow's sternness and the promise of some financial help from Malcolm Heaton were spur enough, just about, and eventually he took a lease on a tiny house in Hammersmith. He said it would be ready in time for Jennet's return to London in October, but it was scarcely furnished and had not been cleaned when he took her to it from the station. She opened the front door onto a narrow hall, encrusted quarry tiles, paper hanging off damp walls. We'll paint it, Bird, he promised. We'll paint flowers and trees and birds of paradise in every single room. There were only two rooms downstairs and two up, and a lean-to washroom; through the party wall a woman shouted at someone to stop and then a child wailed.

*

Benedict was born on 25 January 1948 at St Mary's Hospital. David was in Paris then, he had two paintings in a show and wanted to be there for the opening. Recently he had taken on a part-time teaching post at the Royal College of Art, in addition to his two days a week at Stockwell, and he was beginning to win a serious reputation.

Is there anyone more lonely than a woman in the final stage of giving birth? When Jennet looked back she saw icebergs, islands, reefs of pain. But then the company of Benedict in full possession of his perfect limbs and proving the capacity of his lungs. David, when he turned up at the hospital, inspected his new son with pride. Clever Bird, he said. A fledgling. I wonder will he be as well endowed as me?

It was good to be in the maternity ward. The suckling babies, the smell of milk, the slow gait of unhurried women and their heavy, naked breasts reminded Jennet of her Cornish cows and their undemanding warmth. She had no duties but to eat and sleep and feed her eager son, and she spent the mandatory ten-day stay in a drowsing haze, half wishing away the visitors who came at their allotted times. Margaret Metcalf, expecting her own child then, anxious for a blow-by-blow account of birth. Barbara, wreathed in righteousness because, if not for her, this lovely child would never have been born. Dermot and another friend from art school; their maleness and their voices, the city scent on their winter coats, anomalous in this women's world. And Corinne, anomalous as well in the sharp lines of her tight skirt and her red mouth and her sophisticated hat. She brought a bunch of hothouse roses, smoked a cigarette and only once glanced at the baby. Jennet in her milk-stained, crocheted bed jacket, her lips dry and pale, felt like a blurred outline, a failed pastel drawing, next to Corinne.

In the hospital Benedict was exemplary, the envy of all the mothers. He slept and fed at well-ordered intervals as if he had read the manuals, and he seldom cried. Jennet thought that life with him would be idyllic. He would smile and coo and kick his little heels while she serenely painted. But from the moment he went home to Cardross Street he was a different child. All day it seemed he wanted food but would not feed, or fed and then was sick; he drew his feet up in distress and opened wide his pink-ridged mouth and howled. All night he howled too, and Jennet, dragging herself out of brief, deep sleep like someone at the bottom of a well who can barely find the strength to swim up towards the light, would stumble out of bed and try to soothe him at her breast while David tossed and cursed and slept. In the mornings all three of them were pale and drawn, Benedict's eyelids veined with blue and Jennet's nipples so swollen-sore that to insert one between the baby's greedy gums again required a martyr's effort.

The tiles round the hearth in Cardross Street were pink, with a curious gold lustre, like the scales on the belly of a mullet. The carpet on the stairs was worn and the carpet in the sitting room dark-brown and dirty, patterned in swirls and curlicues of cream. After Benedict was born, the house was full of the ammoniacal, raw smell of nappies soaking in their buckets, and the steam that rose from them as they dried on a clothes horse by the stove. The only heat in Cardross Street came from that stove and it was permanently tented in wet cloth, which in a rainy season took days and days to dry. That winter was a hard one and too cold for Ben to sleep alone in his unheated room. Jennet kept him in her bed with David and was glad to; the damp, oatmeal smell of her small, snuffling son mingling with the beer and whisky on his father's breath.

Jennet listened to them breathe, the two of them, and drowsed and woke while the baby slept, and the nights were like dark passages of water too wide to cross alone. It seemed to her the walls of 77 Cardross Street conspired with each other to inch closer every night, until one morning she would wake and find herself imprisoned. She had dreams of narrowing tunnels and passages underground. All around her in the streets of London was evidence of walls collapsed: in bombed-out houses she could see fragments of carpet, the patterns on wallpaper, flights of stairs still standing. These houses were like the dolls' houses of childhood, open for inspection, their rooms exposed as if their façades had been hinged. There were objects in them, broken basins, fire-places, sticks of wood. In nightmares Jennet saw a giant's hands peeling off the front of her house too, while she and Ben and David huddled inside..

When Jennet woke, as she did so easily at every sigh of Ben's, at David's snores, she sometimes had to struggle against panic, against a sense of being held down by an enormous weight, of being paralysed or drowning. She had to tell herself that she could breathe, was breathing. She would flail around in the tangled sheets to retrieve Ben, to check he was alive and not suffocated in the dark.

In the mornings it was better, and then spring came, and summer. Ben moved into his own cot. There was a miniature patch of garden at the back of the house, and as Ben played on a blanket on the grass, Jennet scraped the varnish off the furniture she had begged or borrowed: a table, dented chairs, utility chests of drawers. Then she painted them in vivid colours; the chairs became vermilion, their mouldings touched with gold. An entire farmyard spread over a child's wardrobe: ducks and lambs and Jennet's favourite Friesians. They helped to keep the encroaching walls at bay, and the dusty streets, the long pavements, the phalanxes of brick and burnt-earth tiles outside.

All that survives from the year and a half that Jennet Mallow spent in Cardross Street is a handful of pencil drawings. She did no other work. Apart from the pressures on her time – and she could not have realised before Ben was born how all-consuming these would be – she had no space for it. The four rooms of the house were cramped and dark, and as the kitchen was always full of washing, there was only the front room left for friends. And the friends came in great numbers, David's friends, migrating down to Hammersmith, squeezing edgeways through the hall to pass Ben's pram, piling in after evenings at the pub, clutching too many bottles. Sleeping where they fell, on the floor or sofa. Artists and artists' models, would-be poets, a man who lived in a gypsy caravan in Cornwall, two wild Scots in love with one another, both of them called Robert, an Indian with the soul of a school prefect seeking to lose his inhibitions, young men who planned to open galleries and bookshops, teachers and students from art colleges, with their girlfriends – pretty and childless – draped around their necks. And Corinne.

In this vociferous company Jennet felt as she had done when the older, louder men and women had crowded into the Art School: reticent and watchful. The glow and confidence she'd briefly possessed as David's lover was dulled now that she was a wife. Other women asked her well-meant questions about babies but did not stay for answers, and Jennet knew that in comparison to theirs, her daily life was boring. But David never bored them. He needed their applause and he obtained it. Alone he could be sullen, but in company he sparked and fizzed, kept witty conversation skimming airborne like the most skilful of jugglers; was clever, beautiful and funny. It's no wonder that they love him, Jennet thought.

Some nights, when it was late and the party showed no signs of ending, Jennet would slip out of the room unnoticed and go quietly to bed. She would lie there, half asleep, hearing the London sounds, the city note of permanent unrest, the distant trains, the crescendo of laughter coming from downstairs, and music, until irate neighbours banged on the walls. She thought in pictures then, saw them swim behind her eyes, felt them take shape beneath her fingers, felt the longing in her fingers for paints and brush, for the chance to bring these pictures out for other eyes to see. The need to paint became a hunger in her, like the need for love.

First light would often break before David came upstairs and woke her. He would be flushed with drink, and blurry, but excited. Sometimes he would fall as abruptly into sleep as a small child, but there were nights when he would take her hand and fix it on his cock or slide his hand between her legs to make his own way ready. Then, as time went on, he'd mutter things which Jennet obeyed when she thought she had to. Dig your nails in. Harder. Hurt me with your fingers. Harder. Hurt me.

He did not say such things, though, in the mornings. Then he would make love to her quite gently, smile at her and tickle Ben, and on many mornings the sun shone and Jennet would remember she was happy.

But then another winter. Even in great cities in the autumn, there is sometimes a fleeting breath of mist, of woodsmoke and salt water, and although it may not be the scent of home, it is the scent of homesickness. Perhaps it is that scent that summons the returning greylag and conversely calls the swallow to take wing. Do wild horses on the shrinking moorlands lift their heads from grazing to fill their nostrils with this stir each year, and dream of unbounded plains? Wandering with her child by the river in October, Jennet also scented this nostalgia, blown into London off the water, from the distant marshes, and she wanted to be somewhere, anywhere, as long as it was not here. She didn't know if it was Yorkshire that she needed. Often she would think of the West Riding and the sweet air of her childhood, but there was melancholy muddled into these memories too: Richard mumbling his sermons to no one in his study; disappointed Lorna, with her mouth growing thinner by the day. So, if it wasn't Litton Kirkdale that she wanted, what was it? She couldn't tell, but she was full of an inchoate aching to be at home in a different place, to go back to somewhere that she had never known before.

The beguiling autumn air soon disappeared into the fog and rain of a London winter, but Jennet's longing grew. November, December: incessant rain, Ben's warm breath a vapour in the cold of Cardross Street, and every night his coughing. Terrifying fits of croup, when he would gasp and choke and she would boil kettle after kettle to fill the already moisture-laden air with steam. A new scent in the house of Friar's Balsam. The child's eyes dark with fear, his ribcage heaving.

Enough, she cried to David, on the morning of a new year: 1950. A new decade. Enough. Enough of Hammersmith, the mean streets, the smog, the soaking nappies, the grey mould creeping up her kitchen wall. Enough of tired women queuing in the doctor's surgery or at the butcher's, enough of rationing. Enough of counting out one's life in coupons. Enough of cabbages and swedes and the pervading smell of frying. Enough of the thick and sticky orange juice that was doled out to babies and which some mothers mixed with gin. Enough of gin. Of empty bottles lining up along the kitchen table and overflowing ashtrays and drunken conversations and David's beautiful long fingers shaking as he lit the first cigarette of the day.

Enough of brick. Enough of rain. Enough of Corinne. Enough of the sluggish river with its sad cargo of barges and its desperate leavings on the mud flats at low tide.

All right, said David, equably. We'll go and live in Spain.

Spain. A country that in David's mind was yellow under brilliant sun, red with the blood of the passionate young men who had laid down their lives for freedom in the International Brigade, black with the veils of widows and the hides of slaughtered bulls. He had never been there and did not know its language, but the country spoke to something in his imagination. He was excited by the seeming remoteness of it in its isolation after war. Besides, he was still smarting from something said about him in the *New Statesman* in October 1949. Having praised David's technical ability, the critic had been scathing about what he saw as his over-reliance on the traditions of the past. A peculiarly English form of high romanticism characterises Mr Heaton's pictures, the critic wrote. Outmoded. Heavily dependent on the pseudo-mysticism of William Blake and the visionary landscapes of Samuel Palmer. That turgid chiaroscuro, those distorted forms . . .

David did not see himself as a particularly English painter, which then, by definition, was provincial: he preferred to be perceived as cosmopolitan, and so had reasons of his own to look for change. It was timely, therefore, that applications for the Sickert Fellowship, which included a sum of money set aside specifically for travel, were being solicited by the Royal College. David put in an application, and he won.

But Franco? their friends all said, appalled. Margaret Metcalf and Richard Benjamin especially were shocked, for memories of the Civil War were vivid. Some of their own comrades in the Party had survived it; everyone knew of others who had not. And after the suffering, and the bitterness of defeat, so many more years of the fight against the Fascists, whom David and Jennet now appeared to be condoning. Don't you see, Richard asked, that by living in their country you legitimise their regime?

We do not, said David, lightly. We shall be living shoulder to shoulder with the poor. We shall be their champions. Through our art we will save them from oppression. Which is what you always say art's purpose should be, don't you, Benjamin? A moral purpose. Social responsibility. Our brave new world.

But in fact, why? Why Spain? To Jennet the destination was in some ways unimportant; what she needed was respite, and sunlight, change. This was not true of David. In the past year he had begun to feel the mark of greatness on him. It was not something he discussed, even after a bottle of whisky, although he did confide it to a notebook that he kept intermittently at the time. Nevertheless it was a conviction, and he knew that in order to realise his goal he must first broaden his horizons and his market. The *New Statesman* piece had stung. David saw that in this post-war world, with its new borders and its new demands, little Englanders would swiftly be forgotten. Already there was talk of revolutionary painters in New York. David had considered joining them but in the end he decided that his future lay in Europe. His intention was to be the most famous artist of the twentieth century, in the vanguard of a new movement in European painting. An obvious first step would have been to go

46

to France. But other painters had got there first, or indeed been born there, and David did not want to court comparisons. He must avoid the shadows of Picasso or Matisse. On the other hand he wanted what they had as their birthright: Naples yellow, viridian, cadmium red, ultramarine blue light. A new palette, in other words, not the northern one of greens and greys and earth. He could have found it equally in southern Italy or Greece. But Spain whispered to something deep in David, seducing him with its harsh history and skies, the crimsons of spilled blood.

David and Jennet gave up the lease of Cardross Street and prepared to move in June. Lorna came to London to say goodbye. She looked around her at the mould and shabbiness of the little house and said: Your father's stipend is very small. I hope you're not expecting us to give you any money. All this waste of brains and education. It's all your fault. You could have done much better for yourself. But she cheered up that evening when David came home from his studio in Baron's Court, accompanied by friends, including Corinne. A party! Lorna said. Suddenly she had a mysteriously husky voice and a thrillingly deep laugh. With eyelids lowered and a cigarette held upright between artfully angled fingers, she coiled herself into a corner of the sofa and set out to entertain.

Life at Litton Kirkdale, which had never seemed to have much room in it for comedy, was in Lorna's party-piece account transformed into a tinkling stream of anecdote, peopled by simpletons and bumpkins. Listening to it, Jennet felt a stab of guilty love. Her mother, fifty-one that year, encircled that night at Cardross Street by the confident and young, was both pitiful and valiant in her remade pre-war clothes and bright gash of ruby lipstick. Bowed, but not yet daunted. Disappointed and yet fractionally hopeful. She blew smoke rings through puckered lips at the young men. Would you like to paint me, David? she was saying. I'd volunteer to be your model. Near her, next to David, Corinne laughed. What a tale to tell the Mothers' Union, Mrs Mallow. The day I took my clothes off, all for art.

Narrow alleyways criss-crossed by rough stone arches, with a tumble on both sides of dilapidated buildings, ending in a strip of shingle and grey sand. Not much more to the village of Santiago de las Altas Torres than a bar, a baker's, a cobbled market square and an ochre-painted church. To the west, the ruins of a Moorish fort; behind it, in the silted estuary, fields of rustling cane; beyond it, in the distance, the Sierras. Snow on the highest peaks, even in the summer.

It was hard to believe in snow, Jennet thought. She, who had never been out of England, had never felt heat before like the August heat of Andalusia. She was transformed by it, loosened, she swam in it as if it were her element, breasting into it at the beginning of each day, letting it recede in the small hours of the night when it surrendered to a light, salt breeze.

It had been a long journey there for Jennet, David and the child: by boat to Santander, then train and a series of slow buses. They paused for a while in Seville, then Cordoba, where David, ravished by cloisters and fountains, wanted to remain until reminded that he had agreed with Jennet on the imperative of sea. Some vague cousin of David's close friend Dermot had connections in the town of Salobreña, east of Malaga, and through him the Heatons found a little house to rent in Santiago. It was more of a hovel than a house – three square rooms and a steep, stone staircase – but it was freshly whitewashed, there were beautiful old tiles on the ground floor, and framed in an upstairs window was the sea.

How strange they must have seemed, this foreign couple, to the fishermen and their families in the village. Santiago then was cut-off and remote, its back turned to the outside world, still shuddering from the hurt of sixteen years ago when its brief, hopeful uprising was crushed by Falangist tanks and warships shelling from the sea. Nothing had happened in Santiago between the departure of the Moors and the horrors of the Civil War, and nothing since; the people lived as they had always lived, precariously, scratching out a living from the inhospitable soil and the unpredictable sea. Tourists were beginning to discover Spanish coasts, but none had got as far as Santiago. There was nothing there to lure them.

At first the villagers were guarded, even hostile; they peered at Jennet from behind their shutters when she went to get bread, or to buy vegetables and meat on market days, and young men stood in clusters, staring like uneasy bullocks from under lowered brows, wherever David went. It was Benedict who won them over. At two years old he was irresistible: fearless, trusting and, with his tangle of gold curls, as exotic in this place of dark-haired children as a tamarin in a clutch of kittens. Soon small girls were vying with each other when they found him on the beach, tempting him with shells and dried-up starfish, seizing him around his fat little belly, lifting him up and staggering across the sand under his solid, laughing weight. Then their grandmothers allowed themselves to yield to the seduction of his curls, touching them to see if they were real, and younger women tentatively offered smiles. David soon acquired his own seat at a table in the bar, and by the summer's end the Heatons were no longer objects of suspicion.

That summer it was as if time had been suspended or

become a transparent membrane in which sunlight, space and water, brightness, whites and blues gleamed and were refracted and the other world – the world of London, Litton Kirkdale, anxiety and frustration, made by contrast shadowy, unreal. No one visited them from England; they were left alone, the three of them, father, mother, child, in a new environment of simplicity and calm. Just before they left for Spain Richard Mallow had sent them a bank draft for five hundred pounds and David had sold Peggy Guggenheim a painting. With this money, and the money from the fellowship, they had enough to live on, in a life with few demands.

Jennet loved the paring-down of needs. Warm wheels of rough bread in the mornings, tomatoes, the sharp taste of sheep's cheese, bitter olives, eggs. Vinos del terreno straight from great oak barrels, and the deep, strong scent of black tobacco in the cigarettes. Ben, gold and brown and naked on the beach, and her own feet bare on cool, blue-patterned tiles. David's body, hot and hard, beneath a cotton sheet. Sitting on the front steps with him in the evening, after Ben had gone to sleep, listening to the village sounds and the sough against the shingle of the sea.

She felt there was a rightness to this way of life. They had nothing in their house that was not needed, no extra knives or forks or clothes or furnishings, only the books they wanted, wooden bricks for Ben, paper, canvas, paint. Theirs was the decorum of a convent cell: each possession in its ordained place and every thing essential. And beautiful as well. Jennet had never had that satisfying sense of absolute rightness in the past. In the West Riding the landscape seen through diamond panes of window had been lovely, but within, the house was dim and full of dusty books and sadness. Oxford's stone symphonies had been overlaid for her by foreboding and the smell of disinfectant. Even in Cornwall there had been jarring notes of corrugated iron and barbed wire. But here, in Santiago, despite the poverty of its people and the ramshackle houses, she saw a careless beauty. Scarlet geraniums growing in old oil cans, the stripe of light and shadow on a white-painted wall, a basket full of tiny silver fish.

Perhaps she was romanticising. Perhaps it was that sunshine hid the flaws. Of course she knew that life was hard for those who had to live in Santiago and depend upon the little they could grow or catch. When inclined to think that she had matched the socialist ideal of a contented and communal life, she always heard Richard Benjamin's sardonic laugh. But still. Those first months in Santiago stayed in her mind as a time of happiness, and they mark the start of one of her most fecund periods as an artist.

There was money enough to live on but not to spare. David's, then, was the lion's share of expensive art materials. This was fair, Jennet conceded; she had made nothing from her painting but David had, and was on the brink of making more. His professional world encompassed dealers and collectors; she was nowhere near this stage. But in Santiago she had time, now that Ben could play on his own or guarded by adoring girls, and space, in the cool square room she shared with David. Although his nearness could be intimidating and his critical presence sharp, Jennet felt free enough to paint again for the first time since Ben was born. To start with she let David keep the canvas – it was pricily shipped out to him by a colleague at Stockwell – and instead made use of whatever she could glean: cardboard, bits of broken boxes, driftwood. On these she painted the green jug they used for wine, a blue bowl full of lemons, the upturned hulls of fishing boats, the slither of a net of anchovies and, over and over again, the sea in all its nuances as she saw it through her upstairs window.

Windows. Always for Jennet these windows. The stone-mullioned windows at Litton Kirkdale; the rough square of the window, an unframed opening in the wall, in the house in Santiago. Within it the horizontals of grey sand, of sea and sky, in varying shades of grey and green and blue. Indigo, ultramarine. A pewter-grey before a storm; an oyster sheen when the storm was clearing. The sea tranquil or angry. Empty or bearing up the outlines of fishing boats. Or seen through something else: the slats of wooden shutters, a trailing strand of grape vine, a vase of wild flowers.

Perversely, perhaps, David seldom painted out of doors in Spain. The subject that filled his canvas at this time was Jennet. Jennet naked on a bed, the pale of skin kept unrevealed against the tan of skin exposed, her three dark triangles of hair. Open your legs, he ordered her one night. Priggish not to, he went on when she demurred. You're beautiful in there. No need to splay them, just open up a little, yes, and he reached his brush across to paint a straight, deliberate line along her flesh.

David liked to paint at night. He liked the play of candle-light or oil lamp on skin, the glow and shadow they afforded. His studies of Jennet naked, which had begun in a dispassionately realistic style, became more intimate as they developed, as though his paint were married to her body. He uncovered with his brushes what he would never do with his fingers: the shapes beneath, the rhythms, the intersections of bone and nerve, Jennet's shyness and her want. These pictures David made in Spain are difficult. Observers now cannot escape a feeling of complicity, as if they were being brought into the paintings too, made voyeurs by the artist of a woman vulnerable; and that woman not anonymous but the artist's wife.

Jennet herself was ambivalent about the paintings. Sometimes she could look at them, at the extraordinary brushstrokes, the way that David with a flick of opaque white revealed a contour or, in exact shades of rose and brown, the vulva's folds, a slope of neck, a nipple, and still preserve her distance. She knew that these were brilliant paintings. But at other times she'd see herself in David's work and feel a sense of violation and of dread that other people, strangers or, worse, people whom she knew, would see her too: brazen, shameless, thrusting out a peculiar invitation. The unwelcome thought would come to her of Richard Mallow wandering innocently through the corridors of a museum, to be ambushed by his daughter, entirely recognisable, with one leg folded underneath her the better to display what should not be shown in womanhood to any father. The prospect of being assessed by any man in her uncompromising nakedness was worrying. Jennet was well aware that the response to David's paintings would inevitably be complex. The woman in them, at once available and evasive, victim and conspirator, her body on offer but her face turned away, was a complicated icon. She felt that ambiguity in her own response. Offering herself up to David's minute scrutiny, admitting his invasive eyes, capitulating to his image of her, was both disturbing and arousing. Lying stretched out in front of him, Jennet searched instinctively for the protection of a sheet and at the same time ached for David's touch, his lips against her proffered breast, his hands on her directly, rather than at one remove through the caresses of his brush.

David was aroused by the act of painting too. Afterwards they might make love; fiercely, quickly and in silence. And often, that first year in Santiago, while the village slept, they would slip quietly from the house and go hand in hand and barely dressed across the shingle and the sand into the waiting sea. Warm water in the starlight, its insistent undertow, its tug and pull and whisper, washing off all trace of paint and love, and later, the taste of salt on their cool skin.

It was cold in Santiago in the winter but the days of rain were balanced by days of brilliant sun. Jennet, waking to the sun on an early January morning in the whitewashed cube of her bedroom, watched the lines of light with pleasure, imagining herself inside a block of ice, clear and clean and hard. In February the scent of orange blossom drifted on the air and by midday the air was warm. With the spring came visitors, the same crowd that used to drink with David in the pubs of Hammersmith and Soho, now translated here to Santiago in groups of two or three. Dermot and his girlfriend, the two Roberts, a poet having a doomed affair with a politician's wife, Corinne and her elusive husband. No one seemed to know about this man, Victor, who was much older than the rest of them and rumoured to be rich. David said he had been released last year from prison. Something to do with currency deals, he thought, during the war.

The coming of the visitors changed things that spring and second summer. It reopened the gap between the Heatons and the people of the village that, after a shared winter, had almost completely closed. Jennet found Spanish easy and spoke the local dialect effortlessly after only a few months. Ben was growing up bilingual. Being able to talk on equal terms to one another and having spent dark afternoons in each other's firelit rooms had made Jennet and the village women friends. Jennet had begun to gather groups of children of a morning to paint with them or make little shapes out of clay, in an informal art class. The London women interrupted this casual comradeship. None of them could speak the language, and with their northern skins and their holiday clothes, they looked more foreign than Jennet. They rarely stayed for longer than a fortnight but, even if they had, they could not readily be absorbed into the village.

The same was true of the English men. David had not been assimilated into Santiago quite as comfortably as Jennet. Being a young man without apparent occupation he was too mysterious, and he did not have the advantage of daily meetings with the mothers of small children in the bakery or on the beach. But he had his own friends in the bar – fishermen and farmers who, after a while, had acknowledged his presence and would sometimes share a jug of wine with him. These men did not take kindly to the company of strangers.

As the Heatons' house was cramped, their guests would take the only available rooms to rent, which were above the local bar. The patron, therefore, had far too close an insight into their unconventional habits; the shortage of wedding rings for example, or two men evidently lovers. And, most dismayingly, their drinking. David, in his months alone with Jennet and Ben, had been drinking much less than he had done in London, but his party spirit was swiftly reawakened. To the visitors the cheapness of unrationed Spanish wine was cause for celebration, and day after day would spin away in a long parade of bottles that ended with brandy in the evenings, the potent, burnt-caramel tasting kind, drunk in quantities around a fire lit on the beach.

As word spread back in London of the easy life in Santiago and elsewhere along the Mediterranean coast of Spain, more and more people came, the Heatons spent less time alone, and David did less painting. He was partly resting on his laurels. Under an arrangement made with the Redleaf Gallery, the work that he had already done in Spain had been shipped to London and had sold at once to great acclaim. An exhibition was planned for that autumn. In the meantime David felt that he had earned a month or two of holiday in which to be hospitable to friends and enjoy the country, discovering its pleasures and the local wines. But for Jennet the holiday was over. These visitors, even when they did not sleep at her house, wanted food and entertainment. She found herself once more in the position of domestic skivvy: David's adjunct, his obliging wife. Few of his friends imagined she was painting. Also she was pregnant. She was glad of that – it was time, she thought, for Ben to have a brother or a sister – but she had not expected to feel so sick and wretched. As spring surrendered to the heat of summer she grew more and more uncomfortable, until it seemed the only moments of relief came when she let herself sink deep into the cool, embracing sea.

But David, sinking too in vats of wine. That summer he was soaked in it: Montilla in the morning, rough reds in the afternoon, brandy late at night. He drank with friends when they were there or, in the intervals between them, on his own; with them he was buoyant on the whole, alone he was morose. He looked at Jennet with blank eyes as if she were a stranger. He did not paint her or make love. He did not paint at all. There was only an hour or so in any day when he was clear-headed; at other times he'd fly unpredictably into a rage or into wild excitement. He'd yell at Benedict for the mildest of mistakes, or else he'd hug him far too hard, tossing him up into the air or spinning him round and round until the child was dizzy. A cautious, assessing look began to cloud Ben's gaze. Left to make all the small decisions of the day alone, Jennet felt for the first time the want of a close friend.

She could tell no one about David. Once, waking at

sunrise and seeing that he was not next to her in bed, she got up to find him sprawled and snoring on the stairs. He had evidently tripped, and was lying at full length, apparently unhurt. But he was barely conscious; no amount of calling or shaking him by the shoulder could bring him to his senses. His eyelids would flutter open, but then close, and, after trying ineffectually to tug him up the stairs, there was nothing Jennet could do but leave him there. Until he woke she watched beside him, fearing that otherwise he might slip down to the tiled floor below or suffocate in vomit. When at last he opened his eyes and they stayed open, he stared at her without expression and said nothing, only pulling himself slowly upright and stumbling to bed.

Why? she asked him later, why? He did not appear to understand the question. What's your problem, Bird? he said.

Jennet's baby was due in early December, and David's exhibition at the Redleaf opened in October. Because Jennet wasn't up to the long journey, David went to London on his own. He took two of Jennet's window paintings with him, and her blue bowl full of lemons, on the off chance, though it was slight he said, that he could sell them. His dealer at the Redleaf, Ivan Whitehouse, was not interested in still lifes or semi-abstract landscapes, but it was worth a try. By then, after more than a year in Spain, money was running short. His travelling fellowship was at its end and they were living on the proceeds of his painting.

Years later Jennet would be asked why David had not been more encouraging about her work. In retrospect he seemed so unsupportive. Was he jealous? the interviewer would prompt. She had to struggle to remember. No, it was not jealousy, she thought. More that David had such confidence in himself. In spite of all his secret demons. He was a shining comet destined to reach the utmost heights, and he admitted nothing that would interrupt his path. He knew he was a genius. Besides, he was a man of his own generation, paying lip service only to ideas of change. The self-sacrifice of women was expected; Jennet was more useful to him as his wife and the mother of his children than as a rival artist. There were other women artists working then, of course, but with one exception, none in England yet belonged in the first rank. It did not occur to David that Jennet Mallow could. At the time she was so inextricably bound up in his own painting as a model, or as his crucial inspiration, that in many aspects he was blind to her. He simply did not see Jennet's potential.

Jennet was not anxious about David's going. She felt entirely safe in Santiago and the month he was away passed sweetly, gently, in a chain of autumn days encircling her, her unborn child and Ben. Ben was inquiring, entertaining, learning how to read; she was discovering new interests as a mother. Not by nature especially maternal, she was pleased by the increasing independence of her son. She began to like him as a friend. And in that month she painted with a sudden surge of energy and insight: whereas once she had perceived shape first as an object, now she saw object as pure shape. In her great painting of that time, simply called *Santiago*, the foreground is a block of saffron broken by a line of deepest blue, above which is a band of blue that is even darker, so dark it might be black if it were not for the light contained in it which magically shines through. Against this blue are five uneven verticals of palest lemon tinged with palest blue, the sails of a fishing boat, perhaps, against the gathering darkness of an autumn sky in the livid light before a storm.

Without David at her elbow, in her whitewashed cube of

space, Jennet for the first time gave her picture scope. Her paintings until then had been domestic in their scale, ninety by sixty centimetres, say, and small enough to prop up on a kitchen chair or spread out on a table. *Santiago* is three times as large. She worked on it all through October, and it took form together with the baby in her womb, both of them developing while the sun splashed through the uneven squares of window and the grapes on next-door's vines turned from green to gold.

It was not with unreserved gladness that Jennet welcomed David home. She had been happy with her child in that uneventful calm. But she was optimistic. Having had a rest from her and Spain, David would be better, had to be, would want to paint again. They might move, she thought, to somewhere larger and more permanent; she could have a studio, Ben a bedroom of his own. Soon he would be starting school in Santiago; he would be a Spanish child then, not a foreign one.

David was drawn and tired but peaceable enough when he arrived, and he said his time in England had been productive. He had stayed in Portman Close with Corinne. The exhibition had been an out-and-out success, after a rather rocky start when it seemed it might be closed by the police. Ridiculous assertions of obscenity. They had to have it pointed out to them they might as well ban Goya, Boucher, Titian. In the end Ivan Whitehouse compromised by hanging David's portraits of Jennet in an anteroom where they could not be seen by passers-by. Needless to say the scandal drew crowds. Many of the people who had bought pictures in the past had lent them to the Redleaf for the show; it had been a comprehensive look at David's work. Spectacular reviews. Even the bloody *Statesman*. He brought a copy of the catalogue for Jennet, and it remains among her papers now, a little tatty; all those searching pictures of her youthful body there in reproduction.

He also brought four hundred pounds for Jennet. Ivan Whitehouse, as predicted, was not especially enthusiastic, but he did suggest that David show Jennet's paintings to Patrick Mann, who had just opened his own gallery, the Heron. Mann was captivated. He bought all three for his own collection and told David he would very much like to see more of Jennet's work. 'If, as I take it, she is not yet re-presented by any other gallery in London?' David explained to Mann that Jennet would soon have her hands full with the baby and could hardly be expected to produce more work. But Mann's invitation stood, for what it was worth.

This approbation was a spur to Jennet – Mann's was the first money she had made from painting since she won the Whistler Prize at art school. And ironically, although he did not suspect the implications, it was thanks to David that this turning-point occurred in Jennet's life.

Margaret Metcalf wrote in shock after she heard that Jennet was intending to have her child at home in Spain. She herself had had two children by then, both boys, was expecting another, and could not imagine giving birth without the wonderful new National Health. Do think of coming back, she wrote. You could stay with us. But Jennet was not worried. Women in Santiago were delivered by the local midwife all the time, and Benedict's birth had been straightforward. She had obscured the memories of pain. Her sole concern she did not share but tried to laugh away as one of pregnancy's delusions: that the baby might be horribly deformed. She dreamed of hydra-heads. A month before it was to be born this child seemed enormous, and possessed of

60

extra limbs; it was restless and moved constantly so that she was never sure whether the bumps she felt were its bottom or its head. An antenatal check at the hospital in Malaga would have been a good idea, but somehow Jennet never got around to it. There was a streak in her of the fatalistic. And private hospital appointments were expensive. The money from Patrick Mann would be better spent on fuel and food, she thought.

She did submit, however, to a visit from her sister. Lorna had been adamant. If Jennet was too stubborn to give up her foolish way of life, she must have in attendance a thoroughly trained nurse. But Barbara isn't a midwife, Jennet protested in a letter. No. But she does know about hygiene, Lorna answered, and she's English. So Barbara took a month of unpaid leave and arrived in Santiago on 30 November, the day before the twins were born.

Carmela, with her straggling grey hair and apron rusty with old bloodstains. *Empuja*, she hisses, *Eso es! Vamos!* Barbara, pinky-pale and puffy, peculiarly dimpled little hands divided by a fold from plumpy wrists just like a doll's, giddy still with travel and the shock of rural Spain, also issuing instructions. Carmela glares. Both of them are miles away from Jennet on her cloud of pain, although even from a distance she can see them clearly. Carmela's broken thumbnail; an orangey snake of powder caked in the curve of Barbara's nose. She can smell their separate but mingling breath. Fish and toothpaste, tobacco, garlic. The two women, one on either side, lean over her towards each other; they would look like this, she thinks, if I were dead. Two women fussing over her prone body – Barbara with torn-up strips of cotton sheet wrung out in cold water, which she keeps plastering on Jennet's head. Swaddling bands or cerements; the napkin that was about his head, not lying with the linen cloths, but rolled up in a place by itself. Jennet is in a place alone and sealed there in icy clarity, each thought entire and separate and perfect as a raindrop but none of them connecting or making contact with the earth. She could speak, perhaps, her mouth might move, but she has no desire to. I may be dead, she thinks.

The sliver of flesh torn out of her is smeared and wet and also, possibly, dead. But then it moves a little, feebly, like a landed fish; its mouth is open and it gapes. Carmela rights it, pats it smartly, sticks a finger in its mouth, bangs it on the back again and then it cries. From her far-off plateau Jennet watches and thinks how easily Carmela might have wrung its neck, the little thing; one quick twist like a Sunday chicken, a practised backwards flip to break the spine.

There is no ebbing to the furious pain, no quieter space in which to breathe or rest. Still the massive, thumping urge inside her to expel an alien form; the pain, if anything, grows worse. Carmela thrusts the wailing thing at Barbara, also open-mouthed, and probes and pokes and presses one hand down on Jennet's belly. *Me cago en Dios*, she remarks. *Uno mas. Vamos, mujer. Empuja! Vamos!*

It takes almost an hour for the second to be born. By then death would have been as welcome as a lover's gentle touch. The baby is impossibly tiny, still and blue. Carmela lifts it to her face in both her hands; it is so small her hands cup it in a perfect cradle. She covers its mouth and nose with her mouth, breathes softly into it and stops and listens, breathes again and stops, and breathes. Each time she stops the silence is immeasurably deep. Even the other baby stills her wail to watch. Jennet, a broken thing tossed back to land from shipwreck, watches too, but does not know if she is dead or dreaming. Carmela breathes and stops and breathes. The baby's quail-like ribcage flutters briefly then subsides. Carmela breathes. And, after hours, or minutes, or a lifetime, the matchstick rib bones heave again and sink, but rise a second time and now the baby also breathes. Shallow, panting breaths, but breath that comes and goes all on its own. Carmela holds the little scrap upright against her shoulder, turns her face aside and spits. At last Carmela smiles. *Gemelas*, Carmela says. *Ya está. Bravo, mujer, bravo.*

Two girls. Sarah and Vanessa. Sarah thrives but Vanessa is sickly, small; in the womb she must have yielded her share to her sister. She is so pale she might be made of candlewax: minute, pinched, translucent nostrils; a frog's delicate, splayed feet. She will not feed; she has no strength to suck. Frantic, Jennet plugs her to the nipple and a little milk goes down; more spills in sprays across her face and neck. Carmela comes to see the baby every day and shakes her head and mutters words about the will of God, but Vanessa is tenacious, succoured on thin drops of milk, she will not do what everyone expects her to and, uncomplaining, die. Instead over the weeks she slowly grows a little stronger and learns to use her tongue and the muscles of her throat. Barbara sends to London for Farley's milk and rubber-teated bottles: meanwhile a wet nurse with some milk to spare is found to supplement Jennet's inadequate supply. Even so. Avidly sucking Sarah. Vanessa's puny, bleating cry, a high-pitched and desolate sound that slices into Jennet all through each night and day. Ben, not yet three, bewildered by these interlopers and their commandeering of his mother, begins to suck his thumb again and wet his bed and whine. The expression in his eyes is like a dog's, expecting to be hurt.

Three children under three, Barbara in a constant fuss and David, repulsed by women, sickness, seeping breasts and sodden cloth, spending his whole day somewhere else. Barbara does not care for Santiago, it is primitive and dull, she says, and David does not care for Barbara. Marshmallow. If one were to prod her, David says, which God forbid, sink a finger in her fat, pink softness, there would be a dint left in her flesh. With reason, then, Barbara is no friend to David, but her resentment extends to Jennet too. Even now, Jennet, bleeding, cut, exhausted, weeping, is prettier, thinner, cleverer than her sister. Jennet has a husband, and he is very handsome, even if he is a fiend. Jennet has three children and two of them are lovely, even if the third is sallow and predicted not to live. It was always so. When they were children Jennet had much more of everything than Barbara and she was their father's favourite, it was so unfair. Barbara doesn't have a husband, has never even had a lover, next year she'll be thirty, wasting her life with nursing, no one ever paid her to mess around with paints and paper. What she gets at work is blood and bedpans, and now she is expected to spend her holiday and Christmas with more of the same, unpaid. But although she is a grudging nursemaid she is extremely competent: she cleans and wipes and cooks, and Jennet is very grateful.

On New Year's Eve people from the village came with presents. Quince cheese, a loaf of bread, a fish, tiny scarlet knitted hats for the two girls, *las niñas*. Carmela had made marzipan. That night, in the intermission of a storm, when at last the children were asleep, Jennet opened wide the shutters to let in the clawing wind and listen to the wild sea, to count her blessings and make her resolutions. Her family will come safely through the coming year. They will stay in Spain. And she will do more painting. Much more painting: she will be profligate and brave, assured, experimental. There was a song the fishermen sang in Santiago about the voices of the sea. Ghosts were in the storms, they sang, and in the clarity of water, but the sea might also sing with the sweet voices of the dawn.

Perhaps it may seem strange that 1952, which was in many ways the most testing year of Jennet's life, should mark the onset of her time as a serious, committed painter. She never explained it. Precedent would have suggested she do no work at all – when Ben was born she had no time for painting; now, with three young children and one of them unwell, she might have been completely daunted. On the contrary, Jennet worked that year with fierce determination. Beneath her quietness, Jennet Mallow had always been persistent; now that the odds were stacked against her she would fight against them rather than let the waters of defeat close over her head. In that year's strenuous activity, and in the following decade's too, there are signs of steely desperation – as if she knew her chance was then or not at all. In London she had ached with a hunger that had only just begun to be satisfied in the past few months in Spain. Her need to work was powerful and she refused to thwart it once again. Ambition had taken hold of her. That, and the fear that one day she might need her independence, might be compelled to make a living and support herself, together with her children. Under the weight of her children's needs, Vanessa's ailing and David's increasing sadness, Jennet might so easily have surrendered. If she had not fought on, twentieth-century art would have been much poorer.

Patrick Mann played a large part in Jennet's new won confidence. He was a young man then, with a new gallery, and greedy for repute. But he was not a mere promoter: he had taste and a good eye, and from the start he knew he had struck gold with Jennet. She would not elude him. He wrote to her in Santiago, repeating the offer he had made through

David, and in June 1952 he turned up on the doorstep. Just passing through, he breezed implausibly. He was a fat little thing in a pair of rimless glasses, and for his Spanish trip he wore a new straw hat. As David said, he looked more like a functionary from Antwerp than an up-and-coming dealer; he could have stepped straight out of a picture by Magritte. All he needs, David went on, is a dove tucked in that hat. But David liked him. Everybody liked him; he was extraordinarily appreciative and polite. Puffing and sweating in the heat, he praised the beauty of the beach, the children, the architecturally unremarkable village church, Jennet's tomato salad. On the evening of his arrival he allowed himself to be cajoled into the sea by Ben, whereupon he told them he couldn't swim. But the water, of course, was absolutely marvellous, and Benedict so expert a swimmer that Patrick felt quite safe. He's one round bouncing ball stuffed with superlatives, David said to Jennet. If you show him any paintings he'll explode.

In the event he was remarkably contained. Jennet was using a neighbour's shack to store her pictures; she took Patrick to see them in the morning. She showed him *Santiago*. She and David had had to take the shack door off to get the painting in; there was barely space for it. Against a wooden wall, in the daylight from the doorway, it appeared to glow. Luminous in blues and saffron, like treasure lit by dragon's fire or an altarpiece by myriad candles. In the dusty, fish-scented shack Patrick Mann gazed at the painting. Jennet had expected him to burble, but for minutes he said nothing. It was years later when he told her that he had been struggling to hold back tears.

Under Patrick's scattergun enthusiasm lay discrimination, expertise and knowledge. And an absence of sentiment. He did not often cry. His interest in Jennet was primarily commercial; he knew the old supremacy of France in modern art was on the wane, that new movements from the States would soon overwhelm the tired Europeans, and that Jennet, unlike most of her contemporaries, could hold her own on the international scene. In her he saw his future.

Jennet had another dozen paintings and some drawings to show Patrick apart from *Santiago*. Not quite enough for a one-man show, he said – or should that be one-woman – but almost. Could you possibly, do you think, get a bit more done before, say, this time next year? Shall we pencil in an exhibition? Launch you with a splash in London? I could start whetting appetites, with one or two paintings, begin to tantalise the best collectors. Would you agree to that? Leave the practicalities to me?

Ferociously well organised, Patrick Mann had crates made up and contracts drawn and pictures shipped to London. To Jennet he was the djiin unleashed by rubbing at a bottle, the fish that grants three wishes to its catcher, a magic creature from a story. Remote from art dealers and art markets, and without a network of her own, Jennet would never have had the early success she did if it had not been for Patrick Mann.

Extract from the draft catalogue of Jennet Mallow's first exhibition at the Heron Gallery in Cork Street with Patrick Mann's own notes:

Child Laughing (Benedict H.) 1952 pencil on paper 12 × 10
Infant Sleeping (i) 1952 pencil on paper 11 × 9
Infant Sleeping (ii) 1952 pencil on paper 11 × 9 [swaddled like a corpse]
Two Infants 1952 pencil on paper 12 × 10
Self-portrait 1952 crayon on paper 11 × 9
Carmela (i) 1952 charcoal on paper 11 × 9
Carmela (ii) 1952 11 × 9

Study of Infant's Hand 1952 pencil on paper 6 × 8
Santiago 1951 oil on canvas 82 × 92
Lemons, Blue Bowl 1951 oil on wood 21 × 30
Green Jug 1951 oil on driftwood 15 × 19
Fishing Boats 1951 oil on wood 28 × 20
Anchovies 1951 oil on canvas 14 × 12
Window (i) 1951 oil on linen laid on board 12 × 22
Window (ii)   "   "
Window (iii)   "   "
Window (iv)   "   "
Window (v)   "   "
Still Life with Child's Cup 1952 oil on linen 11 × 13
Still Life with Wineglass 1952 oil on canvas 11 × 13
Lemons (i) 1952 gouache, watercolour, pencil on paper
     15 × 11
Lemons (ii) 1952   "   "
David 1952 oil on sailcloth laid on board 46 × 35 (male
     silhouette from back, grey against bands of green and
     blue)
Noon 1952 oil on sailcloth 56 × 48 (yellow/orange/blue)
Dusk November 1952 oil on sailcloth 68 × 90 (silver/grey)
Night December 1952 oil on sailcloth 68 × 90 (black on
     grey, white stripe)
In the Clarity of Water 1953 oil on paper on linen 52 × 38
El Muerto 1953 oil on board 78 × 17

El Muerto. The dead man. A painting unlike any other in
Jennet Mallow's exhibition. Coffin-sized, a man stretched
out on a linen cloth. His mouth and eyes are open and his
head is tilted; his hair falls back from it. Whether the
crumpled cloth is laid on bed or board or mortuary slab is
not apparent; the luminosity behind the man and at his head
and feet suggests that he is confined in glass or marble, but

from the shadow over him it seems he is pressed down by something dark.

The hallmarks of Jennet Mallow's early painting are in this painting too: the strong horizontal bands of colour, in this instance the white of linen, the tones of the body, the dark line of shadow, balanced by the verticals of upthrust chin and feet and the two ends of the casket. But this is no abstract, no exercise in form. Instead it is uncompromisingly and harshly realistic; the man's flesh has the hue of putrefaction, green and bruised, a dribble of dried blood trails from the corner of his mouth, his hands are tightened into claws. Jennet's mastery of technique, born of all the lessons in the life classes at Kensington, the hours of practice, all those meticulously detailed drawings of a feather, comes to a pinnacle in this picture of a corpse. Every fraction of it is immaculately painted: the one visible fingernail broken and dirty, the arch of an eyebrow, cheekbone, the corrugated flank, the moulding of a shoulder, each individual toe. The dead man's penis lolling in its nest of curled dark hair, the exact weave of the cloth. The swollen tongue, the black inside a nostril. It is both horrible and beautiful, this portrait, and indebted in many ways to David Heaton. His was the command of flesh, both dead and living, the anatomist's cold eye, and Jennet proved a fine apprentice. Was *El Muerto* then an act of homage? Certainly it is quite clear the man it portrays is David.

A dead man behind glass. An evening in November; wind and rain. All day the wind. And the night before: an anxious wind, sand-laden, whining through the cracks in windows, under doors, its hiss and fret as jangling to the nerves as a blade scraped hard on slate. Sarah and Vanessa are almost a year old. Sarah is crawling now, can pull herself up on to her feet, is saying the odd word, but Vanessa lacks these skills.

69

She is still too small, too light, her bones as frail and brittle as a bird's, her skin too finely stretched, too ashy. Under the skin of the bridge of her nose there is a stain of venous blue, as if she had been dipped in ink. A changeling child she is, made of a substance not quite flesh, a spirit not quite earthly. There is a remoteness in her even as a baby, a disconnection from the outside world. She does not smile much, nor laugh, but she does cry often, still with that same weak, high-pitched mew, that kitten's plea, she had when she was born.

Jennet has been trying hard to disregard the signs of strangeness in her daughter. Vanessa's slow development is easily explained by her low weight at birth, Jennet believes; she will catch up when she's stronger. But on the night the wind blew in from Africa, Jennet, finding the child awake but silent in her cot, looked at her and felt the swirl of fear in her guts.

She brought the child down to David in the room where he was painting. He took Vanessa from her and waved his finger back and forth before her eyes and pressed the little button of her nose until she answered with a squawk. Look at that, he said, look how she follows my finger, how she laughs, there's nothing wrong with her at all. Feed her up, why don't you, with a raw egg yolk and a teaspoon of brandy. In no time at all she'll be as right as rain.

Oh mi vida, Jennet whispers to the solemn baby, using Santiago words of love, I hope your Daddy's right, *mi vida*. That night, the night of plaintive wind, she sees he knows he's wrong.

He had drained a second jug of wine, but that was not unusual, he often did, and sometimes drank a third. Mostly she left him to it, and so avoided the belligerence that could seethe up when he was drunk. He would take his wine upstairs while she used the quiet hours of the night to work, and she would hope he'd be asleep by the time she went to bed. That way she would not have to hear the damage done to love by litre upon litre of red wine. But that night, the night of storm, having blown out the oil-lamps and closed the shutters tight, she comes upstairs to check the sleeping children and finds her husband kneeling hunched up on the floor and rocking to and fro beside Vanessa's cot. In the dull glow of a nightlight she can see he's scratching at his hands, his right hand rasping up and down the clenched fist of his left.

David? she says, cautiously and soft. David? She cannot read his face in the dim light, but she can smell the sour of wine lying thickly on his breath.

There were ants, he says, millions of ants. Or maybe wood-lice. Scuttling things. But now they've gone.

His voice is very loud in this room of sleeping children.

I must get rid of this skin, he says. Where the things were crawling. Underneath there'll be clean bone.

He comes towards her with his hands held out, palms down, and even in the darkness she can see that they are bleeding.

Jennet did not know the words to comfort him, or what to do but gently lead him towards bed. She fetched a cloth and water to wash away the streaks of blood, but he pushed them aside. Long into that night he went on talking to himself, a strung-out litany of mumbled words: ants and bones and barbed wire, Bren guns, searchlights; a long roll-call of names, like a register at school or on a carved stone cross. On and on his muttering and the incessant wind and flicker-ing in the dark, the lit ends of chains of cigarettes.

Jennet slept a little, fitfully, too tired not to and too scared, but woke into alertness when she felt a fumbling underneath her nightdress, a knee levering to prise apart her legs. She tried to turn, but David, rubbing himself stiff with one hand, pushed her back down with the other, held her like that, face pressed into her pillow, flesh beginning to sting and split as he jabbed against resisting tightness, his tears falling. With the strength of outrage she reared up and bucked him off and he cried louder then, wet, gulping sobs, his head against her neck, his arms clutched tight around her, and he begged, through tears, he begged her to let him fuck her bottom. Please Bird, let me, please.

There were bloodstains from his scratches on the bed-clothes the next morning, but David, having fallen suddenly and heavily asleep, in mid-sob almost, slept quietly till lunch-time and said nothing when he woke. Without further con-frontation, which she did not want, Jennet had no way of telling whether his was the silence of amnesia or of shame.

And all next day the wind. Late in the afternoon Jennet left the children in Carmela's care and went out into the storm to walk along the seafront to the harbour. Moored boats jostled on the churning water and a snapped-off spar of fishing crate spun in a tangled mess of weed and rope. Even the screaming gulls were undone and silenced by the wind, huddled bale-fully beneath the cover of their wings. Nothing apart from wind and water moved; the fishermen and their families were battened down in smoky rooms, backs turned to the sea. Their cottages too ignored the storm, squatting tightly on the empty streets, doors and windows barred to keep what little warmth there was inside and stop it slinking out like a turncoat in a siege.

The rain began to fall more heavily as Jennet walked up from the harbour to the main square and the ugly yellow church, which alone of all the buildings in the village still shone with a faint light. On an impulse Jennet turned the iron ring set in its door, not expecting it to yield. It swung open so smoothly she almost fell inside.

She had looked into this church before, but had not explored it. It held no intrinsic interest, and besides it was always full of praying crones she would have been embarrassed to disturb. However much she felt at home in Santiago, she still felt like a stranger in its church. In any church, perhaps: she had not stepped far inside one since the day she married David.

That Litton Kirkdale church so intertwined with her childhood. Its scent of stone and dust and damp, each word on every monument known; the smudged vestige of medieval fresco and the later stained glass in its windows as familiar to Jennet as her home. To this day she could recall each carefully stitched hassock, and her fingers trace the stone knight's enlaced fingers, the links of his chain mail and the haunches of the crumbling greyhound at his feet. As a child she had no choice but to be there every Sunday, and it was to while away the tedious hours that she had learned its fabric by heart. She had had a brief burst of fervour, imagining an early death and flights of angels, Lorna having to admit that her daughter was too holy for this world. But later she grew sceptical, and when she saw the failure of faith as a consolation for her father, she lost what little she had left of it. As a young woman she would have said she was indifferent to God.

This foreign church had another scent from the one she knew so well in Litton Kirkdale: not stone nor damp, but old incense, tallow candles, polish and the marsh smell of stale water. Flowers were hard to come by in Santiago in November, but someone had placed a frond of tamarisk on the altar, and there was a pot of white chrysanthemums beside a statue of the Virgin. The fringes of the petals were beginning to turn brown; the flowers had been bought, perhaps, for All Souls the week before.

Jennet closed the door behind her, having seen that there was no one else in the church. The silence was profound. On the altar there were two candles burning as if in readiness for Mass, but no priest whisked from the shadows to question

Jennet's purpose, no old woman veiled in black. Feeling like a trespasser but glad of the shelter and the silence, Jennet went in further and sat down on a bench. Rain slid off her hair and down her face. A cold, salt sting like someone else's tears. She sat until her eyes were used to the darkness pricked by candles; candles on iron stands in front of statues, a small light in a red glass hanging on a bracket by the altar.

It was a mean, impoverished church, no finery on show. Life-sized saints in crudely coloured plaster, paintings too dull to see by candlelight. Jennet crept up the north aisle and stopped before the altar; there was nothing on it but the tamarisk, the candles, a white cloth and a cross. She resisted an obscure impulse to kneel. Off the south aisle there were two side chapels. One was locked and barred as if a prisoner were in it, the other dark but open. Jennet lifted a lit candle from its stand. What it showed her made her start.

A dead man behind glass. Yellow, waxy, emaciated; knee bones, thighbones, ribs. Lying on his back, a frill of lace across his groin. Thorns rammed into his head, blood in trickles on his face, bloody gouges in his side, on his hands and feet. What is this, Jennet wondered, threat or promise, this image that repelled and drew her to it? In the guttering candlelight she could think the man's eyes moved. Suddenly exhausted, she leaned her forehead on the glass and watched it streak with raindrops from her hair.

Jennet Mallow did not attend her first exhibition in the summer of 1953, but in an ecstatic letter Patrick Mann told her what a sell-out it had been. Amazing. Absolutely without precedent. Every drawing and painting sold within the first ten days of opening; *Santiago* to the Tate. Two buyers had almost come to blows over *Still life with child's cup*, and a rich family in Baltimore had bought both *Noon* and *Night*.

Any number of commissions if she wanted; an eyebrow or two raised over *El Muerto* – uncharacteristic of Miss Mallow's work? – but it went anyway to an anonymous collector. The new gallery in Halifax bought *In the Clarity of Water* and three of the drawings, including the self-portrait; its acquisition men were intrigued by Jennet's Yorkshire background. And, finally, all five of the *Window* series were snapped up by one private buyer, a chap called Leonard Kaspar, who was now on at Patrick to fix an introduction to the artist.

Sucked teeth in the old school, predictably enough; old codgers chuntering on about formlessness, meaningless abstraction. But don't forget it was those selfsame arbiters of taste who warned their students off Matisse and Picasso at that first English exhibition, at the V & A in the winter after the war. The newer critics were bowled over. Lewis Delafield, a bright young spark who was fast making quite a splash on the wireless and in the more highbrow newspapers, had written a piece in last month's *Horizon*, the like of which Patrick had never seen. This is how it ended:

Is this young artist's work a mere flash-in-the-pan, fool's gold, a one-off flowering of glory never to be seen again? I don't think so. I think she will reach even greater heights. Keep a watch out for her name. One day, I predict, it will be very famous.

With his letters and reviews and snipped-out pieces from the papers, Patrick Mann also sent banker's drafts. These were what Jennet wanted most. David had sold nothing in the last six months. Nor had he done much work, only some charcoal drawings and a painting of a crow – sad recompense for the hours spent in front of canvas, hours of anxiety, of painting and then painting out. His increasingly black moods loured over Jennet, and there were fewer lulls between them as the months wore on. Winter had come and gone, and Jennet had prayed that David's spirits would lift with spring; and so they did, but then he whirled from gloom to frenzy. Through the bright hot days of May and June David had woken at dawn and shut himself away in the room they called their studio, from which Jennet and the children could hear the sounds of laughter, singing, David talking to himself. He ate almost nothing, but drank deeply, and late at night he'd go for walks alone on the beach, staying out so long that Jennet would often go in search of him for fear that he had drowned.

Nothing calmed him except drink. Even after his night prowls he'd fill another jug with wine and sit hunched over a piece of paper on which Jennet would later see a scribble of crossed lines like tangled ropes, or single words, meaningless without a context. Hue. Nail. Burlap. Fuck. Fuck. Fuck. Then he would want Jennet with him. You're lovely, Bird, he'd say, you're lovely; but his conversation made no sense, and there was a note in it that menaced. When he touched her she was repelled and frightened.

Beautiful David with his dark eyes and his sharp wit and his mouth all stained with purple, his upper lip drawn back in what might have been a smile or a grimace. Spilling wine across his paper, scrawling thick black marks on it. What are you looking at, Bird? he'd ask, shaking her awake if she dared to fall asleep. Falling asleep himself with his glass still in his hand, and Jennet always half on guard in case he slumped across it and it broke. She saw the crescent of sharp glass slice through the taut skin of his cheek. There were too many nights of vigilance for Jennet then: listening for a child's cry, listening for David to come home, and once he was home and had been persuaded into bed, listening for his choking snore and the strange things that he said in sleep. Night after night of lying awake, and worrying alone. For Jennet these were nights of fear, when she thought of what might lie ahead.

By the summer of Jennet's exhibition it was clear they could not stay in Spain. Their happiness in Santiago, their security and future, was predicated on a sense of shared endeavour. With David unreachable, marooned in some dangerously far place, Jennet was too much on her own. She had never asked for more than casual friendship from anyone but him. Now she saw that the sort of friendship or acquaintance she enjoyed in Santiago would not be enough. Without David there was no one she could turn to.

This, she knew, was not only true in Spain. A faltering marriage anywhere enforces isolation. Codes of self-respect and pride bind unhappy wives, and Jennet would never have wished to be the object of friends' pity. She had long tried to hide the quantities that David drank. The man who kept the barrels in the wine store used to tease her about the constant need for refills, but she had learned to tease him back. Otherwise she was furtive, and she did not think the women of the village knew. If their husbands drank too much Jennet did not know it, nor if they made despairing and inconclusive love. She did not confide in them, and they did not share whatever secrets they might have had with her. She did not expect it to be otherwise in England, but at least there'd be less need for secrecy than in this small community, there'd be a wider net of strangers.

If people later wondered why she had not abandoned David to his wine jugs then, and called time on the marriage, Jennet never told them. These were not the sort of questions she would have countenanced. But if she had, what would she have said? That no one who had children without a steady income would even stop to ask? That she would always remember the sea-taste of David's skin, its coldness against hers in the salt water? That she believed, as he did, in his genius?

But whatever her true reasons were, they were overlaid that summer by resentment. It was David's fault they could not stay in Spain. It was because of him that she could not afford the train fare back for her own exhibition. He was so unreliable as a father in any case that she could not have left the children with him. And, worst of all, it was David's disengaged and empty stare that Jennet sometimes saw in her delicate daughter's eyes. Vanessa, at twenty months, was the other reason why they had to leave. Although eventually she'd learned to crawl, she still could not walk and she spoke no words at all. There was no point pretending any longer that she would catch up with her sister: she would never be a normal child. David's obstinate refusal to admit this or to think about the future was fast turning Jennet's feelings of anxiety to anger.

They made a forlorn, bedraggled bunch, Jennet recollected, huddled round their few belongings at the station, shivering in the English air like survivors of an earthquake or a battle. If leaving Santiago was hard enough for Jennet, who had called it home for over three years, it was even harder for her son. Ben knew nowhere else. He could not remember England. In the one act of rebellion that was open to him, for a long time afterwards he would speak only Spanish. Pretending not to understand a single word of English, he forced his mother and father to interpret this new world for him and so preserved his sense of being somewhere else. We'll go back for holidays, Jennet used to tell him, you'll see Paco and Antonio, all your friends, again. But Ben would not be comforted; he was old enough to know by then about promises unkept. What Sarah and Vanessa felt remained a private matter, they were both too young to say, and one of them still speechless.

The Heatons, off the boat train on a chill morning in October with no destination planned. David had agreed to leave Spain quite readily but would not say where he would like to go. Wherever you want, Bird, he said. It makes no difference to me.

But we must choose somewhere, Jennet pleaded. Somewhere with good doctors . . . where we will both have space to work . . .

London, I suppose, then, David said.

Before they looked for somewhere to live they went to visit David's parents on the outskirts of Wolverhampton. It was the first time Jennet had been to Overlea, an ugly Edwardian house with flowerbeds full of blue hydrangeas and on the lawn a monkey-puzzle tree. Knowing David now, she found it difficult to see him as a child in that welter of Staffordshire firedogs and china shepherdesses. So many meaningless, unpleasing objects: occasional chairs and sofa tables, petit-point screens and cache-pôts, brass things, commemorative plates, inscribed silver boxes. Sludgy pictures everywhere: sunsets, engagements at sea, four-legged animals in fields with little boys and hayricks. And David, tall and angular, in an over-feathered nest like a heron brought up by a pair of dabchicks. That Overlea was home to him in many ways, his books and his old clothes still in his room, each horrible ornament familiar and all its routines known, was further re-enforcement of Jennet's sense of separateness from him.

And yet it was arrogant of Jennet to presume that David had left his childhood as far behind as she believed she had left hers. She thought that she'd been purged of bourgeois desires by Santiago and that David had been too. In his parents' house she passionately missed the windows open to the sea, the feel of cool clay tiles beneath bare feet; but he did not mourn them with her nor complain of airlessness and eiderdowns, or the superfluity of meals. He accepted thick cream in his coffee after dinner while she dreamed of blue seawater and the white cube of her room in Spain.

This discrepancy of tastes also made her question the influences there had been on David's art. He was vague about them: there had been a teacher who impressed him during his unhappy years at Lancing, and he had had a year or two at St John's Wood Art School before the onset of the war. It was the war itself, though, that had taught him, David used to say; especially the years he spent at Stalag 383, when he had had to paint with his shaving brush or tufts of his own hair. That's why I like jagged lines so much, he once told Jennet: I got used to seeing things through the zig-zag of barbed wire. But except in jest, or in his nightmares, David did not talk much about the camp. Now, in the stuffy rooms of Overlea, Jennet began to see layers beneath the surface of the man whom she had married. To the young man so hungry at the end of the war that his kneebones and elbows almost broke his skin, the fatty lamb of childhood's lunch-eons must have been remembered as delight. Something of the boy whose growing into manhood was distorted by the cruelty of war would forever remain at home behind the safe red bricks, the interlined dark velvet curtains of the house where he was born. And which, in due course, he'd inherit as the Heatons' only son, together with the dreary paintings that he might mock now but which had been the landscapes of his youth.

Among David's drinking friends, the poets and the artists, there was often talk about the sense of place. About how vital such a sense was to an artist, and the effect that place had on their work. But even after an extravagance of conversation this sense stayed nebulous in concept, difficult to define. Was it inborn, acquired, or wishful thinking only, a nostalgia for the future? Did it exist in the artist's conscious mind or was it a projection of the reader's or the viewer's? Without it was an artist lost for anchor?

Adrift and homeless after leaving Spain, Jennet thought hard about these questions. They were urgent now, not theoretical; their resolution would make all the difference to her work. If she had been alone she might have given chance the right of answer; let herself be blown to harbour haphazard as a seabird in a storm. There were times when she dreamed of freedom, but then she'd feel the trust assumed by a podgy hand slipped into hers, and she'd know she couldn't have it. Not yet, at least, although to herself she made no promises. Meanwhile, where should she make her home? There were landscapes of memory and landscapes of desire. The lilt and thrust of the Yorkshire dales, moss-green fields and the soft russets of dry bracken; lark song and the curlew. Or the outline of sea-grasses incised against an evening sky, spindrift on a Cornish sea taking wing and turning into bird. Or rock and sand and water bleached of all colour by the harshness of the sun, shimmering in the heat-hazed air. All of these and other landscapes known to her imagination only, from other people's pictures, other people's words. Flat expanses of white sand where Celtic saints heard God in wind and water; hot days scented with ripe peaches in the south of France. Colours of bone and pewter or lapis lazuli, chrome yellow. A promontory in the Aegean, her naked body swallow-diving into clear, deep water; the pure blue and white geometry of Greece. Jennet wanted all of these, was greedy for them in her work, for she was well aware that much of its meaning came from her response to stone and water, light.

*

All these places discovered or remembered, but never in her mind's eye London. London in memory was bleak and lightless, filmed with coal-dust; it smelled of beer and cigarettes and reused cheap fat frying. It was not a place for delicate small children or for vast canvases of pure colour. It was the place for David, though, he argued: it had schools where he might teach again, studios, other artists. Reanimated by England and excited, suddenly decisive where before he had been inert, David announced to Jennet that it was time for a new start. I know I've not been altogether satisfactory, he said in a moment of closeness that reminded her she loved him, but I'm going to try my best . . . As soon as I've found somewhere I can work I'm really going to get down to it . . . I'm going to make up for lost time. There was too much sun in Santiago . . . it made my eyes melt in my head.

He arranged for them to stay with Corinne. There she was, rattling around in that great big house with Victor, desperate for company; she would practically pay to have the Heatons. Rent in London was expensive, everything was expensive compared to Santiago, and the money Jennet's sales had made would very soon run out. Jennet felt she must concur. She was being careful not to upset David's new equilibrium, and besides she had no better plans.

Corinne is enthusiastic, hospitable at first, in her tall, thin house off Portman Square. She has made a nursery for the brats, she says, there is a rocking-horse, it is on the topmost floor where they won't be heard. Churlish it would be of Jennet to point out that her children will not play alone, five floors above their mother, they will keep coming down and then they will get in Corinne's way. Jennet fears for Sarah and Vanessa on the stairs. But she holds her peace and tells herself that this stay is for a short time, it is only till they save some money, find a house, get themselves sorted out.

Meanwhile. On their first night Victor uncorks bottles of Château Langoa-Barton and Corinne cooks a dish she calls paella. When they are with David, Corinne is lovely to the children. She flirts with Ben and is only slightly put off by his answering in Spanish; she picks up and hugs Vanessa. For a second Jennet, watching Corinne smiling up at David with Vanessa in her arms, fights the urge to snatch her daughter back. It's the fashionable thing, Corinne announces, living in a commune. It's so middle-class to want a front door of your own. A stupid little patch of garden. So much better to share everything, stop being so grabby and possessive, don't you think?

Share everything? Share your husband? Victor asks. Corinne only laughs and lifts her glass to toast the first evening of their commune, which will soon expand, she says, let's each invite someone we love. Who will you have, David? she asks him in a voice that thrills with challenge, and the candlelight glints off her golden hair.

Later Jennet lies awake on the left-hand side of a double bed in the room that she and David have been given. It is not the room in which they first made love. She can hear the laughter from the kitchen and the scrape of glasses, but she cannot hear her children. In Spain, in the room next to hers, she could hear them breathe. Now she would only hear if they called out very loud. Come and wake me, Ben, if Vanessa cries, she had instructed him, and he promised that he would. But still she cannot trust herself to sleep, and she misses the soft sound of them, and the voices of the sea.

83

Dr Hellier, magnificent in his morning coat, shone little lights into Vanessa's eyes and knocked her knees with hammers. He told Jennet to undress the child, down to her shamefully sodden nappy. The smell of urine filled the room, and Vanessa, wobbly on the doctor's scales, twisted in his hands and howled. Jennet struggled not to howl as well. One more sympathetic smile from Dr Hellier and she would not be able to stop herself from crying. She could so easily collapse on to his hygienically sheeted couch and weep into his pinstriped shoulder. She thought of the slug-trail of mucus she would leave on the dark wool. Tiredness was making her feel ill. Be serious, she told herself. Be brave. Transmit soothing, psychic messages of comfort to your child. But it wasn't easy. She had to choke the tears back while the doctor listened to Vanessa's heart and stuck instruments in her ears.

She is considerably underweight, he said at last. Her muscles are a little weak. Slightly delayed development, perhaps? I can see no other cause for worry.

No other cause for worry? Jennet has attempted to describe Vanessa's vacant eyes to Dr Hellier, and the first general practitioner she saw, but she knows they do not understand her. They think the child is just a little slow. Their examinations of her eyes indicate no malformation; she is merely underfed, quite possibly neglected. Jennet senses their unspoken accusations. Born in the south of Spain, this little girl? Has never seen a doctor? Underdressed for autumn and has had no vaccinations. And her scruffy mother, who looks about nineteen, with her hair scraped back and her suntanned feet in unsuitable old sandals. No permanent address? What Vanessa needs is at least a pint of gold-top milk a day and red meat and cheese and butter. Vitamin supplements. And eggs. And exercise. Make her walk, don't push her in a pram, is Dr Hellier's advice.

What else could Jennet do but nod, put Vanessa's clothes back on, dumbly accept the advice the doctor gave her? To some extent she must admit the truth of Dr Hellier's unvoiced allegations. Like a kindle of wild cats her children have been fed on whatever came to hand: bread and fish and olives, not the milk of Jersey cows or the flesh of their plump calves. Except in the middle of winter, they wore hardly any clothes. And now they glare at her reproachfully, lined up like small, cross animals behind the white-painted balustrade at the top of Corinne's stairs. Three resentful figures diminishing in size, clutching the wooden rails with stoic fists, their faces fading fast to sun-starved pallor. Reproachful because, although they lack the means to say it, they do not want to be in this bare nursery, in Corinne's house, in London. They did not like their grandparents' house near Wolverhampton either. They are penned in, hushed up, told to go away and play, kept quiet. In Corinne's house, especially, they are made to feel like the children of a persecuted people in a country under occupation. As soon as their mother hears Corinne or Victor's footsteps she bundles them upstairs and makes them tidy up all trace of their presence. Their meals are improvised and hurried; they eat things out of tins, because Jennet is embarrassed to cook in Corinne's kitchen. Corinne is always wandering in and out of it, watching Jennet's every move, wincing undisguisedly if one of the children makes a noise or spills food on the floor. She sticks a finger in their food and sucks it with distaste. Between the two of them, Corinne and Jennet, they smoke so many cigarettes the children smell like ashtrays.

So what else could Jennet do but bow her head and hide her fear that it would take much more than full-cream milk to cure Vanessa? In her heart she knew only full-time, dedicated mothering would do it. Vanessa needed hours spent in coaxing her to talk, to eat, to co-ordinate the movements of her fingers. Hours of patience and attentiveness that Jennet did not have. Instead she had a fierce desire for time alone, and space. Time to transform the thoughts and images that flickered in her mind to distract her from the everyday into significance on canvas; space to breathe and move and be absorbed into unlimited light and colour. She loved Vanessa, of course. But how could she explain to Dr Hellier that the worst aspect of the child's ailing was the threat it promised to her work?

Corinne's husband Victor arrives and leaves mysteriously at odd hours of the day and night, in a camelhair overcoat. He is a slight, dark man with a small moustache, much older than his wife. David thinks he has been married before. Both he and Corinne are vague about where Victor goes and what he does, something to do with property, or financial speculation, Corinne says. Certainly it seems he has a lot of money. When Corinne asks, he gives her wads of it, clean notes unfolded from his wallet. And he commissions David to paint two portraits, his and Corinne's, a matching pair to hang over the two fireplaces at either end of the drawing room which runs the whole depth of his house.

These fireplaces are beautiful, late eighteenth century, crisply sculptured, pale grey marble. Victor owns other important things – a Canaletto, a Bösendorfer grand piano – but even so there is in his house a strange impermanence. Some of the rooms are still as empty as they were when Jennet first saw them in 1947; bare floorboards and paint flaking off the walls. Others, although opulently furnished, have the air of a stage set or the backdrops a photographer might use. It comes as a surprise to feel the solidness of the gilded chairs and the polished fruitwoods underneath one's fingers. Restless Corinne taps in and out of these grand rooms in her high heels, but never finds engrossing occupation. Nothing holds her attention long. There are no calls on her time. Refugees from Poland clean and maintain her house, otherwise during the day visitors seldom come. Corinne describes herself as an artist and has a room equipped as a studio, but Jennet never sees her work. She has offered her studio to David for a time, until he can find one of his own.

It has not occurred to Corinne to provide Jennet with a space to work, and Jennet would not expect one. She could never concentrate in that dark house where Corinne's nerves jangle and disturb the air. But Victor has acknowledged that Jennet is a painter. You like art, I think? he asks her late one night. Well, come and look at this. He guides her upstairs to the room he calls the library, although in it there are hardly any books. There is a desk, though, Victorian mahogany, and on it a clerk's reading light. Victor switches the light on and takes a leather folder out of a drawer. He spreads the folder open flat and with a gesture of courteous invitation lets Jennet see the drawing it contains. Pen and ink, probably sixteenth century, painstaking and very detailed, two naked women and a man, one of the women busy with her tongue, and the hilt of the man's penis visible as it enters her from behind. Its explicitness is a sudden shock. His face distorted in the uplight of the lamp, Victor leers at Jennet. Very valuable it must be, don't you think? I won it in a bet.

We can't stay here any longer, David. Please. Please. We must find somewhere else. We're not even trying . . .

Never mind the sound of Victor's laugh when Jennet excused herself from him that night in the library, trying to look broad-minded and *mondaine*. Never mind the rainy afternoons trailing grumpy children up and down the Serpentine or round the brontosaurus at the Natural History Museum for the hundredth time. The difficulties of getting Ben into a school without any fixed address, the impossibility of controlling effervescent Sarah in a house inimical to two-year-olds. The evenings of too many drinks with Corinne; the nights spent straining to distinguish a child's cry from the creak and snap of joints and pipes and the constant undertone of London noise; the very early breakfasts which she tried to make the children eat in silence before Corinne came downstairs in cashmere and resentment. If all of these were not reason enough and more to leave, there was the sheer waste of time. David had started work on Victor's portrait, but Jennet felt she was suspended between two phases of her life, in parenthesis, inexplicably powerless, waiting for something else to happen. This sense of helplessness was frightening. She needed to regain control, but David, in partnership with Corinne, was peculiarly determined. When Jennet begged him to come house-hunting with her, he told her not to bore him with her worries.

It was Patrick Mann who came to Jennet's rescue once again. Ludicrous, he said, with his eye to the main chance, ridiculous, absurd. That she should be back in the land of the living but not doing any work? When he had umpteen people baying at his door for her, including, and especially, Leonard Kaspar? Well, Patrick couldn't babysit exactly, nor find Jennet a house, but he could lend her the money for a long lease on a studio, and he even knew the perfect one. In an adorable Arts-and-crafty block just by the park in Battersea. No more excuses, darling Jennet. Off to the grindstone with you, now!

But first she took her children up to Yorkshire. She had

not seen her parents in a long time: they had never visited her in Spain. Richard Mallow was on the point of retiring from the living at Litton Kirkdale, and therefore would have to leave the rectory. His parish council, after years of muted grumbling and complaints, had at last managed to be shot of him; his replacement was a younger, keener man. This, then, was Jennet's final chance to show her children the house where she grew up, and besides it was almost Christmas. She could not face the prospect of Christmas in Corinne's house.

People age abruptly, as instantly as children grow. For years they do not change at all and then suddenly, overnight, they seem to shrivel and their hair thins and their skin cleaves closer to their bones but leaves its surplus hanging in weary folds. Jennet hardly recognised her father when he met her and the children at Leeds Station. Until then she had still seen him with a child's eye: tall and broad enough to stop the light from coming in if he stood before a window, commanding in the grimmest of his moods. Even as a failing priest he had had an equivocal authority and had kept something of his military past. Now he had shrunk to half his size and seemed scarcely any taller than his daughter. His hands trembled all the time, and when he spoke he dribbled.

Richard, in December 1953, was sixty-six years old, Lorna twelve years younger. If her husband had aged shockingly, prematurely, she had clung to girlishness. Her hair was blonde still, if artificially, her lipstick crimson and her face smooth, except for the fine cracks round her eyes and the tightening when she smiled.

Jennet back in Litton Kirkdale, in the same bed, in the same room of her childhood. On a shelf an eyeless teddy, a row of children's books: *The Wonder Book of Nature, A Hundred Best Animals, A Child's Garden of Verse.* The hearthrug on which she'd wiped the charcoal from her fingers, the headboard against the wall where her drawings first took shape, the casement window opening on to a view of fields, and beyond them in the distance the sweet rise of the hills. Staying in that childhood room returned her to the state of being a child. She felt once more the old admixture of boredom and excitement, the uneasy sense of marking time on the threshold of a new world, exasperated that it was so difficult to cross. Dependent on her mother once again, having to comply with her house rules, to ask permission for a drink, Jennet's fellow feeling for her children deepened. Then she saw how hard it was to have no voice, no say in the decisions that would shape one's life, no power over future choices. Many of childhood's choices are trivial, of course – damson jam or golden syrup – and can safely be left to mothers, but others change the course of life. She had not asked Benedict in advance if he minded leaving Spain, she had taken his helpless co-operation as a given. But if the Heatons had stayed in Spain much longer, Ben and his sisters would have gone to school there, become completely Spanish.

This new access of sympathy made more comprehensible the listlessness of the past two months. As if the icy moorland wind had blown away the fog that had engulfed her, Jennet saw where she was going wrong. She had to put an end to helpless drift. Adulthood, she realised, was not absolute, but usually contingent on the point at which a person stood. As Richard Mallow aged so startlingly he became less of an authoritative father and more like a needy child. In relation to her children Jennet was grown-up, or she should be; but until then she had preserved a child's sense of destiny, a belief in the world's beneficence, in the story's happy ending. Something would turn up; out of the forest's unending depths an errant knight would ride with the key to a new world bolted to his armour.

In the realisation of her children's utter dependence, and her own concomitant and wholly adult obligation, was the crux of Jennet's problem. Freedom from personal obligation was in the world's eyes vital to an artist who intended to achieve the highest, the most transcendental of ideals in their work. It was that freedom which David Heaton had conferred upon himself. A freedom which was essentially childish by nature but without the drawbacks of a child's powerlessness. David could never be entirely adult if he were to succeed as an artist. So was this the stark choice Jennet faced: responsibility to the people she had brought into the world or truth to her vocation?

In many ways a child's faith is justified. Considering the lilies of the field is not entirely futile as a philosophy of life. Until then things *had* turned up in Jennet's world: scholarships and prizes, marriage. Corinne had shortcomings as a host, but she had saved the family from homelessness. Patrick Mann, a somewhat portly and improbable chevalier, had ridden to Jennet's rescue twice. Nevertheless. A lily does not last, despite the beauty of its flower. That Christmas time in Litton Kirkdale, Jennet, in her childish bed, put aside her childish things. Until then she had seen the years to come as if in a glass darkly; now she saw them clearly, cold-eyed. No one would be there to hold her hand. She could not rely on David or on anyone else. She was on her own but encumbered by her millstones, and unlike the great artists of the past, almost all of them male, she had no choice but to shoulder them, to drag them with her with into the material of art. She used to dream of alchemy, but that was in another time. She did not imagine then the rawness of the stuff she would have to transmute later into gold.

Christmas Day at Litton Kirkdale. Holy Communion at eight o'clock. A handful of parishioners, Ben already sick with disappointment and anticipation, the little girls restive and wriggling on their mother's lap. The nativity of Our Lord, or the birthday of Christ, a babe lying swaddled in a manger, a dead man behind glass. In the words of the Epistle, 'They shall all wax old as doth a garment; and as a venture shalt thou fold them up', and Jennet listened to her father's voice with a new quiver in it. Praise be to God for peace, he said, especially in Korea; but he sounded doubtful – he had prayed for peace for sixty years, but somewhere there was always war. If the world's heartbeat were suddenly to stop, Richard had written in his notebook, I wouldn't call for it to be restarted. There has been altogether too much pain.

Richard's parishioners would never know how the voices of the dead still spoke to him, as they still spoke in different accents to his son-in-law. Their pestering had tired him out, eroded all his faith, and perhaps it was that loss, as if the faith had weight and substance, which explained his dwindling size. With his size he had also lost the shadowy prestige he had once had as rector of the parish; now after far too many doomed and blustering attempts to hide his fears, he was more of a laughing-stock. As he slowly slid down the steps of social desirability Lorna slid down with him, clawing as she went, frantically trying to hold on. Hence the blonde hair and the garish lipstick; keeping a brave face on it, she would have called it, with a jaunty, brittle laugh.

There was not much left to get her nails into. Anything that Richard Mallow had inherited from his father had long ago been spent or lost in ill-advised investments; now he had only his stipend, which one day soon would shrivel to a pension. If she did not keep on her brave face, Lorna would very quickly crack at the thought of the years ahead, eking out a life on that exiguous sum. As it was, the lid on her emotions was not difficult to lift. Some she would not admit to: frustration, for example, even though it stripped her bones. But anger was a different matter. Anger was a bright emotion, brave and vivifying, and Lorna let hers show. Like a child, she stamped her foot because she had never had the things she wanted. Her life had always been unfair. And like a child she still believed in the rainbow's crock of gold, the tall and handsome stranger, the potential in her life for total change. While she waited for the change to come she turned a blind eye to the day-to-day realities that stared her in the face.

Brown stains in the lavatory, silverfish in the kitchen, a constant faint smell of gas. The house at Litton Kirkdale had always been dark and dusty, but now the dust was mixed with grease. A finger brushed along a lintel would remove a fat caterpillar of grey fluff. Peggy the housekeeper had left years before and had not been replaced. I was not brought up to cook and clean, Lorna used to say, with the hot sting of tears that always came when she thought about Jamaica. But she made an effort of sorts that Christmas Day, for the sake of her grandchildren. Cigarette clenched tightly in the corner of her mouth, she leaned over vats of Brussels sprouts and mashed potato and she got up at crack of dawn to consign a goose to the temperamental kitchen range.

How pitifully few they must have seemed, Jennet realised when she looked at her family around the table and en-visioned the Christmases when she had not been there. Richard and Lorna and Barbara Mallow, keeping up the mask of cheerfulness as they watched the pale blue flames of burning brandy struggling feebly to compete with daylight, even at the dull end of December. At least she had multiplied their number, however little joy she'd brought. Ben, with a new sense of occasion and, in the absence of his father, struggling manfully with incinerated goose. Sarah, round-faced, tolerant, happy with whatever she was given. And Vanessa, who in the few days of her being there had formed

93

an unexpected bond with Richard. At the station he had made to take from her mother, struggling with suitcases and children. Daddy, she won't go to anyone, Jennet had warned; but Vanessa had stretched out her arms to him and when he held her she was quiet.

Will there be snow? Ben had asked, again and again, before they went to Yorkshire. There had been no snow in London yet, only rain and smog, but he knew about it in the abstract and Jennet could well understand how much he yearned for the whole grey world to be transformed into a magic field of white. The force of want in children is so strong that it is almost unendurable, and what Ben had wanted ever since he'd learned that it existed was an untouched expanse of snow. Describing it to him reminded Jennet of the sound-lessness of snow, its mysteriously silent coming in the night, of waking to an unmistakably different light.

She had not been able to paint for months, not since anxiety about David and the business of leaving Spain had driven away every thought of work. Returning to the land-scape of her childhood restored her vision. She had not known before how much it mattered, Litton Kirkdale, as a place.

There was no snow for Ben that winter. But on the day before Jennet and the children left for London they woke to sunshine and a frost so deep it had stopped the river and turned the reeds into saw-blades edged with ice. Jennet took Ben on the longest walk the five-year-old could manage, uphill to the tarn where she used to swim in secret when she was a girl. A long climb above the limit of the fields and the line of loose-stone walls, across and down a little, slithering on icy mud, through bracken stems and bramble thorns to where the tarn was, glacier-glinting in its spinney of leafless ash. Be careful, Jennet told her son, the ice is thin and the water deep, and she held onto his hand as he stamped his small boot on the frozen water's edge and the sheet ice cracked and splintered into diamonded spars.

Ice. Not the deep Antarctic sort, crystalline, blue-tinged, but thin ice, nothing much more than a membrane separating the water from the air. Ice that comes so suddenly it seems to seize the moment – arresting on the seashore a wave just on the point of curl, imprisoning the rising bubbles in a mountain tarn. How to show that thinness, that colourlessness full of colour, the way that ice in sunshine is both mirror and source of light? White light. Purity and danger.

Jennet Mallow's paintings of the London period from 1954 are, unlike the earlier works in Spain, unrelated in direct ways to the place around her. Jennet was never a true artist of the city. After the barren months of the past year she began to work quite cautiously, proceeding step by step in her new studio at Battersea like a convalescent learning once again to walk. The frosted tarn was her first subject. She did not try to paint until her muscles had remembered drawing; the preliminary studies are in silverpoint on pale grey and pale blue tinted paper. Not that they are tentative; indeed they show her confidence, for silverpoint precludes all second chances. Once on the page it cannot be erased.

When she began to paint with oils again, the brushwork was equally confident, but paradoxically her subjects over the following three years suggest a narrowing of horizons. *Pool in Winter*, a painting of the tarn on canvas, was followed by two further studies, both on wood. The first is still recognisably a depiction of the subject; the second, *Ice on Water*, is a breakthrough. With it Jennet had discovered how oil colours rich in resin could be combined with layers of tinted glaze to create a luminosity so rich that one might think the paintings in a pitch-black room would give off their own light.

Ice on Water is built up of wash upon thin wash of translucent white, titanium white, bluish-grey and the faintest tinge of manganese cerulean. Beneath the surface is the ghost of what lies under frozen water: the bubbles and the weed and the small creatures in suspended animation. Its triumph is the way in which it is both faithful to its inspiration, a painting that is clearly of a place observed at a particular moment, and magically abstract: luminescence, whiteness, an image of the living world holding its icy breath.

That extraordinary and original achievement should by right have given birth to a whole line of radiant paintings, exuding calm and happiness. But Jennet turned her back on it, and her next work was the first of a very different series. Oddly, it was based on the same vision of the frozen pool, but in it the leafless trees become the focus. *Spinney* is again in oils on wood, but here the translucent water is beset by thorny branches which begin to overwhelm the light. In the second of the *Spinney* paintings the branches form a closer mesh, and in the third the ice is visible only as a gleam beneath a thick cross-hatching of blue-black.

There was no view from Jennet's studio, but she was not complaining; it was a relief to have it and to work. And Patrick Mann was right that it was near a park. Near the river too, where it runs between Battersea and Chelsea, and the river gave Jennet respite from dirty brick and meagre streets. Often she would stand on Albert Bridge and watch the water; she did not love London any more than she had when she left it for Santiago, but she was older now, and stoic.

On her return from Yorkshire, armed with her new firmnesses of purpose, Jennet set about the task of finding somewhere to live. Portman Close was too far away from

Battersea to go to and from with children, and she was in any case determined to claim David back from Corinne. David had not wanted to go to Litton Kirkdale for Christmas, and she had not minded that, she understood; but she found to her surprise that she missed him, and the children missed him, while they were away. Perhaps it really was the fault of Spain, she thought, his unhappiness. Spain with its black edges and its blood reds, its stark, harsh colours, its Goya-ghosts, the sharp blades in the belly of the bull; Spain which had resurrected his memories of war. He will get better now, she thought, back in the grey ambiguities of England, and we will be all right again, as far as any two people, separate souls and separately ambitious, can ever be. It was his wryness and his ironies she needed, his ways of making her laugh. These and the deep warmth in his hands, the recipro-cal warming of his body. His loving of her was not every-thing it might be, but it was something: without it Jennet was afraid there'd be no love at all.

Jennet had no sense of London as a whole then: she knew one small part of Hammersmith, the streets in Maida Vale around the hostel where she lived when she was a student, the neighbourhood of Kensington next to the art school. Now, searching for a house, she tried to learn it better, criss-crossing the city alone like a determined ant, from Highgate to Lewisham, Marylebone to Chiswick. Street after street of grubby houses, in some of which the damage done by bombs was still unmended. Margaret Metcalf, her old friend, had bought a house in Barnsbury with Richard Benjamin, and thought Jennet should move there too; there was no better place to live, she said. But the north of London was a long way from Battersea, and Jennet felt safer when she was closer to the river. In the end she found a little house at the furthest extreme of Chelsea, in the area called World's End. She liked the name especially: bathetic, apocalyptic. There was not much else to recommend the place, which, in the 1950s, was depressed and down-at-heel. The house, in Poole's Lane, was a typical early nineteenth-century workman's cottage, brick-built, semi-detached, three tiny rooms upstairs, two, not much larger, down. But, unusually, it had a bathroom behind the kitchen, and there was a square of garden. The studio was a few minutes' walk away and, most importantly, the rent was cheap.

Later, when the prices asked for Jennet's work had soared beyond the reach of ordinary purses and David's fame was also at its peak, no one would have credited the extent of their impoverishment then, even with allowance for Jennet's overstatement of it. It lasted for a year or two at most, that time of worry, when to Jennet it seemed that the next pair of children's shoes, the next meal even, was a constant problem, but it left a deep groove on her way of thinking. Money would always be a source of anxiety to Jennet, even when she had more of it then she could ever use. In reality, her children would not have starved in their little house at World's End; David's parents would have lent them money, even Lorna Mallow, always penny-pinching, would have intervened. In fairness to Jennet though, it must be remembered that the income of an artist is erratic at the best of times, and materials are expensive but essential: without them there can be no work.

David never saw the point of exchanging Corinne's spacious rooms for the poky little Poole's Lane house, but he did not trouble to argue the toss, and Jennet was encouraged by this absence of resistance. Whatever keeps you quiet, Bird, he said. She had been right, she hoped, that David would be happier in England; he was not looking quite so gaunt, and he was woken less by dreams. In the spirit of joint enterprise he returned to his old job at Stockwell, teaching painting four afternoons a week, thereby ensuring some steady income. The job also brought renewed contact with other artists. In the meantime he would go on using Corinne's studio, where he was busy on her and Victor's portraits. Several patrons from the past were swimming back into his vision, and his dealer, Ivan Whitehouse, was eager to see more of David's work.

The pieces of Jennet's new London life were beginning to fall one by one into their places, and a rhythm established. Ben started at a local school, still doggedly monolingual but succumbing slowly and against his will to the presence of another language all around him. He began by conceding he could understand it, and finally he answered: by the autumn he forgot he ever could speak Spanish. The twins were still too young for school, and private nurseries too costly, so Jennet took them with her to the studio, pushing Vanessa, pulling Sarah, up and down Lot's Road and Cheyne Walk and Albert Bridge. Once there, she could amuse Vanessa easily enough with Farley's rusks and coloured crayons; but Sarah was a small, destructive whirlwind, tearing paper, spilling paint, chewing precious brushes. As soon as she was making money Jennet hired the daughter of a neighbour, a sweet-natured girl called Mabel Harris, to come with her to the studio and guard Sarah. After that it was much easier to work.

Was it some prophetic impulse that stopped Jennet selling *Ice on Water*, even though she needed money at the time? She sold the first two studies of the tarn and the *Spinney* paintings easily through Patrick Mann. Leonard Kaspar, who had bought all five *Window* paintings at the 1953 show, bought *Spinney II* and told Patrick that as he was going to be Miss Mallow's foremost collector, it was time they met. He invited them both to dinner at the Dorchester, and when

Patrick told him Jennet was married, he extended the invitation to David too.

Leonard Kaspar with his narrow head straight off a figure on a wall in an Egyptian tomb. Crescents of black hair streaked back and parted in the middle, gleaming and reflecting light like his patent-leather evening shoes. Shining bars of black at top and base and in between the liquorice matt black of his dinner jacket and its silk lapels. The precise parabola of his bow-tie and, as immaculate in contrast as the clean keys of a new piano, his blindingly white shirt. His eyes black too, and glittering; he had a small moustache.

If David ever owned evening dress he had long since lost it, but he did still have a suit. Jennet Mallow looked at them, the three men with her at the table: Horus-headed Kaspar; tubby, genial Patrick, also in evening clothes, and in rubicund enjoyment of Kaspar's choice of claret; David in his veteran dark jacket. David's face pale and beautiful and angular; Kaspar's smooth and sallow; Patrick's pink and round. If I were to paint them, Jennet thought, this is what they would look like: three verticals in shades of white and grey and black, three ovals in ivory, rose madder, ochre, and the table, white and silver in candlelight.

She will never paint them; she knows that at the time, they are not gathered together for a portrait but for a transaction of another kind. Still, the painter in her narrows her gaze, squints to get the scene and its purpose into vision. With her painter's eye she strips fold on fold of fabric off the men to assess the underlying structure. David's loose-limbed body she visualises as intimately as her own, Patrick's little Buddha belly was on unembarrassed display when he floundered in the sea with Ben at Santiago. She has a notion Kaspar's skin will be all one shade, undifferentiated, tidily pinned on to an even layer of flesh, wrapped around his neat, light bones. There would be a yellow tinge to him, his toenails, and the sparsest stipple of black hair around his penis.

White bowls of clear consommé, dead game birds under silver lids, champagne later in a dewy, silver bucket, these are not the props that Jennet is used to. In Corinne's house the grandiose goes hand in hand with the haphazard; she and Victor are like thieves who, having stolen someone else's silver piece by piece, will never have a set of matching spoons. They do not dress their table with starched linen, their meals are improvised, perfunctory and unpredictable; the necessary tedium of food obstructs the long parade of bottles. There was silver at the rectory and silver of a dreary sort in wartime Oxford, but however often it was polished it was always overlaid in Jennet's mind with a trace of tarnish.

Although these surface sheens are novelties to Jennet she recognises them for what they are: Leonard Kaspar's tools of barter. She is as much for sale as the grouse that they are eating, and the glitter is a compliment, Kaspar's way of saying that Jennet is worth a fortune. Other men in black and white bow and hover around her, solicitously lifting silver lids, pouring wine and water; they are the buyer's accomplices, his conspirators in trade. Buyer and dealer, Leonard Kaspar, Patrick Mann, drawing up the most civilised of contracts. Up and down their hands go in a rhythm, holding long-stemmed glasses, their knives glint brightly in the light. They talk of provenance and ownership. Kaspar has refused a Braque. But the prize of his collection, he tells Jennet, are her *Window* paintings; he would not exchange a single one of them for even the most beautiful Cézanne. What he has in mind, he says, when the evening is over, what he hopes for, longs for, is for Jennet to accept a new commission. He has acquired a house in Mount Street, it is bare and lightless, would Jennet please, please come and paint directly on its walls? My wife is not a decorator, David points out hotly, but his indignation is considerably undermined by the quantities of Kaspar's alcohol he has drunk. No, no, murmurs emollient Patrick, but Raphael, the great Florentines, the ceiling of the Sistine Chapel . . . Kaspar names a sum of money then, and Patrick and David both say yes to it, as one.

How long does it take to peg out a load of laundry, having washed it first by hand, and then to bring it in again when a morning's hesitating sunshine has given way to rain? How many hours of a woman's day are swallowed up by washing, cooking, cleaning, getting children dressed and feeding them, walking them to school, collecting them, scrubbing mud off carrots, scouring grease off pans, swabbing down a lavatory floor? As many as there are, perhaps, by the time she's fed the adults of the household too and shopped for food and planned it. Ten minutes queuing at the butcher's, longer at the bank, a slow walk home with heavy bags and dawdling children, and then there are the other things; please would you send your child to school dressed either as a duckling or a rabbit.

Jennet did all these household tasks when she first moved back to London, with no one else's help. They seemed to take much longer than they ever had in Spain. Something in the London air, particles of smoke perhaps, or atmospheric pressure, weighed her down, she thought, made her move more slowly. She stumbled through the day like a deep-sea diver on an ocean floor. Up at dawn, or what passed for dawn; it was hard to tell the time on days when the morning sky and the midday sky and the evening sky were all the same, the washed-out colour of whey. Vanessa was always the first to wake, but Sarah the first to clamber out of bed and start out on the trail of cheerful havoc that she would follow until her springs of energy gave out and she fell asleep abruptly, almost where she stood, or in mid-mouthful, her head tumbling to her plate.

But there was, even in the hardest day, the promise of reward. As the diver groping through the murk sustains himself with images of pirate's gold shining though the dark bones of a shipwreck, so Jennet clung to the prospect of the time she set aside for work. She used to play a private game: points scored for no mishap or time saved by some cleverly cut corner; five points if Sarah did not spill her drink, eight if Vanessa's sheet was dry, ten if the preparation of a stew today would do for soup tomorrow. An extra minute earned for every point, on a good day a whole hour won to add to those she let herself spend painting. Mabel Harris was part of this private deal as well; the money Jennet paid her justified if it bought time for work, which in its turn would earn enough to generate more time. That the argument was circular she knew, but she saw no way to break it, unromantic and prosaic as it was. The notion of an artist starving willingly for art might make good fiction, but it was never Jennet's. Jennet was a realist, saddled with three children who had not chosen to be born and must be fed and clothed and shod, and a husband who did not always want to share the burden. These were not ideal conditions for an artist. But, however sorely it was tried, Jennet kept her faith in herself, quietly, doggedly and in the meantime cooked three meals a day and cleaned her little house, painting in every spare second she could find.

These pressures on her time, and on her working space, were the reason she agreed to Leonard Kaspar's proposition. At first she was reluctant to accept it, unwilling to be branded as, at best, a mural painter, at worst, an interior designer. In the end, though, Patrick's powers of persuasion ('think Vanessa Bell, Giotto') and the lure of Kaspar's cash – an immense, absurd amount by Jennet's standards, five hundred pounds a painting – overcame her scruples at the end of a long and dreary March when the sun had disdained London completely and all three children had been ill with measles. Sickroom days and broken nights, poor Vanessa forfeiting whatever small reserves of strength she'd gained. The smog-stained London rain for hours on end, no sign of spring yet in the city, and the sky abjuring blue, sticking to a palette of slate and pewter, coal-dust, smoke. Then the thought of somewhere far away from children, a tall house with expanses of white wall, became alluring. If she were to work there, she imagined, she would be connected over centuries of time to those craftsmen painters who, secluded in their quiet spaces, drew saints and devils, God and sinners, on church and chapel walls. They may not have worked in peace, of course – all the village might have come to watch them, and small children stuck their fingers in the pigments, messed up the wet lime-plaster – but Jennet liked to think of them as akin to wandering hermits, carrying the secrets of their craft with them from place to place and leaving behind like a benediction their own visions of their universe: sky and earth and hell and heaven, each element in its rightful place. Visions in colour to light worlds so often monochrome; how glorious their blues and reds and yellows in a fenland village deep in winter. Did a tired woman of the village slip from time to time into the church to get away from clods of mud and turnips, to dream before the painter's scenes of child and mother, blue-robed and gold-haloed? Jennet remembered the fragments of fresco which remained in the church of Litton Kirkdale, almost indecipherable now, but which had once conveyed a message, however crude or simple.

In Jennet's mind as well, when she was thinking about

Kaspar's invitation, was a friend's description of the Chapel of the Rosary at Vence – the great culminating project of Matisse, consecrated four years ago. The death of Matisse himself, earlier that winter, had saddened the English artists, even the many who had never met him, as he had been a beacon for so long, acknowledged as a sorcerer of colour all their working lives. Jennet knew his chapel paintings were on white ceramic, not on plaster, but her imagination was fired anyway by the idea of the blank white space Matisse had had to fill. Virgin walls which, once they had submitted to the artist's command of form and colour, were miraculously changed from mere stone to something sacred. In Matisse's chapel there were other elements as well – the ultramarine and bottle green and lemon yellows of the stained-glass windows, the black-and-white habits of the nuns, the sound of voices praying – but all these together formed a whole which had its origin in the artist's mind. It was the ultimate creation, Jennet thought, a consecrated space where there was only emptiness before.

In no obvious way did Kaspar's house bear any likeness to a chapel. It was immensely tall but narrow, spliced between two earlier houses, and its staircase ran up the centre, leaving on each half-landing a windowless structure of wall. The banisters were painted black and a modern chandelier hung like an avalanche in the hall. Kaspar took Jennet straight up to his bedroom when she arrived for their first meeting to discuss his plan. (Is he a white slave trader? David had joked. Later it turned out that he was a banker, and Corinne's husband knew him, but David's calumny persisted, and among their friends Kaspar was called the Slaver.)

This is what I want to show you, Kaspar said, opening the door. A room with sea-grey walls and a charcoal carpet, an enormous bed austerely covered with a dark grey blanket, three beautiful sash windows punctuating one wall and the others bare except that above the bed hung Jennet's second *Spinney* painting. There was nothing else in the room, no books or clothes, no mirror, but at the foot of the bed a white marble column, curved like a swan's neck perhaps, or like a phallus.

I re-did the room for you, Kaspar said. It was blue before. There were more things in it. Now I just want you. And the Brancusi. I did the dining room as well. Would you like to see it?

The dining room was white: white-painted panelling, full-length white curtains, a long table of the palest wood and, set in the alcoves of the panels, Jennet's five *Window* paintings.

They look well, don't they? I had the panelling made especially.

Jennet was not used to revisiting her paintings; she looked at them with fondness, but also with respect, as if they were old friends, inconsiderately lost. They brought back a rush of memory – the salt taste of the sea, the outlines of a grapevine, dark green on a sapphire sky – and with it, a sudden need to be back in Spain again.

Is there sunlight in this room? she asked.

No. I keep the curtains drawn because the windows face an ugly wall. That's why I hung your paintings here. They are the real windows.

It is very flattering. All the effort you have made to hang them . . .

Exquisite possessions demand an effort, Kaspar said. Come and see the rest.

Leonard Kaspar had a Giacometti and two Mondrians, a late Cézanne and a painting by someone Jennet had never heard of, a Russian, Kaspar said, dead some twenty years.

Malevich. No one knows much about him, but there is a superb example in New York.

Jennet looked at this painting for a long time. It showed a black square slightly tilted on its axis, occupying three-fifths of its frame; the surface of the paint was slightly crazed, and there was something in the painting that profoundly moved her, although she could not have said then what it was.

I buy things and I sell them, Kaspar said. I don't want my collection to be static, with the exception of the pictures you are going to paint for me, on my staircase walls. They will be immovable, you see. And permanent.

Did you have something particular in mind? Jennet asked. She had worried about this. It would be strange enough to work to a commission without having the subject of the work dictated too. On the other hand she had no experience of working to architectural constraints, and she was intimidated by the challenge.

No, I don't think so, Kaspar said. Except that on the fifth floor I would like a full-length figure. Of a woman. Nude.

Any woman? Someone you know?

Well, said Kaspar with the merest hesitation. I thought a self-portrait. I would like it to be you.

How seductive to be promised permanence. What artist could resist indelibility? Jennet knew that Kaspar's was a hollow promise, that at any time his walls could be re-plastered or removed, but even so there *was* a promise. A wall is much more lasting than a piece of canvas. And the old technique of painting walls, with watercolour on fresh plaster, fresco, is more lasting than the modern methods: oil or tempera as a surface can easily be scraped away, but fresco pigments sink into the wall. When the new plaster dries it

107

sets rock-solid, and the paint dries with it, an integral part, inseparable.

Jennet and David's friends advised her against fresco. London is not Tuscany, they said, here it is too wet. And fresco is too complicated – all those scale drawings, and the plastering is difficult – but Jennet was intrigued by it and characteristically determined. Thrilling, the thought of being part of a continuous tradition reaching back through thousands of years and onwards to paintings as yet unimaginable in the years ahead. In the British Library she read about the history of fresco painting, how the Minoans decorated their domestic walls, how in Etruscan tombs the long dead still celebrate at funeral feasts, how in Pompeii the art survived its burial by dust. There, in the house of Julia Felix, a glass bowl full of grapes and pomegranates glows; in the Villa of the Mysteries a naked woman dances, while another, with a beautiful, impassive face, looks on as a kneeling third is scourged. Lampblack, bone black, green earth, Egyptian blue, the colours of the Roman fresco palette; native oxides, native earth.

Kaspar gave her a free hand. She had tried to coax him. Tell me, she had said. If not somebody special, then somewhere? Somewhere you remember as a child? He had smiled at that. I doubt if the places I knew when I was growing up could be described as picturesque, he said, but he would not be drawn. So Jennet invented a landscape for him, a dream-like place such as might conceivably be seen from the windows of an eighteenth-century house, although not one in the middle of Mayfair. In the foreground the balustraded parapet of a formal garden, parkland beyond, a winding river, and in the distance low, rounded hills, stylised in the manner of early Renaissance painting. She would paint the same scene, she decided, on each of the first three landings, but in them the time would change from dawn to evening through midday. Kaspar looked a little doubtful when she described this scheme, worried about being short-changed maybe, paying for three versions of one painting. But this way there will be consistency, she told him. Otherwise there'd just be a muddle of random scenes. My idea is that the pictures will be like windows on the stairs. So each must give on to the same view. But I also want you to go back and forth through time as you go up and down the stairs; it will be dusk outside your bedroom, morning when you come down to the front door.

The technical problems were engrossing. Jennet had never worked on such a scale before. *Santiago*, her largest painting so far, was over seven feet wide, but Kaspar's walls were twelve feet high and the widths uneven. She had to make a separate cartoon, or preliminary drawing, for each wall. Pushing aside everything inessential in her studio, she unrolled great sheets of decorator's paper and tacked them to the floor. Now, kneeling on her work, or crawling over it, she began to inhabit it in a new way. The act of drawing at an easel or a table implied a distance, however small – the length of an arm – but in the course of clambering on her drawing she came closer to it, as if she herself were in the landscape. In that way she began to feel the whole space of the drawings, and was able to lay them out with a better understanding of the viewpoints. A painting hung in a gallery or drawing room is usually looked at from a stationary point, but the viewer of her frescoes would be nearing them from every step, until they came face-to-face with them at the turning of the stairs. In such circumstances the perspective and the scale were hard, and it took Jennet a long time to get them right.

She could not afford to get them wrong. The medium she had chosen for its permanence was not at all forgiving, and would not leave much scope for second thoughts.

Having assembled her preliminary sketches, Jennet drew them all again to actual size in outline on detail paper, the strong yellow paper engineers and architects use for maps and plans. Then she made separate drawings, also to scale, of each square yard of these plans. A yard, she calculated, was as much as she could realistically hope to paint in one day's span. When all the drawings were done, she perforated their outlines with a metallic cutting wheel. Each one was rolled and numbered. She also painted colour charts and labelled them, as she knew she would be working against time.

The next stage was the preparation of the walls. Crucially, they were well above ground level and not damp. A surveyor confirmed that they were sound, and a builder hacked off the existing plaster back to the original bare brick. After the brick had been washed with water and a wire brush, the landing walls had to be re-plastered to the exacting specifications for correctly executed fresco. Here Jennet had a stroke of luck. Talking about the project one day to her old Kensington friend, Dermot, she discovered that his brother-in-law was a master craftsman in plaster. Roddy MacNamara had learned his trade in Dublin restoring Georgian cornices and roses, was looking for a change, would be open-minded. He needed to be: a wall is normally plastered to be as dense and to dry as rapidly as possible, but a wall prepared for fresco must stay porous. Roddy had to un-learn his accustomed rhythms, the long, graceful stroke of his right arm, his float-ing of the surface, and throw plaster on the wall instead, spreading it with pounding thumps.

From the beginning Roddy always understood the point. During the time they worked together in the house on Mount Street he and Jennet were a dedicated team, alternat-ing between them the roles of master and apprentice, scien-tist and technician, high priest and acolyte. Jennet had always loved the material processes of art, the feel and smell and textures, and this shared endeavour required more practice of material skill than most. Her research had necessarily included the technical aspects of fresco – lime plastering, and mixing the pigments – and she described the first to Roddy. Together they tracked down a building supply merchant who kept a store of slaked lime putty aged at least a year. Roman plasterers used lime that had been slaked for three years to stop their walls from cracking, but in twentieth-century London that was a perfectionist step too far. Together Roddy and Jennet mixed the lime with sand and marble dust to make a mortar, in proportions that varied with each coat. One volume of lime putty to three of coarse sand for the scratch coat, finer sand for the brown coat, one part of the finest sand with a little marble dust for the painting surface. Only the purest lime would do, slaked with distilled water. Roddy and Jennet were as strict as surgeons.

Roddy was a quiet man, economical with words; he and Jennet seldom spoke of much apart from work. But theirs was a relationship that went deeper than conventional friendship to a mutual commitment and respect. She admired the sure way in which he worked, his minimal use of energy, his reliability, his patience. He taught her how to apply the plaster by herself, as she would have to do in the final stages of the work, and the clean wet sandy scent of it would always be connected in her mind with gladness and with him.

When the initial plastering was done, Jennet could begin her own part of the work. She started on the first-floor wall, and with Roddy's help pinned her detail paper on to it as soon as the penultimate coat was just set firm. With a little muslin bag of powdered chalk she pounced through the perforated outlines of the drawing in the time-honoured way and then brushed over them with some ochre pigment in lime-water. Now she could see the whole design in its intended place. The next day, under Roddy's tutelage, she stood on a stepladder to cover the top-left-hand corner of the wall with the final coat of plaster. Working as quickly as she could before the plaster had a chance to dry, she brushed on the watercolour paint.

So beautiful the colours, ground as fine and smooth as possible by hand. Morning colours for the first landing: dove colours, palest pink and palest grey, and the new sky rinsed in softest blue. Rose madder, cobalt, Mars black, mixed with pure water, luminous against the plaster's blinding white. On the first day Jennet painted sky and hills, more sky on the second, river and parklands on the third and fourth, garden and parapet on the fifth and last. At the end of each day's work she cut the excess top coat off to make ready for the next day's join; jigsaw work, in many ways, remembering the drawing as it was plastered over, section by section, anticipating lines to come so that the hill's slope would be seamless, the tree trunk whole, not sundered. Although it felt peculiar at first, this sectional rhythm was appropriate, given the underlying image, and to re-enforce it, Jennet superimposed a grid on each painting to suggest the glazing bars of an enormous window.

Roddy came back when he was needed to apply the last but one coat of fine plaster on each landing and to help Jennet with her ladders and her scaffold boards, but for most of the time she was on her own in the house on Mount Street. Kaspar had gone to New York, avoiding all upheaval. Jennet had promised to have the landscapes done by the date of his return. Every morning she left the children to Mabel Harris and escaped, riding her bicycle up the King's Road, across Hyde Park, letting herself in to the silence of the empty house with the keys Kaspar had left her. She worked by arc light in the dark stairwell, and the whole day would sometimes pass without her knowing; the weather in the streets would change from soft May rain to sun and back to rain while Jennet stayed oblivious, rapt in her own created world of changing skies. After the douce colours of the dawn, the brightness of midday – topaz, emerald, azure; and then the final painting of the three, evening – lilac, heliotrope, apricot and amber. At last, when she was too tired to work and beginning to see double in the artificial light, she would straighten, stretch, and strip off her dusty clothing, dropping it in a heap beside her paints and brushes. Then she would walk naked up to Kaspar's black marble bathroom, where he had said that she could use his shower. Long minutes she would stand beneath the streaming water, washing off the plaster and the colours, feeling the sharp sting against her tightened nipples, and her skin glowing in its heat. There were always folded towels, laundered by a maid who came and went without disturbing Jennet; white towels ten times as big as the stiff threadbare things Jennet was used to, and she'd wrap herself in one and wander in and out of Kaspar's lonely rooms like a trespasser, or a revenant.

There was guilt in the pleasure she felt then, but there was more of pleasure. The quiet house in her possession, the Brancusi and the Malevich. Quiet it may have been, but never calm; there was a suspended breath in the house, as in the seconds before an earthquake when every creature stills its voice and waits for something to happen. This air of tension excited Jennet. In front of a tall mirror in Kaspar's dressing room she let her towel fall and watched herself, watched her hand move over her breast and between her legs, and she thought she would accede to Kaspar's demand for a self-portrait.

But in the meantime she must get on with the landscapes. She was pleased with them. In the evenings when she cycled home through the gentle evening light of early summer the sections she had finished filled her mind, and in the mornings she looked forward to the next as if they were a marvellous present. As a surprise for Kaspar, and to make him feel he'd had his money's worth, she decided to include one small distinctive detail in each picture: a fountain, a peacock, a tiny sailboat drifting down the river.

It was while Jennet was working on the frescoes that Richard Mallow suffered his first stroke. Lorna wrote to Jennet, for some reason not even trying to telephone from the semi-detached brick house in Sherborne where they'd moved after Litton Kirkdale. Sherborne had been Lorna's idea, it was to be her stepping-stone, the place she had gone to when her father died and the only other place in England that she knew. She and Richard had bought an ugly house there with his savings; her mother, who died in 1949, had remained in Sherborne with her sister all those years, but the aunt's house had been inherited by cousins.

Reading Lorna's letter, Jennet knew she ought to go to Richard, but the rhythm of her days was so addictive she could not bear to break it. Someone else's front-door key, and childless hours and good reasons not to be diverted; the routine of leaving her own house every morning, not coming back till evening, and working in between in an Arcadian world of light and shade and colour. Why should that have to be disrupted? Besides, there was also Kaspar's deadline, and the final painting still to plan, and her father would get better and when the work was finished, well, she would go and see him then, but just not at the moment.

*

Leonard Kaspar came back early, letting himself in unheralded, walking quietly up the stairs to the third landing, where Jennet was tidying up, screwing the lids back on her jars of paint. The last corner of the third painting was undone. His footfall, before she saw him, scared her.

I was not expecting you, she said.

I was impatient, Kaspar answered. He looked up at the almost finished fresco: evening light, like the evening outside. Have you seen the others? she asked. No. Not properly. I didn't look. I wanted you to show me.

All right, she said. I'll just go and wash my hands, shall I?

Jennet went downstairs to the cloakroom. To use Kaspar's bathroom would have seemed too intimate an act when he was in the house. She shivered at the memory of being in it naked. Somehow his presence compounded the odd silence of the place; the noise of a tap running was like a cataract. She checked herself in the cloakroom mirror: hair dishevelled and escaping from the string she used to tie it back with, four faint streaks of lilac where she'd rubbed an eyelash from her eye with paint still on her fingers, paint and mortar on her shirt. One of David's shirts, cast-off, once white and smart, with a separate stiff collar. It must have been a school shirt, she found herself thinking inconsequentially, postponing the next encounter for as long as she could stand there, running cold water on her fingers, a Sunday uniform school shirt. Now it felt like a piece of armour, David's breastplate, lent for her protection. She had not seen much of David over the past few weeks; he had taken to staying late at Corinne's, wanting to make the most of what he said was a fertile period of work. From Corinne's house he often walked home by way of his favourite pubs, and by the time he got home Jennet, deliciously exhausted by her day, could no longer

115

stay awake. In the mornings, when she got up early, he was always fast asleep, and she would leave him, mouth gaping open slightly like *el Muerto*'s, tangled up in blankets, beautiful and vulnerable even in the vapours of sleep and last night's whisky.

There were mornings when she wanted to climb back into bed beside him, to wake him with her lively body, drawing the drowsy warmth of his into her own, waiting for him to open his eyes, to smile at her, to slide into her in response to her unambiguous invitation. But she never did. There were always children calling and breakfasts to be started before Mabel arrived to take them over, and, most irresistibly, the lure of the pictures in the quiet of the house on Mount Street. This was no time for making love, she told herself, but she was glad in any case of David's sleeping body in her bed and obscurely comforted, on the evening when Kaspar arrived early, by the feel against her of his old white shirt.

Kaspar was opening a bottle of champagne when Jennet came out into the hall, his fingers gently probing round the small bulge of the cork. A christening, he said. My private vernissage. He had turned on all the lights, and having handed Jennet the wine in a glass so fine and fragile it seemed as if the pressure of a lip might snap it, he offered her his arm. Absurdly, as if they were a couple processing down an aisle, Jennet and Kaspar ascended the short flight of stairs to the first landing. Kaspar examined the fresco closely but said nothing. Jennet finished the champagne. Kaspar took the glass from her and set it down on a stair. Then he moved his arm so that her hand slid into his and led her up the next flight to the second landing, where he stood for a long time, silent still. On the third landing he lifted her hand and kissed it. Suddenly, shockingly, he fell to his knees in front of her, his arms clasped round her thighs and his head pressed to the paint-smudged hem of David's shirt. The two of them were frozen for what felt to Jennet like endless minutes, and when in the end he raised his head she saw his eyes were shining. I knew I was right to put my faith in you, he said, but you have outstripped my expectations.

London in the dog days of July; the Heaton children panting, listless flies too tired to buzz, dying on windowsills. Jennet begged a stay of time from Kaspar for the final fresco and spent his money on the summer lease of a house in Cornwall. She remembered cobalt seas and longed for them intensely, lying sleepless on hot sticky nights, imprisoned in the city. It was a large house, the one she took, two miles or so west of St Ives, large enough for everyone: Mabel Harris would come to mind the children, friends would visit, Margaret Metcalf with her sons, even her parents, Jennet thought. She wrote to Lorna to invite them, but Lorna said that Richard was too weak to travel.

Dreamlike, the two months that followed. Day after day unfolding like lengths of topaz silk, glistening days of uninterrupted sunshine until the final week of August brought torrential storms. And then the sea was flinty, foam exploding up towards the sky in arching whips and smoking white beneath the surface. But afterwards another fortnight of clear skies over ultramarine water, and the fields on the clifftops turning gold. All the infinite variety of greens and greys and blues, and her children flowering in the clean bright air. Ben's hair bleached once more to flax, Vanessa's pallor touched with honey, Sarah round and brown and bouncy – delicious to kiss, these children, their silk-smooth skin made sleeker by seawater. Is it some atavistic sense that makes a child swimming so endearing? Their delight in the curling waves, the salt-lick taste of them, their fine hair rat-tailed in the water – all these Jennet loved, and the long lazy days, the evenings without routine, the slow meals and the candle-light, the sheen of mussel shells, the delicate shades of crab claws, the flamboyant iridescence of fresh mackerel. All of these, and Jack, who lived in the town in a one-room cottage and was a painter and walked most days along the field path to the house where Jennet was staying.

The Heatons knew a number of people in and around St Ives. Artists had been living there for half a century, lured by light and landscape and more recently the presence of a famous generation, and others came as the Heatons had for holidays. David's friend from the Soho pubs, the man who lived in a caravan, had left it moored so long in a field below Zennor that grass had grown around its wheels and nettles through its floorboards. The two Roberts often stayed in a ramshackle house nearby, and others of their circle came and went, the same people who had floated down to the south of Spain and who still wandered nomad-like through France and Italy and England, working a little, visiting friends, before washing up again in London, in the pubs and bars to which in season they returned.

Jack Owen was not one of them. Unlike these drifters he had always lived in Cornwall. He was born there, in Truro, where his father was a baker, and he'd come back to it after brief wartime service, a few years as a trawlerman and a failed marriage. Although he had no encouragement as a child, he always knew, he said, that he would be an artist. He was simply waiting for his chance. It came when, tired of the ebb-and-flow life he was leading, he took a job as an assistant to a well-known sculptor in St Ives. She hired him for his muscle, he would say: she needed someone who could haul great trunks of scented guarea wood through St Ives' narrow twisting streets and manhandle tons of stone. Jack Owen, toughened by the massive weight of laden fishing nets, suited her purpose well, and she neither asked nor cared if he could draw or carve. She knew she could teach anyone the little they needed of her craft. Later, though, she saw by the way he used his planes and files on the rudimentary work she gave him how quick his hand was, and how fine. Then she began to train him properly and to pay for classes at the local art school. Her own son, her one child, had long been estranged from her and she may have found a substitute in Jack. Whatever the case, he would always be grateful, and although she was growing old by now, cantankerous and stale, Jack was steadfast and still loved her. He went on working for her while he learned, and at first he believed he too should sculpt, but realised in time that his imagination did not work best in three dimensions.

So Jack Owen, although not part of the London crowd, was embedded in the interlocking Cornish one even if by temperament he kept it at a distance. He knew the local artists and exhibited with them, he taught at the summer school, his reputation was growing fast, his friends were friends of Jennet and David's, and that summer they would inevitably meet.

The hottest day of that whole year, the twenty-third of August. The climax to long days of heat in an England it made unfamiliar, a new country of sandalled feet and people drinking out of doors instead of decorously hidden in the tobacco fug of bars. Richard Benjamin, arriving from London the day before, told of a city turning into Paris: restaurant tables on the pavements, revellers abroad in the small hours of the morning. At Trevenna Jennet and the children had spent the whole day on the beach, and by the evening were brimful of sun and water. Clean as new-bleached bone the sea makes flesh, scoured as smooth and flawless as the secret chambers of a shell. When I am by the sea I feel brave,

119

Ben once said, and Jennet knew exactly what he meant: air and sand and cold saltwater all conspire to strip away the inessential, leaving behind a core that is, at least for the moment, stronger and more pure.

There were other people there that day: David, who had been at Trevenna all summer and was at his calmest, his most loving; Margaret and Richard Benjamin with their three boys; Dermot; Corinne, who was staying with the Roberts; Lewis Delafield, the young art critic who had reviewed Jennet's first exhibition, and a friend of his, Elizabeth Foy, then a disciple of the famous sculptor. And Jack Owen. Jennet had met Jack many times by then and had noticed him, not so much for his Cornish voice or his good looks, but for his extraordinary eyes. So pale they were, diluted manganese, that they were almost colourless in sunshine; yet even then they seemed to exude light, not take it in. Fish-shaped eyes, slanting upwards. There was nothing remarkable about Jack Owen until you caught his gaze. The first time Jennet did so she thought of Botticelli's portrait of himself staring boldly out at the spectator, careless of the Magi worshipping the newborn king. Jack's eyes held the same cool challenge, defiant, almost insolent, and had the same unsettling effect.

As daylight began to fade, someone suggested supper on the beach. They had a sense that the weather would change, and they wanted to drink down the last drop of the summer. Jack and Dermot built a fire of driftwood and broken spars laid on flat stones; there were mackerel wrapped in paper to be roasted in its embers, jugs of beer and cider from the village pub. Deep into the night they stayed there, gathered round a fire they kept on feeding. Elizabeth Foy played a guitar, Richard and David argued about art and life and responsibility, as they always did that summer before the Soviet troops marched into Hungary, when Richard still had

120

faith. 'Art is impossible after Auschwitz,' Richard misquoted. What you do, David, it's too private, it's aloof. And look at what Jennet's been up to. Painting pretty pictures on a rich man's walls . . .

Most often David parried Richard's earnestness with mockery, but he was serious that night. Art is essential after Auschwitz, he said. We are essential. Only artists can make something good out of the disgusting things we've seen.

Yes, says Lewis Delafield, younger than the rest of them, too young for first-hand experience of war. That's what I think, it's artists who show us the truth, pick up the broken pieces, and transcend the old mythologies . . . his voice tails off in some embarrassment and Margaret jumps in. Good artists, maybe, she says. Only very good ones. But even then they are less useful than good dentists. Or good social workers or teachers or . . .

For shame, Margaret, David laughs. We are the very best.

Jack Owen does not say much. Like Jennet he is watchful, tracks the conversations, smiles to himself. But very late, when the night has gone and it is almost dawn, he starts to talk to Jennet about the bird's viewpoint he wants when he is painting. I'd like to learn to fly, he says, I need to look at things from high above. How different the sea must look to an eagle than to a shark. From above or from below . . . or, for that matter, to a swan gliding on the surface . . . I want to paint the sea as a gull sees it . . . did you know that if you fly above this land you can see the ghosts of Bronze Age fields? That's what I want. A high place.

That cliff is high enough, she dares him.

All right, he says, and he disappears in the half light and when she looks around she finds the others have wandered off, back up the path towards the house, and she is absolutely on her own now, on the beach.

She might as well be on her own in the entire world. All at

once there is nothingness around her. The outgoing tide has swept the beach quite clean; there is nothing, no scuttling claws, no resting shells. And everything is still, the slack tide poised, the sway of the sea suspended, the air unmoving as if the whole world were holding its breath. Air and water in an equal stillness, sharing with each other the same scantness of colour, the same palely blue-tinged milky light. Breathless, soundless, formless, and Jennet feels her own boundaries dissolving into blank, white space. But then, from somewhere high above her, she hears Jack Owen calling, calling out her name, and the haze of dawn begins to lift and she can see him clinging by one hand to a spur of rock far up the slippery granite of the cliff. Shall I fly down to you? he shouts, but before she can warn him no, no, no, Jack please hold on, before she can will those swinging legs back to a firm foothold, he vanishes and she is statue-still again, frozen for a moment while she collects the strength to climb the tumble of rock at the cliff's foot and find Jack on the other side with a broken neck.

The rocks are sharp but she climbs fast, scrambling heedless of cut hands, holding on to the vision of his broken body. When she reaches the next cove she remembers that the cliff on that face is not sheer but stepped. Jack is waiting on the sand and laughing. He has a stick and he throws it twirling up into the air as if he were a juggler. It falls back into his hand. Did I frighten you? I'm sorry, Mrs Heaton, I didn't know you cared.

You're an idiot, she says, and he agrees. But look, I told you there were ghosts. And dancing with his stick across the clean-swept sand, he draws the outline of a horse, a giant horse, with its mane streaming and a hoof raised in arrested gallop; Jack's lines swift and sure and strong. There, he says, coming back to where she stands, that horse has always raced along this beach. For a thousand years and more. Come. I'll show you. I'll show you where to hear it.

She follows him up the stepped rock, and where it is steep and overhangs he holds her hand to lead her. At the top there is a tangle of bracken, bramble and gorse with a narrow way through it, tunnelled over years by badgers. Beyond that there is the close-cropped grass, brittle from the weeks of drought but damp now with early dew. From this height Jack's triumphant horse is clear, but beyond it sea-fret still, and cloud on the horizon. Lie down, Jack says. Lie down on the grass. Press your ear to it. There now. Can't you hear the galloping hooves? Well, but of course you can. And the other ghosts? Phoenicians, Romans, tinners . . . and the living sounds, the worms that are just waking up now, in their beds beneath the earth?

What Jennet hears is birdsong, and beneath it the heart-beat of the sea, a suck and rush deep underground as if the cliff edge had become detached, an island or a fragment of an iceberg, or the sea itself were roaring in to undermine it. It makes her feel giddy. And then she sees the blades of grass and the struggling insects, the flowering thrift, the wild thyme, sea-lavender and scabious; she can smell the earth, and if she wished to she could taste it. She turns onto her back and looks up into the clearing sky and into Jack's transparent eyes, as he leans down to kiss her.

Three weeks later Jennet saw David, Mabel and the children off on the train to London and packed up the Cornish house. It was hard to leave it, for it held, she felt, the essence of the summer, their contentment. Not hers alone, but David's and the children's, which Jack with his soft kisses had done nothing to disrupt. The summer had drawn the family together, wrapped it into one again with honey threads, whereas in the stress of normal life it was always fraying. Not since before the twins were born had Jennet felt so close to David. Paradoxically, Jack was part of this. She had seen him almost every day, but not often on his own; all she wanted from him then was the reminder of the amplitude of love. Through Jack she recollected possibility, the luxury of feeling; he rescued her from becoming the efficient and emotionless machine she sometimes feared she was when she rushed from school to shop to studio, counting time in multiples of minutes, counting cash in terms of pennies.

Jack reawoke her sense of promise. For Jennet at the time that was enough. She had always been a realist, and she knew she had to work with what she had, not with what might otherwise have been; and besides, she was by nature faithful. Still it was a wrench to say goodbye to Jack and to sweep the last fine drift of sand out of the old farmhouse, which, in the span of only a few weeks, had become much more than four stone walls and instead was like a hive, containing the translucent gold of happiness in the structure of its cells.

But she had to leave. She had work to finish, David was impatient for his studio, Ben must go back to school. And she had put off visiting her father for too long. So she gathered up the stray socks and the seashells and left the front-door key beneath the doormat and drove eastwards in a secondhand Morris Twelve acquired through Leonard Kaspar to her parents' house in Dorset.

Richard Mallow, like the husk of an ancient coconut: desiccated, hollow. How could a man who once stood over six feet tall shrink so quickly to the stature of a child? Lorna had said nothing to ready Jennet for her father, sunken and shrivelled and confined by chipped white-painted metal bars in a cruel parody of a cot. Why bars? asked Jennet. To stop him falling out of bed, her mother said.

The room where Richard lay was heavy with the smells of baby powder and urine, mixed with cigarette smoke and medicine and sour old man's breath. Jennet kissed her father's concave cheek and held his hand; she saw that his fingernails had been left uncut for so long that they were growing twisted: calcified, yellow nails, with dirt embedded in them. She thought of his fastidiousness when he was a well man, the careful application to his skin of Trumper's Extract of West Indian Lime, the whiteness of his dog collar even when his domestic life was descending into squalor. Now there were food stains on his blue pyjamas. Someone should have clipped his nails, she said. Why don't you do it then? her mother asked.

A series of small strokes had left Richard paralysed on one side but mentally less affected, although Lorna complained that his mind wandered and his speech was stumbling. He goes on and on about the war, she said. His war, not the last one. It's as if he were still there, in the fields of France, he forgets that he's been safe enough in England for almost forty years. Oh God, to think how long I've been his wife! The dreams he always used to have, the nightmares, well they've come back now with a vengeance, screaming blue murder in the middle of the night, calling out in French sometimes, *Pas là, Pas là!* I don't know how I'd cope if it weren't for Barbara.

Barbara was in Sherborne too, having given up her London job to help Lorna with her father. She was so full of anger and resentment that she would not look Jennet in the eye. Every word she spoke emerged through tight-clamped lips. I hope you had a lovely holiday, she said.

That night, after dinner, when Richard had been washed with a damp facecloth and Lorna settled with a cup of tea and

Barbara had told for the hundredth time by deed if not by word her history of sorrows, Jennet slipped out into the empty street and stood a while in the stone coop made for an old monastic well. She lit a cigarette and leaned against the stone, watching the pattern the streetlamps made, a dapple of lit ellipses on wet paving, and she thought how fast the mood of happiness had flown. She had left Cornwall only that morning, but already it was as if the past few weeks had been a dream. And this was the reality: the dying man in his painted cage, dwindling to a pile of bones and only his eyes still bright, imploring. And when he did die, there would be her mother, grim as a camp warden, waiting in the queue for sacrifice. With fat, sad Barbara close behind and Vanessa, blameless, hopeless; and mercurial, maddening David, and so on in a snake of shackles. There would be no unfastening them, nor should there be, perhaps. But that night in the Sherborne drizzle, when Jennet closed her eyes to see again the moment of suspended whiteness on the Trevenna beach, she could not stop the tears.

Bars and grids. Networks, fretworks, screens and veils. It was not only the bars of Richard Mallow's bed that proposed themselves to Jennet when she began to work again after that summer's break, but all their many parallels: the cross-hatching of black thorn on frozen water which she had painted the year before, the window bars of Kaspar's frescoes, the leaded panes of Litton Kirkdale, London railings, the mesh of a fire screen, film of concentration camps, memories borrowed from David, barbed-wire silhouetted on the sky. These grids of Jennet's London period reflect a state of mind. Its seeds were always there: in the landscapes of her childhood, crisscrossed by walls, the views she liked to see through windows, and in those *Spinney* paintings of 1954, but something obdurate grew round them in the following years, an outer casing as if to guard a tender core.

In retrospect the trajectory of Jennet's work is not a perfect curve. Armed with hindsight one might ask what happened to the magical command of light and whiteness that she poured into her painting *Ice and Water*. Did she not listen to that whiteness, not hear the call it had for her? What sadness intervened between the inspiration of the stilled beat of the sea and the expression she gave it in the end? If she were a character in fiction there might be a single answer. Thwarted love maybe. An unhappy marriage. But in real life the answer is more complex. Need, uncertainty and fear come into it; an absence of self-knowledge. Not wilful ignorance of self but the obscured view, the self seen dimly until time or death or wisdom make it clear. Jennet could not have reached that level of awareness then, with so many temporal demands besetting her. These may well have felt like the locked bars of a cage, bars of her own making – anxiety, responsibility, a tendency to pre-determinism, an over-eager surrendering to fate – but there were other elements as well. Jennet Mallow was not a naïve artist, immune from outside influence: she was married to a painter, most of her acquaintances were painters, and they often talked about abstraction and the questions that it asked of figurative painting. Was there anywhere else to go beyond the black square and the empty canvas? Did painting really have a future? To a limited extent, Jennet's London work echoes the arguments of the time. But only to a limited extent. Jennet never yielded much to the prevailing tides, she was drawn to what she had to do, and instinct was her truest guide. What it prompted during that period was grids and bars.

But first she had to finish Kaspar's frescoes. Even then she knew the landscapes were a sideline, a *jeu d'esprit*, although she had enjoyed their making and in their mastery of light and colour they match her finest work. This last painting, the self-portrait was a greater challenge, and it made her nervous.

David Heaton, in the meantime, was recovering his early reputation. The twin portraits Corinne's husband had commissioned were still unfinished in 1955, but he had completed other work, a St Sebastian, a portrait of Dermot in military uniform, and his series of *Crow* paintings – anguished slashes of black paint, the aftermath of Spain – which had been exhibited and sold. And he was popular as a teacher. He thrived on his students' admiration, and he profited from daily contact with professional artists. Jennet had been right to think he would be happier in England than in Spain. He drank himself into unconsciousness most nights, but she put up with this, accepting that he drank as intensely as he lived all other aspects of his life: recklessly and headlong. At least he was no longer as dangerously angry as he had been in Santiago. It saddened her that their waking hours together were so few, but even so there were still times, in Cornwall for example, when he was diamantine, and the embers of her first attraction stirred into flame again.

Jennet filled her studies for the portrait with these moments and with memories of desire. She watched herself in a tall mirror, assessing her own body as an observer might, both dispassionately and as an erotic object. She had seen how it looked in David's pictures: raw and vulnerable, exposed; now she must find out how to paint it in a way that would be neither coy nor exhibitionist.

The murkiness of Leonard Kaspar's motives was not lost on her. She knew that she aroused in him the impure thrill of ownership; but at the same time, and almost unadmitted, his arousal was itself arousing. Jennet could have refused or renegotiated his commission: that she had not, but instead had pondered it when she touched herself in front of Kaspar's mirror and walked naked through his empty house, was disturbingly exciting.

Earlier that year Jennet had been to see a Brazilian dancer at a club in Dean Street. She was there with David and with friends to celebrate someone's birthday, and they all watched spellbound as the woman moved under the irresistible compulsion of a drumbeat, as if her body were enslaved by the rhythm. She stopped dancing when the music stopped and stood, out of breath, accepting the applause. But she began again the moment that the next beat fell, her hands and feet and hips in frenzied motion, light rippling on her dark bronze skin, the thick chains around her wrists and ankles clanking. She wore a theatrical version of African robes to start with, her height and the smooth planes of her face enhanced by an elaborate beaded turban, but as the music grew more intense she threw off each bright layer of silk until in the end she faced her watchers naked except for a scarlet triangle of cloth. Sweat streaked like tear marks on her skin. Jennet felt the accelerating urgency of the dancer and the men who watched her, she shared it as the woman stripped, and she shared the moment of extraordinary lust and equal shame when the dancer raised her beautiful, defiant chin and stared out at the mesmerised crowd as if to say that in spite of her bound ankles and her naked breasts they still did not possess her.

To look and to possess. The ambiguous relationship between the image and its watcher. Does the man who owns the naked portrait own its subject? These were the questions Jennet asked in direct response to David's portrayals of her and Kaspar's implicit claims as purchaser: to what extent should any body be beholden; who did that body, once exposed, belong to?

Details from the studies found their way into Jennet's later paintings – the precisely outlined breast for instance, drawn behind a torn veil – but the fresco she made for Kaspar was the only time she pictured herself unclothed, and even then she eluded confrontation. The nude in her painting is seen in full only from the back; her face and the right half of her body visible but blurred in the reflection from what might be a steamed-up mirror or a darkened window. In her left hand the woman holds a man's paint-stained white shirt. On the right of the painting is a doorway, in which a man in evening dress is standing. Light slants on to the black cloth of his jacket and his patent leather shoes, but his face is hidden in shadow.

Bald description does not convey the unsettling quality of this picture. That lies in its dualities perhaps: the naked woman and the clothed man who might be either lover or intruder, the contrast between the woman's misted frontal view and her articulate, seductive back. That her sexual parts are indistinct forces the viewer to decide between sympathy and disappointment. In itself it is a challenge: would you, if you could, force the woman round to face you? The viewer's sense of somehow being included in the painting is strengthened by its ambivalent internal viewpoint. Is the woman looking at herself or at you in the mirror? Is the man in evening dress, whose eyes cannot be seen, watching the naked woman also, unobserved? The minutely painted detail – the frayed sleeves of the shirt, for instance, the faintly reddened skin in the cleft of the woman's buttocks, and the fact that the figures are lifesize – also make the viewer feel that he has opened a door into a room he did not know existed when he climbed to the top landing of Leonard Kaspar's house, and into which he has no right of entry.

But leaving to one side its erotic and confusing elements, the painting is also very lovely. Jennet used the same gentle fresco colours – apricot, amber, lilac – in its background of wall and curtain as she had in the three landscapes, and the skin tones and the woman's hair, coiled loosely at her neck, are entirely convincing. When Kaspar saw it finished he reached out to stroke the outline of the woman's spine from the top to bottom.

In February 1956 Vanessa, running a high temperature, suffered a febrile convulsion that temporarily undid her already shaky hold on speech and left her very fragile. She was admitted to the children's hospital at Great Ormond Street for tests and observation. While she was there Richard Mallow had a final, devastating stroke. Lorna broke her usual rule and telephoned to tell Jennet that she should make haste to Sherborne if she wished to see her father while he was still alive. Unable to leave Vanessa alone, Jennet wavered for a day, then discharged the child and, bundling her in blankets on to the back seat of the car, drove down to Dorset with her.

Richard was in hospital in another high-sided bed. He lay like an unwrapped corpse against his pillows, his eyes closed and his mouth sagging as if he had mislaid the strap to hold his chin. His skin was porridge-white and clammy. Only his breathing, rasping and irregular, punctuated by soft moans, proved he was not already dead. Jennet waited through the night with him, aching on an upright chair with Vanessa swaddled in her arms, and it seemed to her that in their shallow breaths – each breath achieved for a reason unimagined by the living, and yet desolate, beyond consoling – the sick man and the girl merged into one mute unity: child and father, begotter and begotten, beyond the reach of speech and reason, suffering to a conclusion long foregone. At some time around four o'clock, exhausted, she dropped off to sleep, and when she woke there was a thin bar of grey light between the drawn curtains. Vanessa had slumped sideways from her hold on to the old man's bed and was lying peacefully against him, her eyes wide open and one hand resting like a reassurance on his shoulder, and her father peaceful too, and dead.

That was the first of her new paintings: a ghostly child's face, seen as if through wrappings of grey mist, beneath a trellis of grey painted bars. The second was two heads in profile, a child's and an old man's, face touching face as if about to kiss or to borrow one another's breath, the fingers of their hands, one pale and small, the other bent with twisted yellow nails, held up as if to lay against the other's cheek. In that painting the splayed fingers make their own network, one that could be either threatening or protective. Jennet would always be haunted by the memory of her daughter cradled by the dead man, the only witness of his death.

Over the following months she painted a series of these enigmatic faces – always with their eyes closed, usually in profile, overlaid by bars. Some of them were portraits – there was one of David and one of Lewis Delafield – many were of children, most of them from her imagination. They are enigmatic because they pose unanswered questions: are they alive or dead, awake or sleeping, real or revenant, imprisoned or protected by the bars? The ones in profile have an almost heraldic quality, evoking medallions, cameos, stamps, or the faces of the dead in a tomb painting. The few that are shown in full face have other resonances too. They might be inmates of an asylum or prisoners in solitary, seen through the spy-grids set in the locked doors of their cells.

After Richard's death, Jennet helped her mother to clear out his clothes and papers, and it was then that she found his collected sermons, the poems and the journals she had never known he kept. Throw them all out, Lorna said, a load of junk, but Jennet took them home with her and read them gradually over the months, mourning a man she realised she had hardly known and had certainly neglected. Reaching back to him through his uncensored writings was to unearth a wholly different man from the one she had taken for granted when he lived. If Richard Mallow had been more prepared for death might he have destroyed his intimate journals? Or would he too have kept them, as Jennet did her own, half-hidden, almost secret, asking to be read but also forbidding access, like a door marked Private or a sinuous sculpture labelled Do Not Touch?

Jennet read Richard's notebooks word by word. As a child she had loved her father, saw him as an ally against her cross, frustrated mother, an even-tempered sharer of books and information, but always unengaged and distant. Richard, born into a Victorian world, was not a man to share his feelings. Jennet had never heard him say the words, I love you. And yet his journals were full of love: for Lorna when she was young, for Jennet, for his grandchildren, especially Vanessa, in whom he had seen a sort of grace, and also, most startlingly, for a young man in his regiment who had died in the Battle of the Somme. There were sonnets to this un-named man, dwelling on his beauty and his wasted youth and that of all the thousands dead like him. There were reiterated outpourings of horror: the mud, the barbarism, the running wounds, the gut-twisting suffocating terror of the war. And there was the painful account of Richard's struggle to justify the dying and re-sanctify his life in the contemplation of Christ's agony, and how profoundly he had failed. Over and over again in his years of ministry Richard had battled to relight the small flame of faith that had led him into priesthood at the end of the war; but he never succeeded. In the end he simply wrote that there was nothing left. Nothingness. Blankness. An infinity of empty space.

Works of art are infinitely solitary, Rilke said, and loneliness is a dominant note in Jennet Mallow's London paintings. They have boundaries, narrowly defined: edges, boxing, frames. And yet the paintings are in no sense costive; on the contrary, their limitations are perversely liberating. Within each separate box or cage is trapped an intensely beautiful, suggestive, isolated image, which beats its wings more strongly because it is enclosed, because the loss of freedom is proof of freedom's existence. A hawk caught in an aviary distils within its sullen body and its cruelly clipped wings the whole ideal of flight.

Seeing the London paintings gathered at the Guggenheim retrospective two years after Jennet's death, ten years or more of work hung chronologically on a spiral, brought music to mind. The *Goldberg Variations*, for example: one perfect and essentially simple tune spun to interlocking and expanding coils, as a glass-blower creates a fragile master-piece with molten sand and soda ash scooped on an iron tube.

There were the faces to begin with, the children and the old man and the identifiable portraits. Features that initially were defined – the Delafield painting is done in such close detail and such translucent colour that it recalls Elizabethan miniatures and makes its subject seem like a melancholic poet trapped by briar roses – yield to ghostlier ones, fleeting impressions like faces seen in dreams. Later, there were frag-ments of a body – Jennet's body as it happened – forearm, breast, neck and shoulder, crooked elbow, knee joint, ankle, each one separate, as if the body had been hacked apart. These were painted in two series, the first one merci-lessly real, the second more impressionistic. In one the dismembered parts are seen behind a painted mesh as if locked in a meat safe; the other has inked overlays of barbed wire.

As the work developed the painted bars and nets gave way to actual ones, stuck or nailed onto the wooden boards that Jennet used, adding a third dimension to the image, turning it literally into a cage. At the same time the paintings themselves grew larger. The heads are on a small scale. The last paintings of the period, the barred landscapes of 1967, completely transcend the domestic scope, being over two and a half metres by nearly five.

With this increase in size, and related to it, although not its only cause, came Jennet's huge increase in reputation. In 1956 she was still relatively unknown; within ten years she had become a famous name. Why? There are several reasons. The least significant, perhaps, is external to her work and merely her good fortune: that her most fecund time coincided with an upwelling of energy in Britain.

Britain in 1956, the year of the Suez Crisis and the Hungarian Rising but also the year of 'Rock Around the Clock' and of *Look Back in Anger*, was a country on the edge of change, excited in anticipation of the new. New clothes, new music, a new Establishment, new art: in January of that year the exhibition Modern Art in the United States opened at the Tate and showed the Abstract Expressionists for the first time. New magazines, and a few years later, the first of the Sunday colour supplements, all with a need to fill their empty pages. Who better on their front covers than a beautiful young woman forging her own path as an artist? And, moreover, a young woman married to a romantically photogenic painter, and so able to supply the human interest and lifestyle angle for those readers who could not care less about the art. David Heaton shared the spotlight in the early

135

1960s; all of a sudden he and Jennet found themselves courted and, more importantly, their work well publicised.

Patrick Mann took advantage of this astutely. He had a genius for making connections and always knew exactly whom to speak to and how to attract the most attention. Jennet's second solo exhibition, at his gallery in December 1957, was the first salvo in a fusillade of sensational successes that Patrick choreographed. To celebrate its opening, Leonard Kaspar gave a party at the house in Mount Street, which led to more commissions than Jennet could ever have fulfilled. She turned down dozens of requests for murals. For the first time in her life she could paint whatever she wanted and be certain that a hundred buyers would queue to snap it up.

But the buyers did not buy because they saw Jennet in their papers. The corporate buyers came in part for Jennet's Britishness – ironically, as she often said she never felt particularly English, and at that stage in her life was not at all sure where she wanted to belong. National identity was nonetheless a selling point for curators spending public money at a time when Britishness was a new concept in marketing, and characterised to some extent by its distinction from American. In the 1950s the big American painters were rolling their great tanks across the world, along with all the other phalanxes, industrial and military, political and economic. Elvis Presley, Coca-Cola, Jackson Pollock, Hollywood. It's no wonder little England, so often told in kindly tones that it would fit nicely into Texas, searched for heroes of its own.

Jennet was an ideal candidate, not only young and female but also working in a style that was all her own yet international in its appeal. David Heaton benefited too from this faintly desperate surge of national pride, but for different reasons: the 'English' quality of his art, which he had tried to lose ten years before when he moved to Spain, now worked firmly in his favour. In 1960 he was the British Council's choice to represent young painters at an exhibition that toured Eastern Europe.

So time and place were two of the reasons for Jennet Mallow's fame. And luck, of course. The good fortune of being beautiful when superficial image was important. But these were not the main ones. The reason Jennet Mallow's paintings sold, and why her standing amongst the greatest artists of the twentieth century remains unchallenged today, is simple: she was extraordinary, and her work was brilliant. Just look at *Clear Glass*. Sheer luminescence, balance, grace. No one else could paint like that.

So. Fame and fortune. Are they not enough? They are no guarantors of happiness, but that is not to say they make no difference. They made all the difference to Jennet, buying for her time and space and, finally, independence. After the success of her second exhibition there was an Arts Council sponsored tour, and in September 1959 her first New York show, at Hagopian's on Madison Avenue. She was now making enough money to pay for the domestic help she wanted and to buy a house. This was important to her, not only to give the family more room but because she hoped to find somewhere which would double as a studio. She needed a bigger space than she had in Battersea for her increasingly large-scale work. After seven years or so of paintings, which, apart from Kaspar's frescoes, would fit comfortably into a drawing room, she had a desire for wider scope. As her work progressed it was as if the grids and bars needed to be balanced, saved from claustrophobia, by sheer size. Size was also a response to the demand from corporate buyers; her early work was made for private spaces, her later for more public ones.

In 1959 David Heaton was still using Corinne Golding's studio in the house off Portman Square. It was convenient, he said, and besides he did not need it often because he had his own space at Stockwell. His life had fallen into a pattern he did not want to change: late mornings, four agreeable afternoons a week teaching adulatory students, enough time in between to do his own work, which now included portraits. Time for friends and for late nights. Especially for late nights. It suited him, but it suited Jennet less. Do you love me, David? she once asked him. Steady on, he said. Of course I do, that's a silly question.

If she could find a house that was large enough, she thought, a house on several floors, a place into which a clean northern light would stream, then she and David could have studios together, spend less time apart. It would be quiet in this house in term-time, the children out at school; perhaps she and David would make love sometimes, of an afternoon, a morning's work behind them. It was so long since they had made love by day. A simple and harmonious life, she dreamed, cloistered hours of intense work in the humming silence of a sanctuary made safer by the sharing, her thirst for open sky and seas assuaged by summers spent in Cornwall, and she and David growing closer as they moved, confident and prospering, into middle age.

Solitude is easy when you're young. It's easy when the open-ended years are full of possibilities and any stranger met by chance might become a lover. It is not, then, to be confused with loneliness. When she was a child Jennet spent much time alone and as a young woman she had been content in her own company. In her mid-thirties she was beginning to learn how short life was.

It had not occurred to Jennet until he died how much she

would miss her father. She had seen him so rarely in recent years; he had become as remote to her as God, if loved at all loved distantly, and infrequently recalled. How shocking then to find in death her father transfigured into a real presence. She sensed him at her shoulder, watching her at work, judging her as he had always done, strictly, but with kindness. She saw him in the corner of her eye. And yet this presence was not a comfort. It was a reproach, a warning, a reminder of how little time there was in any life and how much of that was lost in loneliness. Jennet knew that Richard Mallow had been lonely in his disbelief and that his wife was lonely now, as she had been all through their marriage. Two lives with no bridge between them.

The perception of loneliness scared Jennet. Not so much her own as that of other people: Lorna, Barbara, Vanessa. And David, forever seeking oblivion, burying his nightmares in his paintings of raw flesh. Her father's death was revelation, and it was his voice she heard commanding her to act, to salvage what she had before it was too late.

Flesh and bone and blood and sinew; brain and heart and soul. A whole man, any man, a man in real life, not a man on paper. A man like David Heaton, a mass of complex structures and connections, contradictions, proteins, molecules and cells. Such a man is reducible to words on paper but only at the cost of a dimension. The words in which David Heaton was described depend on who was describing him. Dazzling, his friends might say, but unpredictable. Generous and spendthrift, talented but wasteful, careless of himself and other people. Yes, and unbelievably attractive, lovers might add, until the boozing really got to him; in his prime he could have melted with one look a statue's heart.

Jennet's biographer might choose other words –

destructive, selfish, doomed, for instance – ignoring awk-ward truths. It's a problem, this: how to paint a portrait of a man who changed from day to day, moment to moment, like a chameleon on a rainbow. Jennet herself did it, of course, but then she didn't need to use as imprecise and blunt a tool as words. There are the drawings that she made over her twenty years of marriage: the nude of 1952, the cold face of *El Muerto*, and the 1956 portrait of David behind painted bars. And there is the study of David with a painting of his own in progress, which she completed early in September 1960, just before they moved to their new house. It is the last portrait Jennet painted of him and it reveals her feelings exactly. Tenderness, exasperation, fear and hope. David is sitting on a high-backed wooden chair against a grey back-ground, perhaps his studio wall. His face is slightly turned, but his eyes look straight out at the watcher. One hand, circled by a loose white cuff, hangs downwards from the arm supported by the chair, the other holds a board on which there is a drawing of a woman. At the time of this portrait David had returned to Jennet as a subject, so the woman, presumably, is her. Implicit in this picture is their shared connection.

If the hands in this painting are extraordinary, the long, bony fingers tense although apparently in repose, so lifelike one expects them to reach out of the canvas, the face is even more so. Anybody who knew David Heaton finds it haunt-ing. His uncombed hair, still as dark as woods at dusk, only just beginning to thin off his high forehead. The black eye-brows, the thin beak of his nose. His mouth stern, unsmil-ing, a line of redder skin along his lower lip as if it had been bitten or had cracked. The straggle of dark beard he'd grown in the past year, stark against his upturned collar. One ear showing, sticking out a little from his head. And the eyes as sad as shipwreck, sombre. It is absolutely clear that the woman who painted those eyes, and the expression in them, loved her subject.

Bridge House. No one else wanted the old ruin at the end of Cheyne Walk, it was too decrepit and impractical, half tumbling down, with great holes in its floors. But it also had vast rooms and floor-length windows, a wrought-iron balcony and the straggling remnants of a vine on a pergola in the garden. Jennet loved it. It was a survivor amidst newer buildings, a refugee: it would have been at home in the market square of a French village. Here on the corner of a smoky London street it was outlandish and, though crumbling, defiant. And besides, the greys and greens of riverlight, the silvers and the blues, flooded in through its high windows, making flecked patterns on the walls as if with brushfulls of its cloudy water. There were stone facings round the windows and on some the splintery remains of ancient shutters.

It's such a wreck, said David. Yes, but Roddy will make it good, Jennet assured him, thinking of Roddy MacNamara's steadiness and strength, the clean sand smell of him, his shoulders in white overalls. Who better to restore this house to a place of sanctuary and calm?

Vanessa at the age of eight is as frail as a dandelion clock. Pale hair like gossamer around a small white wedge of face, her eyes the lightest blue. She can walk now and even talks a little; perhaps she would talk more if there were more that she would like to say. Certainly she has no difficulty understanding. But she is habitually quiet, more likely to answer a question with a nod or a shake of her head than with a spoken word. In this way she is her mother's daughter. Jennet also kept her own counsel as a child, but in her case silence hid a mind that was always fiercely working, whereas Vanessa's quiet hints at blankness. But also like her mother at that age, Vanessa is happiest when given paper and coloured pencils: before she learned to talk she liked to draw. It used to be a way of occupying her in the days when Jennet had to take her to the studio, propping her up with a sketchpad and a clutch of fat wax crayons, but even now Vanessa spends hours at the playroom table, covering sheet after sheet with her bright scrawls.

Guilt about Vanessa is one of the constant undertones of Jennet's life. For the past three years the little girl has been at a special school in Sloane Street where she is, as far as Jennet knows, content. She is deeply attached to Mabel, who takes her to school every morning on the number 19 bus and who comes in every afternoon and all day in the holidays. But still, there are so many trade-offs. The school's fees are steep: one of the best things about success is that Jennet can meet them. She tells herself the school is doing her daughter good. She tells herself that saintly Mabel, with her sway of hip and her fine ankles, as solid and as warm a presence as those much-loved and remembered Friesians, is the perfect mother-substitute. Better than the real mother, Jennet allows an inner voice to argue. And yet, there is a look in Vanessa's pale eyes when she is carted off to school each morning that gives that siren voice the lie. Don't make me go, the look says, let me stay with you.

It's a look that Jennet remembers seeing in her son's eyes when he was small and she took him to school. Unlike Vanessa, Ben translated it into words: Don't leave me, Mummy. If you loved me you wouldn't leave me in this cold place, you wouldn't walk away. Ben is older now and has learned to guard his feelings, but she still sees it some-times, the shadow of that hurt look, when she is too busy to give him her full attention or he knows that she is not listening. She knows the look too well. She saw it in her father's eyes every time she went away after one of her infrequent visits; it was there when she said goodbye in Sherborne, the last time she saw him conscious. She has noticed it recently in Lewis Delafield. Some people never have it, though: Corinne, for example. And Jennet's other daughter, Sarah. Sarah is Vanessa's opposite, she has a tangle of dark curls in contrast to her sister's lint, she is always dancing, jumping, shouting; nothing seems to trouble her and she lets nothing stand between her and her will.

Sarah is the one who doesn't care when Jennet is away from home; the other children do. Bring me a present, Sarah says; but Ben grows sullen and Vanessa seems bewildered, as if she were not sure that Jennet would come back. What should Jennet have done? So many trade-offs. She tells herself she's buying security for her children. In 1960 she made two trips to New York, one to Zurich and one to Frankfurt, and in 1961 she represented Britain at the Venice Biennale. The next year she went to Rio de Janeiro and New Delhi. Her life was getting busier and busier. There were openings and parties and official functions. She had to make time for painting. Something had to give.

The Venice Biennale? David Heaton is outraged and for a moment shows it. He is, after all, the most exciting British artist on the scene. An exhibition called New Faces has just closed at the Whitechapel, a celebration of new developments in portrait painting and of up-and-coming painters. David was its undisputed star. There were three recent paintings of Jennet in the show, an affecting one of David's mother, then recovering from cancer, and his matching portraits of Corinne and Victor Golding. Full length, life size, generally agreed to be David's finest work. Victor in a dark-grey suit, Corinne naked. Victor with one elbow on his lovely marble mantelpiece, his Canaletto in the background, a cigarette in his upraised hand; Corinne in front of the twin fireplace, one hand on her hip, the other lifted to her head as if she were smoothing back her hair. Or as if she had a headache, Jennet said, when she first saw this picture.

You're just jealous, David mocked.

I am, a little, she admitted. Why did you paint Victor with his clothes on but Corinne without?

Because Corinne is much prettier than Victor. And anyway, you painted yourself nude for Kaspar.

Jennet was surprised. She had discussed that painting with David at the time, and he had not said it troubled him. How could it have done in any case, when he had made her body public time and time again? At the Whitechapel there she was, crouching on a wooden floor, shivering, with water running down her in a shower; lying on a crumpled bed. What difference is there, she asked, between those images and the painting that she did for Kaspar? Anyone who sees that picture of yourself, David replied, will assume that you were Kaspar's lover. That you are, perhaps. Well, are you?

Jennet thought of Kaspar slinking through the Battersea studio, his soft, hairless hands. Kaspar likes to drop in on her unannounced, and clearly feels he has the right to do so, his sense of ownership augmented by each purchase that he makes. He flicks through canvases stacked against the wall like an expert blackjack dealer. What's new? he asks. He always wants first choice. Jennet finds this truffling through her unfinished work disturbing; it presupposes a closeness that she does not feel. He is not easy company: there are whole areas of his life that are out-of-bounds to her; she knows nothing of his childhood, for example, or what he does in his long absences abroad. She does not know if he has lovers. But she does know that it is not her body in the

144

flesh that Kaspar wants, just yet. When he touches her, when he takes her hand or guides her with an arm around her waist, his touch is that of a possessor, not a suitor. He runs his finger in the same way down the flank of the beautiful bronze dancer by Marini which is a recent acquisition; he likes to touch the things he's bought.

In David's painting Corinne Golding invites touch. She looks very lovely: her high breasts and her long white legs, the brass gleam of the hair between them, the expression in her eyes amused, enticing, her lips slightly parted. At the Whitechapel Gallery this portrait drew many admirers and would-be buyers, and inspired other women to offer themselves as models to David Heaton. The Tate bought the painting of Jennet in the shower. The head of an extremely rich and well-connected banking family commissioned David to paint each member of it, from his nonagenarian mother to his grandson. Thirteen separate portraits: a lot of time and a lot of money. David was on a roll and knew it, but something rankled; he might have been more pleased, perhaps, if Jennet had not matched his success.

Or bettered it. So, Venice? Prestige and honour and, importantly, exposure to the international market, which is what David wanted most of all. The old jibes about his Englishness still stung. Ten years ago David had seen himself as the forerunner of a major movement, a new art in which the long tradition of figurative painting would take on new relevance and say the things that had to be said in a dangerous new world. He might mock Richard Benjamin, but he did not disregard him. In the ruins of post-war Europe, Benjamin would say that art was futile if it served no moral purpose. After such horror and such slaughter – and with every reason to believe the slaughter would continue – what in heaven's name could ever be the point of a society lady's portrait?

When he went to Spain in the summer of 1950 David was

fired with resolution. It was to be his new start, the opening of a fresh page on which the nightmare of his past experiences would be transmuted into universal meaning, as Picasso had transmuted the suffering of the Basques into an image which no sane man could contemplate while still justifying the act of war. David had begun to say something of what he felt in paint, with his Lazarus painting and his dead man in uniform. But these had been dismissed by a slimy critic as parochial. David had meant his art to be supranational. Yet now, a decade later, what had happened? His genius and passion had dribbled away in paintings of naked women, especially of his wife. So much of his vital energy soaked up in the fawns and musk-rose of her skin. David remembered how the Elizabethan poets thought of the sexual climax: an expense of spirit, a waste of precious and finite resources. That's what had gone wrong: instead of spending his strength he should have hoarded it, to blazon the truth in cadmium red and Naples yellow. But he had squandered it all on subtle browns, on the coral-tinted folds and flaps of Jennet's flesh.

Now Venice. Now Jennet, whom by some process not entirely of his own will he'd married, Jennet whom in his own way he loved, mother of the children he loved, part-time painter in the time she had to spare from taking care of house and children, this same Jennet had been plucked out from the ranks of British artists to represent the best of them in Venice. The British pavilion would be a shrine filled with her curiously muted pictures and all their bars and grids. David wished he could feel pride unalloyed by jealousy, but it was hard and he could not.

So Venice in May as pretty as the pictures, and Jennet at the opening of the Biennale in a Jean Muir dress, David taking glasses of champagne from the trays of passing waiters until he could no longer stand. It was Lewis Delafield who caught him when he stumbled; Lewis was there to write about the Biennale and praise Jennet. By the waters of the Grand Canal I sat down and wept, said David, and he did weep there, before Lewis and a porter tugged him up the hotel stairs and got him into bed.

Lewis Delafield, who reviewed Jennet Mallow's first exhibition in 1953, remained her champion and also became her friend after they met in Cornwall two years later. He had been living there with Elizabeth Foy, who was talked of as a very promising new sculptor, but confounded expectations when she later disappeared into a convent. Her acquaintances were shocked: it was such a waste, they said, and besides they knew she was in love with Lewis. But Lewis had married someone else six months or so before, an unlikely woman, Deirdre. Unlikely, in his friends' view, because she was stern and dull and apparently uninterested in art. Jennet though, when she met her, saw that Deirdre was rather beautiful and that Lewis might have liked in her precisely her detachment from the over-excited world in which he worked.

Lewis. A clever, strange and sensitive young man, younger than Jennet by enough years for her to treat him lightly at first, as if he were someone's teenage brother. Too young to have been in the war, although he did do National Service in Malaya. But old enough by the late 1950s to have become a noted critic of contemporary culture who always had something pertinent to say. Lewis had a good voice, a mobile face and the gift of clear expression, without the fault that sometimes goes with it of over-simplification. In 1960 he was asked to make a television programme about Barbara Hepworth. It was well received and Lewis, enthusiastic yet natural in front of the television cameras, began to appear quite regularly as an interviewer and presenter.

There was something in him that reminded Jennet of David, just a little. His dark eyes, perhaps, with their oddly unstable colour, which seemed to deepen when he was tired or angry, or in love. He had David's dark Celtic hair, but unlike David a Celt's build, compact and wiry where David was lean and angular.

Lewis. A supper-party friend in London, someone to say hello to at an exhibition, someone to rely on for an excellent review. A different, closer friend in Cornwall, where he spent much time, Elizabeth having given him the use of her old cottage when she walled herself up with the Carmelites. The cottage was on the outskirts of a village near Trevenna, the house which Jennet rented every summer for ten years, and in those summers Lewis would come and swim with her or fish or talk for hours about himself and painting. Deirdre Delafield did not care for Elizabeth's cottage, which lacked electricity and plumbing, so even after Lewis married he was often there alone.

Lewis, like Patrick Mann and Leonard Kaspar, was one of those who recognised Jennet's greatness even before it found its full expression. Patrick would always say he knew Jennet had the seeds of genius in her from the moment David showed him her two *Window* paintings and the blue bowl full of lemons. Kaspar saw it too, and did much to promote it; it was largely through his influence that Jennet won the World Bank Commission in 1957. Both these men had their own motives: Patrick's frankly mercenary, Kaspar's tangled up in his desire to be seen as a connoisseur of all that was rare and precious. But Lewis Delafield loved Jennet's work for no other reason than itself; he believed she was among the finest painters of our time and, while he lived, he took every opportunity to say it.

One of the things that Lewis often talked about was the hallmark of serious art. His essay on what makes an artwork

148

great, posthumously published by the Oxford University Press in 1968, is to this day the last word on the subject. His argument is that there is a quality, impossible to define but impossible to mistake, that distinguishes the work of genius from the rest, however competent or pleasing. Preference and personal taste are irrelevant to the distinction; it is not necessary to enjoy the work of Malevich, for instance, in order to concede its brilliance. Time and genre are equally unimportant in Delafield's opinion; a bison in a cave at Altamira, Piero's *Resurrection*, a portrait head of limestone found in a tomb at Gizeh, Mondrian's 1930 *Composition*, a clay jug made by an anonymous potter to hold wine, masterpieces all of them, irrespective of period or place. Having said this quality in art was indefinable, Lewis went on to define it, using such terms as integrity, honesty, purity of intention. He steered clear of the word soul because he disliked lazy hints of mysticism, but it hovers anyhow in his work, hiding behind its close relation, spiritual. There was no other way in which he could begin to speak of the immanent spirit of great art. But there were no words, in any case, that could convey completely a matter of instinct and perception. The ones that Lewis was forced to use for want of any better were, he knew, overused, inadequate. The word genius especially. But with what other could he tell what he knew to be the truth of Jennet's work?

Would Lewis have fallen in love with Jennet anyway, if it had not been for that work? Perhaps not: for him the woman and the work were indivisible. He probably did not intend to love the woman, but he couldn't help it, it was inevitable from the moment he lost all objectivity and could no longer separate Jennet from her painting.

On the Riva degli Schiavoni in the opalescent dawn, and Jennet mortified and tired, humiliated by her husband. So many people had been there that night to watch him getting drunk. You don't deserve it, Lewis whispered, and because just then she thought he might be right, because she was so tired, because loyalty was tiring, because Lewis was sweet and by her side, on the Riva degli Schiavoni with the sunlight just beginning to part the wisps of cloud but mist and water merging still in shades of grey and pearl, because of all of these, she put her hands up to his face and drew it down to hers and kissed him hard, until she felt the startle and the answering hardness of his body.

The weary hotel porter unlocked the doors to let them in, to Lewis's room, where Jennet took off her blue silk dress and lay down on Lewis' tidy bed and he made surprised and grateful love to her, which happened rather fast.

David, waking up at lunchtime with an aching head, took himself to Harry's Bar to try to cure his hangover and en-sure tomorrow's, Jennet gave an interview and went to a luncheon hosted by the British Consul, and Lewis took the train back home to London, where his wife told him she was pregnant. Her news shocked him very much: he had been planning all the long way home to say that he had to leave her. Meanwhile at the far end of Cheyne Walk, Roddy MacNamara planed old oak for new floorboards and re-plastered the high walls of Jennet's house. Shall you be painting pictures on them? he'd asked her. Absolutely not, she said. We'll have white paint everywhere, plain old-fashioned whitewash.

Except in the room meant for Vanessa. When Jennet saw

that small square room white-painted, it made her think of orphans' cells, and straight away she went to Peter Jones to buy pink-sprigged paper and material for her sick child's cocoon. The other people in her family could take starkness, but not Vanessa. Almost ten years old now, her fair hair faintly green-tinged, falling in a fringe above her solemn face.

As it gradually took shape under Roddy's command, the old house began to be what Jennet needed: a cool, white, restful space, somewhere that allowed for concentration, filled with waterlight and the cries of gulls. The souls of shipwrecked sailors, the tellers of folk stories say, and they do sound bereft and haunted, those wheeling, searching gulls.

To be so near the river is to be in some way shielded from the harsher aspects of the city, as if the river carried with it traces of the fields it runs through and the promise of the sea. Even in the heat of London the river has a salt smell, clean beneath its topnotes of sludge and sewage. And those who live beside it share the rhythm of its tides, its ebb and flow, in their subconscious.

In the house on Cheyne Walk Jennet came to know the river. She was grateful to it. Like a watery escape route it connected her to places other than the grimy city, and brought her the daily blessing of its light. When she first lived by it, in Hammersmith, in the winter after Ben was born, she had not liked the river. Then its breath seemed foggy and malevolent, laden with disease and sulphur. Now, although on dull grey days it could still turn hostile, crawling cold and sluggish past her door, she had mainly made her peace with it. It was a link in the long chain of compromises she had learned to make: city over countryside, England over Spain, soft light instead of stark, David for better or for worse.

There was a time when Jennet could have combed out separately the various strands of her existence, but now they were all tangled in the complicated warps and wefts of other people's lives. She had had to make adjustments and to shift, and as she had changed so had the river, seeming lighter now, less sullen, as London's air turned cleaner by grace of newly enacted law. Jennet could survive the city now, and even grow to like it, with the help of her white-painted house and the nearness of running water.

Gradually the river made its way into her painting. Although Jennet was never in any real sense an urban painter, she remembered the impression London made on her when she first lived there in 1947. Strong white verticals, horizontal bars of grey and green and brown. Fifteen years later, as she came to learn her own reaches of the river, she began to see its lines more clearly, especially the lattice forms of bridges over water and by buildings. During the 1960s, while she continued to explore the potential of geometric forms, London and its river were a presence in her work.

In the two or three years after Venice, Jennet went on making paintings under superimposed grids. *Late Afternoon: December 1962* shows a smoky sky under a fretwork made of actual branches of bare cherry; two other paintings finished in the same year, *Cell I* and *Cell II*, are both enclosed in wooden boxes faced with wire mesh. The culminating painting of the series, the much-celebrated *Rivergod*, which Jennet made in 1964 and is now in the Philips Collection, is a long streak of greeny-grey flecked with gold, running underneath a set of metal bars painted black like the girders of a bridge.

After *Rivergod* the wire and wood began to soften into cords and thread. The *Chelsea* suite of paintings, in which Jennet paid her homage to Whistler, are studies in grey and blue, each covered in a mesh of fine grey silk. Apart from the use of silk, these works are significant because in them Jennet experimented with techniques of thinning paint, as she would go on doing over the following years.

That other stretch of often-painted water, the Venice lagoon, did not enter into Jennet's work – despite her admiration for Whistler and for Turner's later paintings – except, perhaps, as a private reference in the magnificent *Isola*. It's a possible interpretation, although Jennet would never confirm it. She gave it to Lewis Delafield in 1967. It is a beautiful thing of ghostly pearl and grey, shrouded in a veil so sheer it might be made of cobweb.

These veiled paintings, and the ones that followed, have an iconic aspect, like images of devotion hidden from unauthorised view in temples or in chapels. Their coverings are iconostases, screening the sacramental, or the embroidered curtains drawn across a tabernacle. They have other resonances too, suggestions of fragility, as if the pictures they hid were too delicate to stand prolonged daylight.

Unlike divine or fragile images, Jennet's paintings were intended to be seen, not made invisible by their coverings. Those overlays of net and silk are there to add a new dimension and to deepen the illusion of cloud and mist that imbues so much of Jennet Mallow's painting in that period. And yet these veils are symbolic, as, in later work, would be her tightened strings and wires. Curators in public spaces often hang the paintings with their coverings looped back or drawn half way to reveal the underlying paint and to stop their visitors from lifting the veils themselves. But however transparent they may be, or pushed aside, they still whisper ambiguity; simultaneously revealing and concealing.

Jennet never made explicit the sacramental aspect of her art, but she kept it in her mind. It is clear in her final paintings. In the 1960s though, the metaphysical was there by implication only; the paintings themselves are abstract. They change over the years and on into the next decade, the

153

palette of dawn and dusk colours surrendering to a hundred different shades of white. *Rivergod* has warmth in it and flashes of sunlight, but less than ten years later the 1972 painting *Cliff Face* is frozen, empty, white. There is an iciness in the paintings that ensued. They belong to an Antarctic time, Jennet's own white south.

Ice-bound. All sensation frozen. Salt tears crystalline. Lewis Delafield's first child, Guy, was born in 1962 when Lewis was in a blinding state of pain, desire for Jennet Mallow growing in him like a tumour. While his wife grew heavier by the day, making sweet plans for the coming child, he tortured himself with memories of Jennet. Jennet stepping from her slither of blue silk, Jennet's lithe, brown body. Jennet's breasts, the smoothness of her skin as she lay beneath him, unresisting. Jennet, known from David Heaton's paintings, but so much more beautiful when he had her in his arms. He no longer wanted Deirdre with her breasts blue-veined and leaking milky fluid, he only wanted Jennet. Jennet and her magician's powers, her absolute command of form and light. Otter-slim, kingfisher quick, as fresh and cool on that Venetian morning as the petals of a lily.

But Jennet was not in love with Lewis. She belonged to David and she believed in the promises she'd made to him. She knew that Lewis was lovesick but she thought he would grow out of it, and in the meantime she avoided him when it was possible, and when it was not, she teased him; if she was sisterly, or comradely, she hoped Lewis would stop thinking of her as a lover and return to being a friend. She also hoped he would forget about that dawn in Venice. To her it was a memory that aroused only regret.

In the spring of 1965 Jennet's sister Barbara telephoned her to say that she was getting married. You sound surprised, she said to Jennet. How very rude of you.

Oh no, said Jennet, quickly. That's wonderful. That's the best of news.

Barbara had been working as the matron at a boarding school near Sherborne since Richard Mallow died, and her intended was a master, recently retired. At the age of sixty-eight he was two years older than her mother. He had never before married. Now he wanted to go back to his ancestral home in Scotland with a bride. But that's so far away, said Jennet, so far away from Mother.

Well yes, it is, her sister said. That's why I'm ringing you.

The wedding photographs are in an envelope among the other photographs that Jennet stored in an Aquascutum box. Barbara, fat as ever, in a girlish wedding dress, with the white-haired and already stooping Lionel beside her. Lionel McPhail. Lorna Mallow smiling brilliantly beneath a wide-brimmed hat, David Heaton looking distracted, Jennet in an op-art shift, absolutely of the period, and the children, Sarah, Vanessa, Ben. The girls are dressed as bridesmaids, but without the bond of their identical blue satin it would be hard to tell that they were sisters, still less that they were twins. At thirteen Sarah was well developed, with a round and cheerful face and a mass of dark-brown curls, but Vanessa next to her was wraith-like, half her sister's size. She had been ill for much of the preceding winter with an undiagnosed complaint and even then could not stand for longer than a few minutes unsupported. Ben was seventeen, and taller than his father.

After the wedding Lorna raged and wept. Everyone I ever loved is dead and gone. Oh, Harold, my poor darling brother.

My brother and my father, my mother and my sister, and now Barbara has left me on my own. You, Jennet, you've never really loved me, you've always been too busy with your oh-so-very-special painting, you hardly ever bother to visit, it's so obvious you simply do not care.

What Lorna said was true, Jennet in her heart conceded. She had taken the children down to Sherborne on their way to Cornwall once a year, and Lorna had stayed in London sometimes over Christmas. But months went by without Jennet seeing her mother, and when she thought of her it was always with relief that Barbara was there as her companion. Jennet had shut out of her mind the realities of her mother's and her sister's life. She could not pretend she did not know them. The bridge fours and the cinema outings, the coffee mornings in aid of charity, the local history group. All those sad women still in search of love, even if it had to come in the mildewed form of Lionel. On Lorna Mallow's dressing table was a cut-glass powder bowl with a flesh-pink velour puff, and a purple, lidded pot in which she put the combings of her hair. Jennet opened that pot once, when Lorna wasn't looking, and saw the meagre strands all snarled together like the discard of an untidy bird's haphazard nest.

You could come and stay with us, she pleaded faintly, and Lorna cheered up at once. Now that's a good idea, I've always rather thought I'd like to be in London.

Disarmed by guilt, Jennet could say nothing when Lorna made it clear she had in mind something more permanent than a visit. I'll look for somewhere of my own, she murmured vaguely. When I've had a chance to find my feet. Perhaps I'll go back to Jamaica. Anyway, you have lots of room. And I could be very useful. In your studio, for a start.

Doing what exactly? David asked.

Filling in the backgrounds? Doing little details. I used to

be a dab hand with a brush. It's where Jennet gets it from, I am quite sure.

You must admit there's something valiant about her, David said a few weeks later, watching his mother-in-law in crimson lipstick introducing herself gaily to a BBC producer as the Heatons' new apprentice. Yes, but maddening, Jennet replied, mourning her loss of space. The cloistered quiet of the house on Cheyne Walk was under threat. Vanessa had been too ill to go to school all year and might never be well enough to go again, and now there was her mother. Voices all day long and mouths to feed, all these people, hungry for care, hungry for attention.

That sanctuary of cloistered space. So contingent and so easily defiled. An afternoon in the middle of June, conquering sunshine chasing rain, bright light striking diamonds on leaves still cupping water. A white rose in flower at the gate, and the river sequinned by the sun as if, like Jennet, it were about to celebrate the opening of David's exhibition. His largest and most glamorous yet, at the Redleaf Gallery. Royalty and rock stars expected at the party. Jennet had come home earlier than arranged to a house that she knew, for once, would be unpeopled but for David. She had bought a bottle of champagne. It was intended as peace offering and tribute both, a healing draught that she and David needed.

The past six months had tried them. Lorna's chafing presence irritated David; he especially resented her demands for entertainment, as if she were a passing guest. Vanessa had been ill again, the prognosis for her future was bleaker than before; she would never be self-reliant. Ben's future was in turmoil too: he would be leaving school next week but still had no idea what to do. He had rejected the conventional choices and was talking vaguely of going to be a lumberjack in Canada or taking time out to travel. And as ever, David's response to trouble was to turn away from it, to drown it in the amber depths of whisky.

Jennet's response was to lose herself even more in work. Some would say that she was right to do so. Her most recent paintings, particularly *Rivergod* and *Isola,* had received huge acclaim. She was making enough money to keep her household and to fund Vanessa's extra care without the help of David. She was working on the foothills of a mountain that she now thought she could climb. The plaudits she was winning had not made her complacent, she knew there was much further she could go. She had been forty in 1964, a birthday that felt like a climacteric; she resolved to treat it as a springboard.

But David was in some sense grieving. Jennet's confidence was armour, yes, in the daily round, but never insulation: she was aware, even on the hardest days, of her husband's feelings. How could it be otherwise, after so much time? She had lived with David and had loved him for so long that his moods were like her own, sensed and understood, needing no words to make them plain.

And so she knew that he was disappointed. As a young man he was certain of his genius, but he was so much older now and had frittered it away in portraits whose success was his defeat. Every celebrated picture generated more commissions: he was on a treadmill, and secretly he knew it was his own weaknesses and fears that stopped him jumping off. Fear of failure. Fear of never living up to the promises he'd made his younger self. Fear of comparison with Jennet. He was afraid that she might really be the greater artist. And what would he be then? Merely the artist's husband, a man who made some money painting nudes and fly-by-night celebrities but who came nowhere near the truth of his own vision. Art is impossible after Auschwitz. He remembered Richard Benjamin saying that in Cornwall, as others had done since, and his own assurance that they were wrong. But what would the men whom he'd left dying on the bloodstained sands of Crete now say if they were resurrected in the Redleaf Gallery? Would they be filled again with hope at the sight of David's portrait of the bass guitarist of the Rolling Stones?

That Jennet knew of David's feelings did not necessarily make her sympathetic. In fact she found him self-indulgent. She would have liked some practical support during the bad times, and she was bored of David's drinking. Probably the boredom showed: certainly she had been a little distant. On the day of David's opening, she hoped to close the gap. She was looking forward to Cornwall in a fortnight; there, at Trevenna, she and David would be friends again, and maybe even lovers. Today she'd take a step in that direction. And so the bottle of champagne, and her unannounced return. They would drink to his success and they would kiss and then get dressed together for the party. She had a new dress that David had not seen. It zipped up at the back; she would need him to help her.

It was quiet in the house when she opened the front door. She called out from the hall but David didn't answer. She supposed he must have gone somewhere, although he had said he would be staying at home that day. She was disappointed. Something about this planned encounter in an empty house aroused her, as if David were her lover not her husband. It had been months since they last made love and his absence was frustrating. But she might as well make what she could of it, and get on with some work. She went up the stairs to her studio. A sanctuary designed for peace;

159

whitewashed, orderly, flooded with sunlight on that June afternoon.

The door was open wide. She saw David sitting in the armchair by the window. His eyes were shut: he had not seen her nor evidently heard her light step on the stairs. He was already in his evening clothes: stark contrast of white and black, his hair black still, although threaded now with silver. His head tilted back against her chair, dark against the brightness of the window and the white paint, white too the linen fabric on the chair. And a woman in a white dress kneeling in between his legs, her back turned to the door. Her head rising and falling rhythmically. Her hair fanned out across the blackness of his lap like the gold rays of a monstrance. David's face contorted. And then Jennet must have moved, or perhaps a floorboard creaked, for his eyes opened and he saw her, standing in the open door. Too late, by then. He moans out Jennet's name and Corinne lifts her head and turns to look at Jennet. There is no embarrassment in her face at all, only triumph. Her wet mouth gleaming as she smiles, her fine hair drifting back in place like golden feathers.

Later, at the Redleaf Gallery, there is Corinne again, with her husband, Victor. Victor is a very rich man by now; it is said that he owns half of London. He also has a peerage, for political service rendered – Corinne is known as Lady Golding. She is looking lovely in Balenciaga, and men are clustered round her while Victor looks on with a keeper's eye.

Jennet need not have gone to David's private view, she could have pleaded illness, but she would not let Corinne know how badly she was shocked. Instead she got Mabel Harris to zip her into her new dress and she held her head up high as she stood at David's side.

Lewis Delafield was also at the Redleaf. He had loved Jennet intensely and forlornly for so long that his love was like an injury, a wound in hand or side that would not heal. That night at the Gallery Jennet saw the pain in him because for once she was looking at him closely, remembering a dawn light and incoherent words of love. I shall be in Cornwall soon, she told him, suddenly. On my own most of the time. And shall you? Shall you be staying at Elizabeth's cottage? Shall we meet perhaps? If you would like to meet, then I would too.

A man's hindquarters, greenish in the moonlight, working up and down above her with determined purpose; a terrier's white scut frantically bobbing as it scrabbles at a hole. Lewis is so eager and so abject, so desperately in love. He would do anything he could do to make Jennet happy, but she will not do what he wants her to and fall in love. Instead she falls deeply into guilt, and while Lewis worries away within her she turns her face aside.

Find consolation where you can, she recalls some cynic saying, and she did think she needed consolation; she just hadn't realised its price. She and Vanessa were on their own that summer at Trevenna. Lorna was visiting Barbara, Ben travelling overland to India, Sarah in Italy with friends. David, Jennet thought, was somewhere with Corinne Golding, possibly in France. After the party at the Redleaf and dinner in a restaurant, David and Jennet had gone back to Cheyne Walk together, taken off their evening clothes, lain down on their bed. David had said nothing to her since the moment she had seen him with his cock in Corinne's mouth.

If Jennet could have turned away from the studio door, if she could have gone back down the stairs in silence and walked out of the house, she would have done, but she could not, and so she felt some confrontation had to follow. David would rather have pretended Jennet had seen nothing. If his manner was a little sheepish it was also nonchalant. Not a bad turnout, don't you think, he said, and, as if he were settling for sleep as usual, goodnight Bird. Sleep tight.

David, you have to tell me, Jennet said, after minutes listening to his breathing, you have to tell me how long this . . . how long have you, how long . . . ?

And you have to understand, he answered. He was angry suddenly, and wide awake. It meant nothing, Corinne and I, we've known each other so well, for so long, we're friends.

And lovers too, long before you knew me, Jennet thinks but does not say, remembering Corinne on the evening they first met, her hand on David's shoulder. Remembering the shift in her own world, the newly unleashed arrow of desire she had felt that night when David touched her. Now she can scarcely name her feelings, they are so intertwined and tangled. Shock is there, an inadvertent voyeur's self-disgust, and anger: rage at the despoiling of her tranquil place. Jealousy, of course. But guilt also: a little nagging voice is hissing in her ear about hypocrisy, a hotel room in Venice, soft light on a strange man's body. And she feels a sudden need for change, a desire to precipitate some action in response to all the compromises of almost twenty years.

Why don't you go to her? she said. You can have her, if that's what you want.

All right, he said. I shall. If that's what you want, Jennet.

So now the aching beauty of the landscape and the scouring sea and long walks on her own. Narrow lanes with high banks cobbled a thousand years ago and more from stone and turf and blocks of granite; sweetbriar, rosebay willow-herb, a salt taste on the air. Slower walks with Vanessa's hand in hers: in the sea the girl is as pale as a mermaid, with her floating strands of hair. And Lewis Delafield stealing days away from Deirdre and his children to make anguished love to Jennet and one-sided plans for a shared future.

In August Deirdre and the children come to spend a month in Cornwall. Jennet meets the children then: Guy who is four and square and sunny, and Fabia, two, serious and dark-eyed like her father. Vanessa loves them, wants to spend as much time as she can with them, and they seem to love her too. She has seldom come across a person younger and less strong than her, and Jennet sees her playing with them, drawing with them, contented in her quietness with their chatter.

It is obvious to Jennet that Deirdre loves her husband very much. She is like the stage-door fan who cannot quite believe it when she actually meets the star. A beautiful woman in her way, red-haired and milky-skinned, but unaware of her own beauty, diffident and shy. Dull even, and perhaps an odd foil to her excitable and ardent husband, unless she was exactly what he'd asked for, someone who adored him and would never be a challenge.

Jennet discourages Lewis from talking about Deirdre; there are disloyalties enough, for heaven's sake, without piling on some more. She sees that Lewis does not know what it is he wants. He plays with various scenarios: family man, avant-garde intellectual, broadcasting celebrity, Cornish recluse. At the moment he has thrown himself wholeheartedly into his love affair, and already she can see the dangers. He is too passionate, too desperate. He fights for time with her as if it were essential air. He takes wild risks while she wants discretion: he telephones her at all hours, leaves Deirdre on her own, and stumbles through the darkness to her in the middle of the night.

When Lewis is making love to her Jennet remembers David. Her body remembers David's, even against her will, and Lewis's mouth, his hands, his penis, feel as alien as a broken tooth. She is tense with him, because she knows however hard he tries he will not turn her gratitude and affection into love. And although she also knows she has in consequence the power to hurt him, she tells herself half-truths, which for a time excuse her. This is infatuation, she says. Lewis will recover. In any case Lewis hardly knows her: he thinks she is her painting, he is more in love with his idea of her than with her reality, he is incurious about the past. All the cords that tie her – the children and her mother, her memories of place, her deep connectedness despite herself to David – are like spiders' silk to Lewis and as easily torn apart.

At Trevenna in that summer all Lewis will allow himself to see is Jennet, tender with her wraith-like daughter and free of her dissolute husband at long last. Most lovely Jennet, in mind and body beautiful, and the more alluring because a little distant. Her separateness thrills him. It is intrinsic in his mind to greatness in an artist; when she turns her eyes from his he imagines luminescence in them, a vision of light in waiting, and not the dull preoccupations that cloud the ordinary gaze. Although she drives him to a pitch of desire he has never known before, although he wants her all the time, still when he holds her in his arms he is wondering and breathless.

But Lewis has his own cords too, and they are tightly knotted. He has not told Deirdre about Jennet, who has asked him not to. But Deirdre will of course find out. She may already know: his distracted manner while she was there in Cornwall would have stirred even the most trusting wife's suspicions. When Lewis forces her to face the truth she will be very hurt.

A tense and difficult time then, and at the end of it David arrived one midnight without warning, coming straight through the front door and up the stairs to the bedroom, where Lewis and Jennet were asleep. Lewis did not wake up at first but Jennet was startled out of sleep by the noise that David made. It was raining and his clothes were wet. She could smell the dampness, and the whisky on his breath. He began to pull hurriedly at his clothes, wrenching his jacket off, his shirt, fumbling with the buckle of his belt, and before Jennet could get out of bed he was next to her and pushing his way in. Move up, he said. I'm very cold.

David, stop, she said, but he was butting at her shoulder gently with his head, the cold rain dropping from it on to her uncovered skin. Move up, he said again. And he slid a little further down the bed so that his mouth was level with her breast and in the darkness she could feel him rooting for it like a suckling child. Then Lewis, at last woken, leaped up and seized the lamp beside him. He flicked the light switch on. David smiled up at him, with cracked lips smeared red. He looked and smelled as if he were a tramp.

Get out, shouted Lewis.

Don't be so unkind, David said, still smiling. I'm cold. I'm very sleepy. I'm not doing you any harm. This is my bed anyway. The least you can do is let me watch you while you fuck. Like Victor. Victor watches. So go on, Lewis. Let me watch.

Recovering from his breakdown, David Heaton spent the next three months in a mental hospital in Surrey. Jennet paid the bills. In lucid moments he assured her everything would be all right . . . he would be well again in no time . . . his best work still to come. You'll be proud of me, I promise, Bird. I'll show I'm the tops.

But his moments of clarity were few; for the most part he made no sense and his doctor prescribed total rest. He appeared to be suffering from exhaustion, the doctor said.

165

Brought on by stress and also, possibly, the illicit use of drugs, a combined effect disconnecting in some way the rational areas of his brain. Now his behaviour was, to put it mildly, antisocial. What can you mean? Jennet asked. His speech is inappropriate, the doctor answered primly. There is a marked absence of inhibition.

Corinne, in a coffee bar in Frith Street, appears to have remade herself. Her hair, which used to be cut sleekly, is still gold, but longer now and straighter; it hangs on each side of her face like thick brocade. Her eyes are rimmed with black and she smells of something musky, a compound of sweet oils and spice. Her latest lover is another artist. He is over from New York. Tonight there is to be a happening, she says to Jennet, painting's so *vieux jeu*, my God.

Jennet has asked Corinne for this meeting because she feels obscurely that an inquest is in order; she needs to know what happened to David in the summer and what Corinne's intentions are. But in this new coffee bar with its shiny red machines Corinne only waves her cigarette back and forth, and laughs.

Don't take it all so seriously, she says. But you always take things seriously, don't you? David and I, well obviously I'm very sorry he's gone loopy, but you could say he brought it on himself. Not such a good idea, dropping acid with whisky, but he's not one for moderation; never has been; he walks on the wild side, don't you think?

Corinne leans across the table to light a cigarette for Jennet, and as they touch their hands together, shielding the flame, their two heads bent towards each other, a moment of intimacy is kindled that fills Jennet with disgust.

Is it true that you let Victor watch you when you were in bed? Jennet wants to see the evidence of pain in Corinne, will inflict the pain herself if that's what it takes to shake Corinne's self-composure. Claw marks on her carefully primed skin, her mouth battered and bleeding.

Oh, come off it, Jennet, Corinne answers, world-weary. How Victor gets his kicks is not your business.

But David is. And David's locked up in a room that has prints of soothing seascapes on the walls and bars across the window.

I've said I'm sorry. Of course I'm sorry. But I'm sure he will recover.

And then? Are you going to be with him, are you leaving Victor?

Leaving Victor? Jennet, you are *such* a fool. Do you have the faintest idea how much Victor makes a year? Open-handed, open-minded: Victor is the perfect husband.

October 1966. A pivotal time. That was the month when Ben, who was supposed to be on his way back home from Kashmir, forgot to keep in touch with Jennet. There had been no word from him since the end of August. Jennet had done the things she could – telephoned consulates, sent worried letters – and had received the usual reassurance. Teenagers. Self-centredness. Unreliable post, and telephones expensive. He'll turn up. Don't worry. But she did worry, inevitably, and she played on her mental screen the same repeated scenes: lorries careering round blind bends, feet sliding on loose mountain scree, desperate flounderings in a rushing river. Giving Ben's description to a High Commission official – six feet one, light brown hair – she had seen the younger Ben in her mind's eye so vividly she moaned aloud in pain. Like an image on an overpainted canvas re-emerging, her son looked at her across the years, bewildered but ultimately trusting. She recalled him staggering up the beach on sturdy dimpled legs the first year in Santiago. How small he was that year, how happy. Blond hair like curls of butter, his whole-hearted, rich and rounded baby laugh. She recalled too the wounded look that sometimes flickered like a shadow in his eyes: when the twins were born, for instance, or when his father's moods were particularly black. But Jennet had been able always to dispel the shadows in the end and bring back the laughter. Now she felt her power-lessness most keenly. Of all the children, Ben was the closest to her heart. She should have been connected to him by sheer effort of that heart, but this past summer she had been unforgivably distracted. And even when, a fortnight later, he sent a telegram to say that he was well and he had forgotten how long it had been since he last wrote, she still felt negligent.

She ran the risk of losing Sarah too. Sarah was in love with Italy and an Italian boy, but most of all with a family in whose Sicilian home she now proposed to live.

They're a proper family, she told Jennet. They sit down together every evening. The father is always there and the mother stays at home. She looks after them, she cooks them lovely meals.

Yes, but, Jennet protested, stricken and trying not to show it, I cook you meals, don't I? Anyway you can't just up and go to Sicily. You're much too young. You have to go to school.

But you know I hate it, Sarah said. I'm never going to be as clever as you. I can leave school in any case, and there's nothing you can do to stop me. I don't want to be in London, and that's that. If you loved me you would want me to be happy. Trying to make me stay here shows you don't.

Of course I do. Of course, but would you be happy, really? Happy with this family, happy giving up your future . . . ?

I'd be much happier than you. Happier than Daddy. I wouldn't be giving up my future. That's the future I want, being a proper mother, having loads of children, being a proper wife.

Oh sweetheart, Jennet said. Sarah had always been a wilful child, with her father's recklessness and her mother's determination, but untempered by her mother's sense of duty. They reached a compromise that time: Sarah would stay on at school in London for a year, but still she had the final word.

Just in case you think I will, I'm absolutely *not* going to share my house with Lewis Delafield. I hate him. He has a huge mole on his chin.

Sarah, what do you mean?

Oh don't be so stupid, Mum, said Sarah, scornful. Vanessa's told me all about it. How busy you've been these last few weeks. Do you think Vanessa's blind and deaf? Poor Daddy.

It was also in October 1966 that Jennet Mallow met Jack Owen again, for the first time in five years. He had been teaching at the University of California, exhibiting abroad and travelling, so their paths had never crossed. Every summer at Trevenna she had missed him. She had heard that he had been successful in the States, and there was mention of a second marriage; but Jack was not the sort of man to send Christmas cards or letters.

When Jennet saw him she realised that his absence had hollowed out a space in her that she had not felt until his presence filled it. It was hard to put a name to this strange recognition. She had never known Jack Owen very well and now, after all this time, he was virtually a stranger; yet she felt when she ran into him at Piccadilly Station that she had rediscovered a lost twin. But there was something else mixed in with this emotion, a physical excitement that surprised her, as if a butterfly were trembling at the threshold of her womb.

Well, how nice to see you, Mrs Heaton, Jack Owen said; matter-of-fact and unsurprised, it seemed, in the middle of a throng of people. He was greyer than he had been when she last saw him, and there were lines radiating from the corners of his eyes, which were whiter than his sunburnt skin. Those eyes still clear as sea-glass, and unnerving. He was on his way to see some friends, he told her, and was staying in London for a day or two, doing a little business. Come to supper, she said, could you? Yes, he said. Tomorrow.

On this desk there is a bowl – Korean, glazed stoneware, made in the sixteenth century; it was a present to Jennet Mallow from the potter Bernard Leach. Undecorated, completely simple and completely perfect. But it was not made to be an ornament, it is a tea bowl, and long ago it must have been in ordinary use, its fine lines less regarded than the liquid that it held. What gave it its function and made it desirable to its first owner was the empty space in it, not its outer shell.

Think of the last of Cézanne's Mont St Victoire watercolours, or a Chinese painting of a swallow on the wing. A few brushstrokes and then empty space, but this empty space is full. It's the space that makes the mountain real, as the feather makes the sky. It's the space between the columns of a monastery's cloister that gives a soul its room to pray. Put your fingers in the hollow at the core of a stone sculpture of a mother and her child. That space defines the relationship between them: both separate and indivisibly one.

In the drawing room of Jennet Mallow's house beside the river Jack Owen holds his glass up to the light and flicks it gently with a nail to make it ring. Next to him, on a sofa, Lorna is complaining about the surliness of the conductor on a number 19 bus. When I lived in Jamaica, she tells Jack, the people were always smiling. I can't think why they change so much when they get to London.

At a table by the window Vanessa is threading blue beads on to string. Sarah is watching Jack. It strikes Jennet as peculiar that neither her mother nor her daughters are apparently disturbed by the electrostatic charge that fills the air. She half expects to see scorch marks on the floorboards where she treads.

Jack is too vivid in this pale room. The room is long and narrow, with windows at each end and a fireplace in the centre, before which are two elongated sofas covered in bleached linen. There is little other furniture: a low table between the sofas, Vanessa's gateleg table in the alcove of one window, some Danish wooden chairs, and, at the far end of the room, a piano. David used to like to play it, bashing out jazz chords and singing songs to which he only ever knew some of the words. Jack in American blue denim and a shirt of tartan wool looks like a splash of paint spilled on this backdrop. If he feels awkward, he does not let it show.

When darkness falls Jack helps to draw the shutters. Before they close them he and Jennet stand together for a moment side by side and look out at the dancing lamplight on black water. You've got yourself a lovely place, he says, and Jennet smiles at his Cornish sounds filtered now through California.

Supper drags on far too long. All through it Jennet wishes she were rid of Lorna and the girls, who fence her in at her own dining table, interrupting conversation. Silent Vanessa eats her chicken pie so slowly that Jennet has to fight the urge to feed her with a spoon. And yet, in spite of herself, she sees that safe in the glow of candlelight they might be a family together. With a stab of pain, she thinks of David in his neon-lighted home. He would be eating supper, if he did eat, off a thick green plastic plate with smeared and blunted cutlery; he would be drinking tepid water from a beaker, not claret from a long-stemmed glass. There would be no glass within his reach, nor sharpened steel, nothing with which he or any other inmate might do themselves harm. And Ben, too, what would he be eating, somewhere on the road in Turkey, making his slow way home? Those members of her family who ought to be kept safe within the lighted circle were outside it in the darkness, and Jennet had lost the power to draw them back.

If Lewis had been at supper that night in Jennet's dining room, and able to discern her thoughts, he would have been desolated. In his mind he had already abstracted Jennet from the prison of her family, and all that remained to fix was detail. He did not imagine Jennet would take David back once he was recovered, but he knew that until then no practical arrangements could be made. He knew that Jennet did not love him as much as he loved her, but he was sure that, free from guilt and David, she soon would. And then he would tell Deirdre. In the meantime he saw Jennet whenever she allowed it, and he was glad that on occasion she would let him share her bed. She can't have been the only woman who found some comfort in the arms of an admiring man she could not love.

It was not comfort that Jennet wanted from Jack Owen. Never before had she felt this strange compulsion: to touch and hold and taste and take within. She could not comprehend it rationally but she knew, that evening in her house beside the river, that she had to touch him to make real his re-emergence in her life. Otherwise it was as if Jack were a delusion, brought into being by loneliness, confusion, need.

He made it easy for her. They had been talking during supper about people he knew, artists in New York whose paintings were on such a scale they had to work in warehouses not studios. With cranes and hoists and scaffolding. Jesus, it makes us so trite, he said, with our little easels. There was one man in particular who needed even more space, because he always painted with an audience. Art for him was a spectator sport, quite literally, and a contact one as well: he used his hands instead of brushes; sometimes he used his entire body. Or other people's bodies, all covered in paint and rolled across the canvas.

With their clothes on? Lorna asked. Not usually, said Jack. Oh, said Lorna. I do hope Jennet's not going to do that in her studio, think of the nasty mess.

I'd like to see your studio, Jack said. Are visitors permitted?

Jennet doesn't like people seeing her work in progress, Lorna began to say, but Jennet interrupted. Old friends are different, she said, taking Jack's arm.

Leading Jack up the flights of stairs made the half-open doors they passed on each of the landings unfamiliar: the girls' rooms, Ben's, Lorna's sitting room, David's studio, hardly ever used. Jennet saw the house through Jack's eyes, as if she were the stranger: its whiteness, its faint chill on an autumn evening, her painting of David, which then hung in the hall.

She opened her studio door on to its accustomed neatness and the desecrated chair. She could have moved that chair, but she had not: it still stood by the window like a ritual object. She did not expect to sit on it again. Now she looked at it dispassionately, through Jack's eyes, and it seemed like any old armchair. She saw her brushes, always cleaned and regimented, the primed canvases, the glass jars of bright pigment aligned in spectrum on a set of wooden shelves. Her painting *Isola* leaning on a wall.

While Jack prowled around the room intently, she rehearsed in silence the calming incantations: viridian, sienna, caput mortuum, ultramarine. Larch Venice turpentine, poppy and safflower oils, rough linen, amber varnish. Still, after all these years, these words are her touchstones; she tells them as a nun would tell her beads. They quieten her with magic, but with their solidity also; even now she loves the scents and textures of her craft. The element of mystery stays in the practice of it: there is *Isola*, for instance, achieved by Jennet on her own with nothing but a few hog hairs fastened to a wooden stick that has been dipped into a mixture made of minerals ground and oils pressed from seeds. Earthly things, unremarkable, forged by her into something wonderful and precious.

Jack was looking hard at *Isola*. It's pretty good, he said, at last. Why did you put that lace or whatsit on it?

Silk, she said. Not lace. And I don't know exactly. Lots of reasons. I thought of mist. It felt right. Oh, come on, what sort of answers can I give to such a question?

I like it, he said. It's sexy. Like a nightdress. Half hiding, half revealing. Like you. You're always hiding something, what it is I don't quite know, your feelings? Even when you seem most open. Whenever I am with you I can see the beat of thought going on all the time inside your head, I can almost hear it, it's like the engine of a boat humming away night and day below the deck.

You don't know me well enough, I wouldn't have thought, to know what I am thinking.

I don't know what you're thinking, that's my point. But I'm going to know you better, aren't I, Mrs Heaton?

He got up from where he was crouching beside *Isola* and

moved over to the shelves of paint. Viridian, he said, as if he had been reading her mind, raw umber, indigo.

Do you mix your own paints, then? he asked. It's really good, the way you get that thin, transparent colour. That bloke I was telling you about in New York, the body painter? He uses acrylic, bright colours, reds and blues and yellows. But if you were covered in the paint you use you'd be something different, a will o' the wisp, a ghost. And beautiful. I'd really like to see it.

He comes closer to where she is, just inside the door. His presence fills the big room and it shrinks. Jennet sees a tiger's cage and the great animal pacing to and fro. Every muscle that Jack moves tightens something inside her: this string will snap soon if he does not move fast enough. But now he turns away and picks up something from the trestle table in the middle of the room; it is nothing, a smooth white stone found on a beach in Cornwall. He kneads it between his palms, slowly, rhythmically, like a potter with a ball of clay. I hear you're seeing Lewis Delafield, he says. I'm sorry about David. It is the first time he has mentioned David's name.

How did you know? she asks. She can see no purpose in denial. Oh, there are no secrets in St Ives, he says. You ought to know that, Jennet. Someone saw you, people talk.

Well, it's not important, Jennet says, after a moment's silence.

Good, he says. I'm glad.

And he comes towards her, nearer, until he is inches away and she can feel his heat. Do you remember that morning, he asks, on the cliff? I think about it often. His voice is a little rough, as if his throat were suddenly sore, his eyes less clear now, clouded glass.

Jack, she says, as he takes her hand and kisses it, each finger, slowly, one by one. He turns it, holds her by the wrist, and she touches him lightly with one finger on his mouth.

He bites that finger very gently, and all the time his eyes are fixed on hers. She hears his heartbeat as her own, she hears the stillness in the room out of which all air has gone. In the distance she can also hear a door slamming, and voices in the street outside, but these are a million miles away and in another world. Much louder is that taut string resonating and the pounding of her blood. Jack, she says again, and he puts his arms around her, and those unsettling eyes of his, at long last they are closed.

St Ives is a town that seems less built than grown: like an ant's nest it has augmented layers and narrow passageways, hidden places burrowed out behind high walls, dead ends and unexpected turns. Over the years its inhabitants have made the most of the spaces they could squeeze between the granite-bouldered moorlands and the encircling sea. Tiny squares of secret garden, roof terraces, or just room enough for a chair or two at the top of stone steps leading to a door. A strange place, turned in on itself in some ways, small stone buildings hugger-mugger in the surrounding vastness. But beautiful as well. White-painted walls and grey slate roofs unrelieved by false notes of bright colour, cobbled alleyways, and everywhere, through a break between the houses or at the end of a walled lane, visions of the sea.

It was in one of those stone cottages, minute, a hutch more like, that Jack Owen lived. Waking in his bed, after he was up and gone, Jennet Mallow opened her eyes to a light that she half-knew, a light with borrowed luminescence from near water. It was not the river light of London, nor the sea light of Santiago de las Altas Torres, so clear and un-equivocal, nor even the light of the summer house along the cliff where the surrounding fields lent a certain softness. This was a light that held in it the glisten of cobbled streets in sea spray and the reflection of white walls: an Atlantic light, familiar, but yet peculiar to this place.

If light could have a sound, in St Ives that sound would be the cry of gulls; constant and pervasive, melancholy even on the brightest days of summer. Sometimes it seems as if the birds are the real owners of the town, mirroring its grey-streaked whiteness, claiming its streets, keeping watch over the harbour with their baleful yellow eyes. Lying in Jack Owen's crumpled bed, Jennet listened to the gulls and wondered if they scolded or applauded. The cold air of the morning streamed in on her through the open window like a banner. For once she let her mind give way to her senses: light, sound, air rushed in and through and over her like clear mountain water, waking her completely on a bright new morning.

All her senses, never given such free rein before. Her face a little stung from the scrape against it of Jack's beard, her mouth ripe with kissing, his semen a warm caress, in between her legs. She is wet and bruised there, but she feels the opposite of pain. Her pleasure is almost as fierce in recollection as it was when first experienced, as if her lover's touch were still deep inside her body. Ah Jack, she says out loud. She does not know if they slept at all last night, the hours are fused into one long unfocused passage of discovery: Jack's mouth, his cock, his tongue finding the steeple point of pleasure in her, the pinnacle, the hub to which each of her nerves is wired. She had not known those nerves could sing like that. Revelation: that thought could be stilled and self-consciousness become pure self-awareness, uncomplicated, needing only to receive and give this unimagined pleasure.

Jack's sheets are stained and dirty, and the room in which he eats and sleeps is a mess of papers, bottles, ashtrays, un-washed plates, beer mugs and tangled clothes, bits of an old bicycle he is trying to assemble in a corner. Jennet does not

177

care. She revels in the smell of Jack that impregnates his sheets. When she gets out of bed she picks his clothes up off the floor and folds them tenderly, but otherwise she does not tidy anything. She has a sense that too much domesticity would scare him.

He had seemed surprised when she arrived last night. It was a long drive down from London to St Ives, and during it she had prayed hard that she would find Jack alone. He had not mentioned the wife of whom there had been rumours, and because of that Jennet had dismissed them; he could hardly have forgotten to tell her he was married. And besides, he could not be. From the moment they met he had known that he belonged to Jennet. It was she who had been too blind before to see it.

After the first time, in her studio, awkward on the bare wood floor, Jennet had known she was in love. She had known because her body told her and because she had never felt like this before. Even then, half-undressed and uncomfortable, anxious in case her mother or her daughters overheard, she knew she had to be with Jack. Making love with David, even at its best, had not been as compelling, and with Lewis some part of her had never been engaged. But with Jack she could be single-minded and whole-hearted in a joint intensity of purpose: she felt in him entire acceptance of the moment, and in return, instead of holding something back, she could let herself surrender. The relief of it was overwhelming.

If only you could be here all tonight and all tomorrow, she whispered to him later, and he answered with his mouth against her hair. Soon, he breathed, of course. But tonight there are things I've got to do, I really have to go back home tomorrow. I'll call you. Soon. You could come and stay, perhaps, if you're not too busy.

He did not ring the next day, but she was not dismayed.

She did not expect it. They had an understanding, born on a clifftop on an August morning, sealed with love last night, which soared beyond convention. But still. After three days in which she could do nothing but relive every second of her time with Jack, she could no longer bear to be without him. Cancelling her appointments, including a lecture at the Royal Academy of Art, and confronting Lorna's disapproval, she took off for St Ives without giving herself time for second thoughts. She did not warn him of her coming.

And, although Jack was taken aback, he was also pleased. Mrs Heaton! he said, happily, gathering her up into his arms. He was not at home when she arrived late on in the evening and she was afraid she would have to ask for him in the local pubs. But after only a few minutes of waiting and wondering what to do, she saw him coming up the narrow lane in his paint-stained shirt, carrying a pint of milk. Ah, the smell of him on that blue shirt, the reassurance of it being already familiar.

Are you planning to stay long? he asked her later. Forever and a day, she said into his cradling shoulder. Oh, he said, oh fine.

She had not made a serious plan, how could she? David was still in hospital, due to be discharged in time for Christmas. Jennet had enough compunction left to want him settled gently. But meanwhile, all she knew was that she had to spend every second she could with Jack, and in his bed, and until December there was nothing that would stop her. After that, she thought vaguely, she might try to buy Trevenna and sell the London house. It was so lovely here, in Cornwall; the silver light, the breathing, rippling colours of the water.

Waking then on the first morning she was absolutely happy. Not since the early years in Santiago had she felt such ease and calm. I am at home here, she said to herself in the chaos of Jack Owen's room; I am finally at home.

'Ideas wrought back to the directness of sense, like the solidness of objects', George Eliot wrote in *Middlemarch*. Imagine there was no dichotomy between the left hand and the right; imagine a harmonious fusion between mind and body, intellect and apprehension, experience and logic. A marriage between the beautiful clarity of abstract thought and the deep-seated pulse of feeling. Not the transcending of the sensual by thought, as is the goal of meditation, but a complete union of the two, like one note sung by separate voices or bowed by violin and cello. Imagine if in prayer, thought and word were one. Well, one can imagine; it is harder to achieve.

At art school Jennet Mallow was taught that a thing could not be drawn if you thought too hard about it. About the thing itself, that is, and how to draw it, rather than the concept of the drawing. The bird would only come to life on the white page if instinct drove the artist's hand. On her own she learned, however, that instinct had to be preceded by truthful observation. It was not possible to draw precisely from memory alone. The best drawings came from careful looking: looking and then looking again, before the unself-conscious pencil even touched the paper.

Such truthful observation is an act of worship. But it takes more than that to make a painting great, to differentiate it from a textbook illustration or a photograph. A work of genius is like a prayer that's found its mark. Intention and execution joined; truth matched with originality, sense with rhythm, soul with body, heart with reason. An idea with the reality of an object.

Jennet Mallow's work before she loved Jack Owen was

touched with greatness – with genius even, in the case of *Santiago* or *Isola*, or *Rivergod* – but it could be slightly too schematic and over-intellectualised. Jennet was aware of that shortcoming, 'Sicklied o'er with the pale cast of thought,' she used to tell herself when she stood before a half-made painting and wondered what was wrong. She had always found abandon hard, as a woman and an artist, but now, like Finn MacCool with his golden leaves and his silver foam, she was rich enough at last to fling her carefully stored reserves into the wind.

It would be too simplistic to explain the developments in Jennet's work by reference to what she learned in Jack Owen's unmade bed. But even so, the short time that she spent with him was a watershed.

It cannot have been much more than a month, that time. Jennet did not record the number of the days she stayed with Jack, but she was back in London when David Heaton was discharged from hospital in the first week of December. So, four or five weeks, perhaps, in the early winter in St Ives; rain ricocheting off the sea in diamond beads and pitting the sand on Porthmeor Beach, small fishing boats in the harbour, sea-weed trailing fingers against its granite walls beneath the sage-green water. The black and lemon roundels of gulls' eyes and their unceasing, lonely calls. Washing hung from sticks protruding from the cottages, fish smells, coils of rope, the clumping sound of rubber boots in the early morning, the clink of mugs and glasses in the evenings in the pubs. Above the little town the grassland and its crop of lichen-covered stones, beyond it the steep cliffs of Zennor, the far end of the land. And always the changing light: silver, pewter, moth wing, oyster shell.

Greys in Jack's eyes too: steel, moonlight, unexpected

sunshine seen through rain. What if, she asks him, in the middle of the night, her body pressed as close as it can ever be to his, the sole of her foot against the arch of his, what if we could stay in this bed forever, in this room? I would be happy if we were like lovers in Pompeii when the ash flowed over them so suddenly and made them permanently one. Jack laughs and says, yes, but I think we would get hungry. I would not be hungry, Jennet thinks, having everything I need in this bed, with this man who is world enough for me. But she does not say so, knowing Jack will brush off over-ardent protestations, even though he loves her and she is sure he does.

David Heaton was gaunt and grey when he came out of hospital, but better, evidently, and calm. As soon as he was home he locked himself into his studio, which he said he would use regularly from then on. There was work he burned to do, he said to Jennet. His resources in the hospital were limited but he had managed to do some drawings, preliminary studies in charcoal, mainly, for a new series he had in mind. Gethsemane, Calvary, Judas out-staring Christ at the Last Supper. He showed Jennet the sheaf of drawings: jagged lines, more birds with sharp beaks and talons, men's faces full of pain.

That a woman who already had three children could be pregnant without suspecting it is strange, perhaps. But Jennet had never been especially in touch with the rhythms of her body, which were in any case irregular. When she did not have a period in months she supposed she must be menopausal. If she gave it thought it was only to remark the paradox of her body's ageing just as she was feeling more womanly and more fertile than she had ever done when she was young. She saw that fertility in terms of painting, though, and happiness, not the literal engendering of life. She was careful. She used a diaphragm. She did not want another child.

The diagnosis was unavoidable in the end. It came in February 1967, the child then in the fourth month of gestation. Four months. October. David had been locked away in hospital that month but there had been Lewis, and then later Jack.

On leaving the doctor's surgery Jennet drove to Richmond Park, the nearest place she knew where she could walk in open space for long enough to pull herself together. She could not have gone straight home where David or Lorna might read her face and see in it consternation.

Her panicked first reaction was to get rid of the thing without telling anyone at all. How to explain otherwise, and to whom? So public an embarrassment, so many people from whom it could not be concealed. Gossipy people, relishing a scandal, and her belly swelling grossly every day. A full stop would not have been difficult: a discreet doctor prepared to break the rules if the reward was large enough, no questions asked, an obvious solution.

But as she walked across scrub and bracken in the hazy low-lying sunlight of a February afternoon, she changed her mind. This shock, this news of an unexpected child, brought sharply into focus memories of Ben's unplanned conception and her half-intention to abort him. Nineteen years later it was horrible to think how easily her beautiful and beloved son might never have been born. Something in Jennet rebelled against the taking of a life. Besides, this one was already well established. If she were to kill it, she had left it rather late. A week or so and she would be feeling its fluttery first stirrings. It would already have a face. And that face, she felt quite sure, would look like Jack's. Instinct, if not reason, told her so. Why should she have been surprised that love so passionate had swept away her flimsy defences and insisted on bearing fruit? The surge demanded lasting proof, like a great flood leaving landmarks, stones lifted on to hilltops from the bottom of the sea.

Jack's child. As such it had a home in her envisaged future. It would be a seal on love. The more she thought the more she wished, and could even half believe, it had been conceived on purpose. Jack would be so glad. She longed to tell him, but he was on a visit to America, and this was not news to share by telephone.

Meanwhile she would celebrate her child. A winter blessing, a sign of rightness, new life, a new future. An embarrassment nonetheless, but one she now decided to brazen out.

Sarah was the first person Jennet told. She asked a direct question, a week after Jennet had seen the doctor, while she was still clasping the secret knowledge to herself. They were in Jennet's bedroom, and Sarah was watching her mother dress for a party in the evening. It was something she had liked to do when she was small and still did from time to time: playing with the bottles on Jennet's dressing table, trying on lipsticks, choosing from the jewellery Jennet kept in a box that once stored sandalwood soap. There was not much of a choice. Richard Mallow's watch-chains, earrings, a gold bracelet Leonard Kaspar had given her, a Victorian opal ring from Patrick Mann. Sarah was tossing the watch-chains through her fingers when she said: Ma? I don't mean to be rude, but aren't you getting a bit fat?

So Jennet told her, almost pleased to have someone, even her own daughter, to confide in. And Sarah was disgusted. She was not naïve enough to think this child could be her father's. You're so old, she said. You're far too old to be a slag.

Still reeling from Sarah's reaction, but perversely emboldened by it, the next day Jennet decided to tell David. I'm pregnant, she said, abruptly: no point in procrastinating now. He was sitting at the piano in the drawing room and she had just brought him a gin and tonic; the first drink of the day, the best time, she felt, to break the news. Rehearsal had not helped her to do it. There was no way she could soften it or make it easier for him. He looked at her as if he had not heard. But we haven't been to bed together in a long time, have we? I'm not sure I understand. And then he understood, or thought he did. Delafield's? he asked.

No, she said, determined always to be truthful. I think the baby's Jack's.

Jack's?

Jack Owen.

Later Jennet would wish she had not seen in David's eyes the look she knew he must have seen too often in her own. Contempt. In twenty years of hauling him away from parties when he was too drunk to stand, taking glasses from him before he fell and broke them, hoisting him into bed, Jennet had kept the high ground, but now she knew that in David's view she had fallen very low.

He did not say much. There was nothing much to say. He had no idea there was anything but friendship between his wife and Jack. He did not want to think what Jennet had been doing while he was in the hospital he hated, whose iron-barred windows were reminders of a nightmare: cages, barbed wire, white-faced men imprisoned.

What are you going to do about it, then? he asked.

I'm going to have it. And I'm going to live with Jack. But I haven't told him yet. He's away, he's in Los Angeles. What else can I say except that I am very sorry. David, I am very sorry.

So am I, he said. Sorrier for you than for myself.

And Lewis, already desperate, because Jennet had been away all through November without giving him a reason and he had scarcely seen her since. Every time he tried to meet her she had an excuse. Ben was home, she said, or David coming out of hospital; then there was a play at Sarah's school, and Christmas, and in January she was too busy with her work. She had an exhibition scheduled for that spring. Only once had she been unable to avoid him, at Patrick Mann's Christmas party, where he had forced her into listening to him.

She had never looked so beautiful, he thought. There was a new softness to the usually sharp contours of her face, and she shone that night in a long red dress as if a thousand fireflies danced around her, He took her arm and propelled her to a corner, careless of Deirdre possibly watching, or David, or anybody else. Jennet, he said, I must see you. It's been so long. I'm dying.

Of course, she said, it's just that there's been so much to think about, the children, and now that David's better . . .

She trailed away, wanting him to see without her having to explain that David's being in the house made Lewis's affair with her impossible. An affair was what she called it to herself, wilfully refusing to admit that it was much more to Lewis. He did not see, of course, that David's coming home made any difference. To him it was a start and not an end. He believed that Jennet would leave David as soon as he could stand on his own feet. His mind was closed to other possibilities. The less time Jennet gave him, the more passionately he craved it: his life was meaningless without

186

her. Watching her that night at Patrick's, radiant, unattainable, Lewis burned.

That night was weeks before Jennet knew about the baby. Now the time had come to tell the truth. Jennet knew she should have done so months before: she should have said she did not love him, she should have told him about Jack. But there was a rawness in Lewis, a vulnerability, as if his skin were only newly healed after harsh abrasion. He was easy to hurt, and that made it hard to hurt him. She knew that – she had hurt him many times before. There were nights last summer when she pushed him away. Why? he would beg, pretending to no dignity, standing on her doorstep, clinging to her hands. Why, when I want you so badly? She would plead tiredness or discretion or Vanessa, and even then she knew she was being unkind. This last unkindness would be the hardest, and she shrank from inflicting it on him. She might as well be his executioner.

Having rejected the temptation of telling Lewis by letter, as she had already been quite cowardly enough, Jennet telephoned to ask him to lunch. Her heart sank when she heard the pleasure in his answer. They met at a fish restaurant in St James's, which she had chosen for the privacy of its old-fashioned booths. They pleased him too when he arrived; he may have thought she was inviting his embraces.

Jennet wore a loose dress, but Lewis had a loving eye and when she stood to greet him, he saw at once that she was pregnant. Darling, he said. Why didn't you tell me . . . ? How far gone is it, how are you feeling? You poor thing, so brave keeping this a secret. You should have told me. Did you think I would be angry, that there would be problems . . . ? Well of course there will be, but this makes all the difference, this can't wait. I will tell Deirdre straightaway. What's the matter, Jennet?

To have blurted out so much before he stopped to listen.

187

To have presumed so much on love. And then, after having listened, to remain so undeterred. He was deadly pale but dry-eyed; he heard her out in silence, he even managed to deal with hovering waiters. They both ordered Dover sole, although neither of them ate it. Jennet talked, apologised, explained, told him she loved him as a friend, would always love him come what may, but when she had finished, Lewis said, counting backwards on his fingers, unusually delicate for a man's fingers, five months? October. I was with you then. You are carrying my child. Our child. And what is more, I want it. Which Jack Owen won't.

What do you mean, Jack won't?

Well, what do you think his wife is going to say about it? His wife, the would-be movie star, who can't come to St Ives because it's too far from Hollywood? She wants him to move to California and stay there. Which, by all accounts, he's going to do. There's a market for his crappy pictures there, but no room, I don't suppose, for a baby or for you.

Both of them are white-faced now and sickened, glaring at each other across their untouched plates, spitting out cruel truths which neither will believe because they hurt so much.

Jennet's exhibition went ahead as planned at the end of April 1967 at the Whitechapel Art Gallery. It was on a large scale and included loaned work as well as work completed since the 1961 Venice Biennale. *Isola* was there, lent by Lewis Delafield, to whom Jennet had sent it, without note or explanation, straight after their last meeting. Among the more recent paintings were eight which Jennet had made in six weeks of extraordinary creativity between November 1966 and the following January. She gave this series numbers instead of names, but her notes record that in it she was again exploring light. Light on water, light reflected, light streaked through a marbling of cloud in the moments before sunset on a November afternoon. Sunlight in the winter. They are astonishingly beautiful, these works. Jennet experimented with new techniques in them, diluting her paint to the thinnest possible consistency and in places adding fine metallic powder to it. Silver, gold and pearl. Gold leaf, overpainted, and then varnished lightly, with the varnish in some areas scrubbed away so that the surface of the painting changes as the light which strikes it changes or as the viewer moves. Dancing paintings, with the quality of jewels which emit light and attract it, and in which Jennet had visibly mixed the happiness she felt then into her paint.

There was only one painting in the exhibition made after February 1967. It was *Lot's Wife*, that often reproduced and haunting image, which hangs in the Philadelphia Museum of Art. A woman, life-size, full-length, dressed in a white shift, her arms pinioned against her sides and her face terror-stricken behind the carapace of salt that is her prison. In the story Lot's wife turns into salt itself, but Jennet has a different version, showing the live woman trapped as if the salt had crusted instantly around her and would soon corrode her flesh. Although the expression of fear on the woman's face is unmistakable, her features and her body are glazed over by the salt so that she looks like a ghost, or someone seen through water. There is no colour in the painting except white; many different whites: the woman's hair, her shift, the blue-white of the salt. Minute flakes of mica in the paint make it glitter coldly. Translucent white, zinc white, titanium: if one did not know the story one might think the woman's tomb was made of ice.

The Whitechapel show was followed by a travelling exhibition in the States, arranged through Hagopian's, Jennet's New York dealers. It ended in July 1968 at the San Francisco Museum of Art, where Jack Owen must have seen it: he sent

Jennet an undated note of congratulation that she kept. It was the second note she'd had from him; the first, sent in March the year before, told her that he planned to stay in California for good.

Jennet's son was born on 18 July 1967. He was a slate-eyed, dark-haired child. She called him Adam and, because she did not know what else to do and because David said he did not care, she gave him David's surname when she registered the birth.

In that same summer Sarah left for Sicily and Ben also moved away, to a flat in Redcliffe Square, which he shared with friends while he trained to be a pilot. Flying was his new passion, and he was too absorbed by it to be interested in the baby. Unlike the rest of Jennet's family, he took it for granted that David was the father. Having been away from England while David was in hospital, he did not have his sister's forensic grasp of dates. It was to Sarah's credit that she did not at the time see any need to upset him with the truth. Jennet too maintained the fiction that Adam was David's son, even with old friends like Margaret Metcalf.

On 27 July Lewis Delafield fell off the cliffs at Gurnard's Head in Cornwall. His death was instant, his skull crushed like a gull's egg dropped. As there were no witnesses to his fall, and as he left no note, the coroner at the inquest recorded an open verdict. It is possible that he wanted to be kind to the devastated widow. But Lewis's close friends were sure he meant to kill himself. The path along the cliffs at the point where Lewis fell was not especially treacherous, it had been a bright, clear day, he was in no sense physically infirm; he could not possibly have stumbled over the edge by accident.

In the absence of an explanation for his shocking death,

Lewis's friends cast around for one and came up with Jennet. All they had was rumour, and that rumour was vague. No one knew anything definite about her relationship with Lewis, but after Lewis died, the filaments of tenuous knowledge were stretched and spun together into inalienable fact. Despair killed Lewis and Jennet was its cause. Only despair and a woman's cruelty could make a man who had so much to lose do what Lewis did. Jennet, that star of their generation, admired by other artists, remote perhaps but deeply attractive, now took on a malign aspect: the woman who played fast and loose with a good man's feelings. A Circe toying with him for her entertainment, luring him from a faithful wife, seducing him with magic. Betraying her own husband. Those who had been close to Lewis knew that Jennet's hold on him was born out of the enchantment of her art. His worship of her as an artist had never been a secret. They also knew that Lewis was mercurial, unstable, prey to depression, and ever capable of an unconsidered act. Nevertheless, rather than reproach themselves for not having been observant friends, they laid all the blame for Lewis's death on Jennet.

And Jennet knew that they were right. The morning after Adam was born Lewis had visited her in the hospital. He had been told about the birth by Lorna Mallow, deliberate envoy of the news, despite her daughter's plea to keep it quiet.

Lorna's motives are difficult to uncover now that she's been dead for thirty years. At that time she was utterly dependent on her daughter. Having chosen to live where she had no past or current friends, no independence and nowhere of her own, Lorna needed Jennet for definition. Without Jennet her image of herself was too precarious. With her, while things were going well, the image was gratifying: mother and mother-in-law of celebrated painters instead of disappointed rector's wife; worldly and sophisticated, an exotic with a Caribbean background, no longer dowdy and provincial. Gatekeeper and co-hostess both: she enjoyed entertaining in the Heatons' house. These sensitive young things, she'd say of their visitors, they need someone they can turn to, a friend whom they can trust.

Of the visitors she was particularly fond of Lewis; for his good manners partly, but more for his public face. In 1966 he had a weekly television programme reviewing contemporary art. Lorna liked to watch it with an insider's pleasure, and in the hope that she would find herself quoted on it. Her critical aperçus, she felt, were much admired by her son-in-law and daughter's friends. Or mainly, if she were honest, by her son-in-law's friends: these were the ones who shrieked with laughter at her jokes, lit her cigarettes and filled her glass up for her. Jennet seemed to have fewer friends, and those she did have were faintly dull.

Except for Lewis Delafield, who had fame and glamour. Lorna did not know then that he was Jennet's lover. She did know, though, about Jack Owen, who was, she often said, an obvious bounder but devastatingly good-looking. Scandalised though she was when Jennet scampered after him like a bitch on heat, she had grudgingly admitted that she could understand it. Living in Bridge House she was aware of David's faults, and she felt that he neglected Jennet. But a bit on the side was one thing, a baby quite another, and the shame that Jennet's pregnancy would surely cause greatly upset Lorna.

She aired her worries to Sarah, for want of a more suitable confidante. They had become close over the last three years; so alike in many ways with their love of finery and brightness, their impatience, their restless need for pleasure. Lorna would embroider tales of her childhood for Sarah, who drank in the sloe-eyed women in white dresses, the masked balls and the dancing, the hummingbirds' sparkling wings.

In her turn Sarah too confided. She poured out to Lorna all her hurt and outrage, telling her grandmother what Vanessa had told her about Lewis in the summer at Trevenna. And Lorna, being neither foolish nor unable to understand a calendar, worked out for herself the complications. If David were to divorce Jennet, which Lorna was sure he would, she would much prefer Lewis as a replacement son-in-law to Jack. Jack was just another messy and relatively unsuccessful painter; Lewis was well known already, and there was promise for the future. Who the actual father of the baby was seemed to matter less.

White-faced against the dark wood and the sepia tints of the old-fashioned restaurant where they had met in March, Jennet had told Lewis she would not see him any more. She would have been gentler, she would have said they could be friends one day, that Lewis mattered to her, if Lewis had not told her about Jack Owen's marriage. Sorrow made her brutal. In her heart she knew what Lewis was saying was true. But he went on and on – he'd seen a photograph, someone he knew knew her, she was a real stunner – for misery had made him cruel too. And angry. He and Jennet faced each other across the starched white linen and the cold grilled fish like devastated children whose world has fallen round them. As children do, they wanted to lash out at one another, to pinch and bite and scratch, and they would have, perhaps, if convention had not reined them in. Instead they fought with steel-edged words. Bitch. Whore. Deceiver. Faithless. I never loved you, Jennet said. You deceived yourself. I don't want to see you ever again.

Lewis had not argued then, he'd simply got up and walked out of the restaurant. The next day he sent an armful of Madonna lilies round to Cheyne Walk, with a note asking for forgiveness. It was then that Jennet gave him *Isola*; but she refused all further contact. She would not return his calls or answer his anguished letters, and when he arrived on the doorstep unannounced she sent messages to say she was away. Once, caught unawares, she opened the door to him herself, but closed it again without a word. To herself she said that it was less unkind to insist upon a clean break, to let Lewis pick up again the pieces of his life. As far as she knew he had not said anything to Deirdre. There was no reason why, once he had recovered from his madness, he could not be happy with her and his children.

Lorna knew all about Jennet's cold-heartedness. It was she more often than not who conveyed Jennet's uncompromising answers to the despairing lover, and it was she whom Lewis told when, pitched beyond reason by his grief, he fled to Cornwall. He needed to take a hard look at himself, he said to Lorna, think things through and try to get some sleep perhaps. Excited by this high romance, sorry for Lewis, cross with Jennet, who would persist with her pretence that the child was David's, Lorna made up her mind in secret to let Lewis know when the child was born. If Jennet had been closer to her mother and able to confide in her, Lorna might have been less interfering. But Jennet was numbed by her own sadness then, and had only strength enough to crawl from the start of every day until its end while the child inside her claimed its space.

Lorna sent a telegram to Lewis in Cornwall as soon as she knew the baby had arrived and Lewis caught the night train up to London. Jennet was alone in a side room off a ward; she had gone into hospital alone when she felt the child coming. She saw Lewis at the half-glazed door, preceded by a cheerful nurse who was relieved to find her lonely patient had a friend. He was carrying roses and a soft toy, a white seal, larger than the child. The nurse ushered him in, sure he would be welcome with his flowers and his present. Jennet could not have turned him out without a fuss, and anyway, just then, she did not want to.

The baby was in a plastic cot next to Jennet's bed. He was asleep. Lewis bent over him, touched his closed fist gently, saw the damp mat of dark hair, the tiny face still clenched as if to ward off this new brazen world with all its shocks of light and noise. He thought this child looked exactly like his daughter when she was newly born. Hello, he said, softly, to the baby. He did not know its name.

Well? he asked, turning to Jennet, who was awkwardly propped up on pillows in her institutional bed.

It is good to see you, she said, truthfully. His face was dear in this place of strangers. She had felt so lonely. But even then she still recoiled when he leaned down to kiss her. It was the hope in Lewis's eyes that frightened her, with its undercurrent of pain. She was exhausted after the birth, and irrational, perhaps, but able even so to see that she could not take on herself the burden of this man. There had been altogether too many loads to carry in her life. Now she had a new one: this unchampioned, undefended child. When she was with Jack she had felt a lightness in her being, but Lewis was a dead weight stacked on top of all the others – her mother, her daughter, her melancholy husband – who threatened to drag her down. She did not desire Lewis and she could not love him: she had no right to take his love because she needed someone's, anyone's, then.

The words with which to make this plain to Lewis were difficult to find. She stumbled and she wept and so did Lewis, and while they were clinging to each other, crying, the baby woke and cried as well. In a mess of milk and snot and tears Lewis protested despair and love and possession of his son, but Jennet still would not accede, and in the end he had to leave her. The kindly nurse, coming in on them and

the distressed baby, made them both a cup of tea and then
led Lewis away.

At Lewis's funeral, a small bewildered son in his school
uniform of shorts and a blazer and a daughter in a borrowed
dark-blue velvet-collared coat, too big for her, its sleeves
so long you could not see her hands. She was three years
old, too young to understand what was happening in the
vast dark church or what was in the flower-covered coffin
at the bottom of the sanctuary steps; but she had caught
her mother's mood, and she stood and sat and knelt with
absolute decorum all through the requiem mass. Afterwards
she followed her father's coffin-bearers down the aisle, holding her brother's hand beneath a velvet cuff, both of them so
pinched with shock it was as if a clamp had scrunched up the
soft skin at their napes and pulled it tight across their bones.
Behind them, Deirdre, with her eyes red-rimmed and her
nose pink from days of crying.

    The three of them passed Jennet where she stood, as
inconspicuously as she could, at the far end of a pew. She
wanted not to look, and yet she had to look at them, and at
the coffin, lurching very slightly on the shoulders of four
men in black frockcoats with faces of professional gloom.
Days had passed since Lewis's death: what would he look like
in the coffin now? She saw his body snagged on the granite
under Gurnard's Head, worried by the uncomprehending
sea. She saw him taking Adam from her arms to cradle him
and claim him, the child he knew to be his own. She saw him
naked, arching over her in bed, telling her he loved her, that
he would always love her, imploring her to say the same
words too. When his children passed her, the fair-haired boy
and the dark-haired girl, Jennet stayed dry-eyed but reflex let

the milk down in her breasts, as if she'd heard her baby's hungry cry.

Scouring out a cast-iron pot at the kitchen sink, Jennet stops to watch the reflection of a light above it glinting in the greasy water and her own hands submerged. Out of nowhere a wave of fear crashes over her and she is suddenly quite sure she will never lift her hands out of the water or unglue her feet from the floor. Only her wildly pounding heart is evidence of life. Otherwise she might as well be paralysed, like Lot's wife trapped in salt. Somewhere in the distance there is a baby crying, but Jennet cannot go to it. She cannot move at all. She must stand there forever with her hands beneath the water in the blackened pot.

Lorna Mallow had been wrong to suppose that David and Jennet would divorce. In fact David had no time for such legalities. Marriage is nothing but a bit of paper, he told Jennet. Why pay to get ours unmade now? Although he was in no way pleased by the outcome of Jennet's infidelities, he quite enjoyed the new licence it gave him. Her adulteries brought him more into line with those of his acquaintances who had always scorned conventional marriage. Dermot, for example, divided himself between two women, both of whom were mothers to his and other men's children. The two Roberts were notorious for their plurality of lovers. The Indian poet and the woman who called herself his wife could never quite remember if, in fact, they had ever married. David had always been a little irked by the sheer middle-classness of his household. It was more amusing now. He and Jennet were quits again after his years of unfaithfulness with Corinne. He saw no reason why they should not go on sharing one convenient roof. He was working well in his Chelsea studio. Above the door one day he painted in elaborate mock Gothic: My Name Shall Live For Ever More.

For Jennet, stasis was preferable to change. Indeed she would have been incapable of effecting any change, had she wanted to. Guilt and exhaustion had corroded her away. Her sense of self was as an empty thing, and worthless, fit only to feed her son and tend the daughter who remained at home. The birth of Adam had wrung out the few last drops of strength she had after her humiliation by Jack Owen, and Lewis's death was proof to her of her essential badness. She had been a woman proud of her intelligence and perception. Now she was a creature too stupid to have seen what stared her in the face, and too self-absorbed to stop a man from dying. As this degraded being she was dumbly grateful to David for his forbearance, for giving Adam the protection of his name, for not beating her or slamming the front door on her or leaving her to face opprobrium alone. She clung to David now. Her twenty years of standing by him through every shifting mood were vindicated, he was what was left to her, the only future she could see.

But later on that year David met a German artist, Wiebke Wendt, at the Chelsea Arts Club. In the beginning he made jokes about her, calling her the Youthful Nazi, describing her as the spitting image of one of his camp guards, a woman born in jackboots. Before long, though, he was extolling her potential as an artist. Wiebke was determined and ambitious; she was not impressed by David as a painter but she knew he could be useful. She needed somewhere to stay and he gave her Sarah's room at Cheyne Walk. Instead of paying rent she sat for him; he admired the moulding of her head and the fine rise of her shoulders. She was in her early twenties then, a small woman with a boyish and slim body, an intense face under fashionably short black hair.

Wiebke Wendt described her own work as experimental. She would argue that traditional forms, and painting in particular, had nothing left to give a changing world. The new task was to make reality as it was lived, which photography could do, or film, or her own multi-media assemblages, which used everyday detritus in contrast to iconic image. In a work made just before she came to London, she enlarged a reproduction of Grünewald's *Crucifixion* and glued the words of an advertisement – Dying for a Coke! – on the horizontal of the cross. This showed one form of manipulation being suppressed by another, she explained, and the pointlessness of sacrifice.

When Adam Heaton was about five months old, Lorna Mallow, who was afflicted by claudication, developed a blood clot in her leg. Attempts to disperse it surgically were unsuccessful, and in January 1968 the leg was amputated just below the knee. It was a terrible blow to her, in the year before her seventieth birthday. Only weeks ago she had begun a friendship with a widower who lived a few doors down from Jennet's house in Cheyne Walk. The possibility of courtship had made her sprightly. With the ruin of her hopes, and in continual pain, she became a querulous old lady, an angry and resentful invalid who now relived the memory of all the other cruelties that fate had inflicted on her. And the same silting-up of arteries which had caused the damage to her leg was beginning to affect her brain. There were increasing phases of unreason and forgetfulness, except about the childhood she recalled so often, the time when she was happy, in Jamaica.

Jennet's sister, Barbara, came to help look after Lorna for the first fortnight of her convalescence, but she could not stay beyond it. Her husband, Lionel McPhail, himself an old man by then, had problems with his sight and could not spare her. Because she had to care for him she could not possibly take Lorna back with her to Scotland. Jennet understood. Poor Barbara was grey-haired now and dressed like an old woman. All too clearly Jennet could imagine the bleak years that stretched before her; she would not make them bleaker yet by lumbering Barbara with their mother.

A sickroom smell crept through the house in Chelsea. Lorna could not manage stairs: what had been the drawing room became her bedroom. There was a lavatory on the ground floor but no bathroom, so Lorna was bathed with flannels soaked in bowls of water. The smell of disinfectant, misery and urine. In the time it took to heal, Lorna's stump had to be cleaned and dressed. A pucker of raw, shiny skin. Barbara showed Jennet how to dress it, and after Barbara had gone this was her task, together with the washing and the emptying of the old commode that Lorna used when she could not reach the lavatory.

A paid nurse could have done these things instead. Was it perverse of Jennet not to hire one? Probably. But, as she shuffled from cot to bedside, wheelchair to pram, bandages to nappies, young child to sick old woman, she knew that she was living in the only way she could. It was a form of penance.

And all through this long, exhausting time of meeting needs, denying her own, there was sad Vanessa. Sixteen the month before her grandmother's operation; a pale, moth-like presence in the house. She did not need feeding or dressing: in such things she was self-sufficient. And she could talk too, if she wished to, although she never said more than a few words at a stretch, except to Sarah, whom she must have missed. Sarah was the only one who behaved as if Vanessa were as robust and cheerful as anybody else. Without her sister, Vanessa withdrew even more into herself. She was too old for school and obviously unfit for work, and so she drifted through the days like someone who had found herself washed up in a stranger's life by some mistake.

The same constricting pain that Jennet felt when she let herself imagine the loneliness of Barbara seized her with much stronger force when she thought about Vanessa. Only two things gave her daughter pleasure: painting and the baby. Jennet had been afraid at first that Vanessa would not have the strength to hold the child. When Adam was new-born she would only let Vanessa cradle him when she was safely seated, as if Vanessa were a small child too. Images of the baby slipping out of her frail fingers on to the unforgiving floor, of his small skull crushed, as Lewis's had been, flashed through Jennet's mind. But in fact, Vanessa held the little boy securely, as if from deep instinct. He responded to her too, would smile at her, go to her, apparently content. Sometimes Jennet found Vanessa kneeling next to Adam's cot, crooning to him in a high voice, talking to her brother without words.

Vanessa had had the same instinctive confidence with a pen and pencil since she was a little girl, and it had never left her. To Jennet that was reassuring. The pictures Vanessa made were formless still, tight masses of scrawled lines in colour, but it was enough that in their making Vanessa could be happy. Happiness was otherwise in short supply.

David Heaton's fiftieth birthday party, in the long gallery at the Stockwell School of Art. There are photographs of it in Jennet Mallow's cardboard box. David still good-looking, lean, but with something hectic in his eyes. The day before he had returned from a visit to New York. David's father, Malcolm, a wizened figure in his nineties; his wife had long since died. David's sisters. Ben Heaton with Joanna, the girl he later married. Sarah, with her Italian boyfriend, home for the occasion. Vanessa in the dress that Jennet had bought for her from Biba, silk in a gentle violet, fading in the background of the photographs as if she had strayed into them from the distant past. Jennet looking thin and tired but beautiful in black.

Buying new clothes had been important, a brave act, the only thing that Jennet had done for her own sake since Adam's birth and Lewis's death. She wanted to look fine at David's party. It had been a pleasure to run her hand along the racks of silk and velvet, to stand before a mirror and watch herself turn back into an attractive woman. The dress she finally chose from Xandra Rhodes was lovely: self-patterned silk in rich matte black, cut to fit beneath the breasts, long, open sleeves like a medieval queen's. Dressing for the party, making herself up, putting on her high-heeled shoes, was like preparing for a battle, Jennet thought, but it was also essential. She had hardly left her house in the past year. Blaming childbirth, she had cancelled all her normal obligations. This night, David's birthday, was the first time she was prepared to face the outside world.

All the old friends, and the new. Corinne and Victor Golding, Corinne's lover Abe, Dermot, the Benjamins, Ivan Whitehouse; cases of champagne, balloons. A great stir of excitement caused by David's new commission, the cover of the Beatles' next LP. Some of David's latest work showing in the gallery, markedly different from the work he had done before and while he was in hospital. His Calvary project temporarily abandoned, he was working now in vivid colours, acrylics instead of oils. Fewer shadows, flatter planes, form implied by blocks of colour, spray-painted in some instances to avoid marks of the brush. A life-size painting of Wiebke Wendt nude, with poppies growing from the cleft between her legs. Wiebke herself in a state of celebration because her first exhibition was about to open soon, under David's sponsorship.

Although Wiebke clearly had some power over him, there is no evidence that she was David's lover. Her own account, given in an autobiographical essay in 1997, suggests that she was not, or at least not more than once. David, she asserted, was not really capable of performance at that point in his life, but he liked to watch while she made love to herself or to other women. Women were her own preference, although she would have accommodated David happily enough if he had wanted her. She did not object to sex with men.

If they were not lovers, David Heaton and Wiebke Wendt were something more dangerous to Jennet: they were conspirators together. When Wiebke lived at Cheyne Walk she was not much in Jennet's way, being out most of the time and coming back quietly in the night. She took no part in the life of the household and, as she often said, she actively disliked small babies. She worked in a friend's studio, somewhere east of Tower Bridge. Jennet found her theories of art tiresome, but seldom had to hear them. She herself was not working at all then; from Wiebke's point of view she was just a housewife who would probably never paint again. What Wiebke felt for Jennet, if anything, was pity.

Or that is what she claimed, when afterwards she talked about her exhibition. Pity and irritation. Jennet Mallow, Wiebke would say, like so many women, was throwing all her gifts away, squandering them on home and children. Wiebke Wendt was in hot revolt from the *Kinder, Küche, Kirche* mantra of her mother's generation, loathing it as part of Nazi ideology. It made her furious to see, as she thought she saw, a woman who was better than most men, and certainly much better than her husband, waste her time on nappies. Even though she did not care for painting,

Wiebke Wendt had to concede that Jennet's work was good. More than good. Unlike David's, it was original, compelling and enduring.

Wendt's exhibition opened in April 1969 at the Redleaf Gallery. David had talked Ivan Whitehouse into it. Neither man gave Jennet any warning; she was invited to the opening, and she went, out of politeness. Wendt no longer lived with her by then, but she was a friend of sorts, and Jennet thought it was discourteous not to show support for friends.

The exhibition filled two rooms. In the first were variations on Wendt's Crucifixion theme: several well-known works of art in reproduction, with slogans or the cast-off stuff of everyday life fixed to them. The *Mona Lisa* with a new collar made from the packaging of a depilatory cream, Michelangelo's *David* with a helmet and swastika tattoos, Van Gogh's chair with a crumpled, greasy sheet of newsprint and an empty Woodbines packet glued on to the seat.

The second room contained six large squares of white-painted chipboard on which were mounted scraps of paper, torn-up photographs, postcards, domestic rubbish – all related in some way to Jennet Mallow. The boards were labelled. The first was *A Portrait of the Artist as a Girl*, and it had childish things on it: a colouring book, heart-shaped pink and yellow sweets with mottoes, several undressed plastic dolls with drawn-on breasts and pubic hair, a Ladybird *Book of Churches*, half a photograph of Jennet as a child, a matching set of pants and vest with a pink lace trim which Jennet recognised as having once belonged to Sarah. Wiebke Wendt must have taken them from a drawer in Sarah's room. The second board, *A Portrait of the Artist as a Lady*, was covered with the things a woman might keep private: underwear, a diaphragm, balls of dirty cottonwool, a pink nylon belt intended to keep sanitary towels in place and a stained sanitary towel as well. Half-hidden under that was a photograph of Jennet's 1947 self-portrait. There were labels from gin bottles, cigarette packets, lipstick-stained cigarette butts and, inked directly on the board, a nude in the style of David Heaton.

So it went on. *A Portrait of the Artist as a Mother* combined a Filippo Lippi Madonna with used nappies, smeared bibs, a pair of plastic breasts and a reproduction of Jennet's painting *Santiago*, torn up and glued in random scraps across the board. *The Artist as a Mistress* was a collage of Goya's Maja reclining on a coffin, with a skull propped up against her thigh. *The Artist as a Housewife* rather decoratively combined a mophead, the cardboard packaging of various brands of washing powder and a photograph of a woman with her face concealed by a white lace apron. The final assemblage of the series was called *A Portrait of the Artist: 1924–1969*. It was covered with a nylon curtain of the suburban-window sort. Lifting the curtain revealed a woman photographed from behind, unidentifiable, except that she was wearing a long-sleeved black silk dress. In the background were fragments of Jennet's paintings, again cut up and haphazardly reassembled. *Rivergod, David, Pool in Winter, In the Clarity of Water*. Above them were the letters R.I.P.

Patrick Mann thought Jennet should sue, but she knew there was no point. Every image in Wendt's exhibition had been tampered with to the extent that she could claim it as her own. When challenged, Wendt said that she intended the exhibition as a tribute, an act of homage. Only the stupidest of critics could fail to see that juxtaposing Jennet's work with that of Michelangelo or Goya was to put her on a pedestal with them. The tragedy, in Wendt's opinion, and the reason why she had written R.I.P., was that Jennet had allowed her mundane business as a woman to interfere with art. She had put a brake on her own progress by having another baby, refusing to hire nursemaids, doing her own cooking. She could have gone so far, Wiebke Wendt lamented. But she sold out, just like other women. Which is why there have been so few woman artists. Until now. My generation, Wiebke said, we will not sell out.

In public Jennet Mallow laughed off Wiebke Wendt's show, pretending that she shared the joke. In private she was hurt, and the small steps towards recovery she had made at the time of David's birthday were reversed. There was enough truth in Wendt's accusations for them to hit their mark. And the parody was cruel. Net curtains, lace aprons: Jennet could see how her pictures could be made to look ridiculous. Worse was the fact of David's trickery. Only he could have been the source of some of the photographs and papers Wendt had used. It made Jennet writhe to think how much he must have loved their plotting. Like a child anticipating the result of a successful tease, he probably did not intend to be unkind. And like a child, he would have revelled in the details. Among the rock stars and the bankers, the photographers and the actors David Heaton was now meeting, there were those who held that all means justified a commercial end. Who cared how it was made, if in the last resort it was a memorable image? In New York David had met Andy Warhol and he admired the slickness of his operation: the multiplication of the image, the ways in which the most banal objects were made iconic.

Here was the future, David said; but Jennet could not agree. She believed the singularity of an image was important. What Wendt had done was to turn her life into a production, simultaneously mocking and respectful, distanced and over-familiar, as Warhol had done to other famous women. Jennet could imagine how quickly David had been persuaded that there was an artistic purpose to all this. As he entered the second half of his own century, with his anxieties and torments still clanking round him like a set of rusty leg-chains, he was easy to seduce. The singers and the drugs, the alcohol, the adulation, the company of younger women: these were powerful seducers. Terrified of death though he was, David had not bargained on old age. He hated all reminders of his advancing years, such as being the father of a son who was old enough to marry. Spending time with the young set he was encountering in Chelsea bought him a stay of execution. When he was himself a young man in the studios and bars of Soho he had found some comfort in the company of friends, some measure of oblivion. Many of those friends were old or dead now, but David needed comfort still, as much as or even more than he had before, and his new coterie was there to give it: in the form of pills or snow-white powder, or from the same familiar bottles.

Not much comfort though for Jennet. Some, yes, in the small, warm body of her child, his eagerness for her, the sureness of his growing. Some, a stern kind, in her mother kept clean, her children fed, a house well run. But none in David's being danced away by sirens. And none, absolutely, in the impossibility of work. There were commissions lining up, an impatient Patrick Mann, the touring exhibition in the States, people beginning to notice Jennet's absence. How could she explain to them the numbness that stopped her hands from working and made the brush fall from her useless fingers? Day after day she went to her studio and stood there, staring into white space, into blankness. *La page vide que sa blanchesse défend.*

Beyond the window the river runs and evening comes, and morning; somewhere in the house her son calls out, but

Jennet cannot answer. Ice crystals are flowering on her, sealing her mouth and eyelids, making frozen pillars of her bones.

If the opposite of joy is not sorrow but the absence of real feeling, Jennet Mallow was indeed paralysed. For a long time her heart was like a stone. But slowly, very slowly, small signs of life began to stir. Bare branches have green thoughts, and the birds sing. To Jennet, waking to them one late February morning, they were like familiar voices hoping to revive someone in a coma. Some trick of the sun's renewed light made three bright slashes on the wall, like rips in canvas, and it dawned on Jennet that escape routes might exist. The same routes, the old ways, which worked for her before, when she had felt the cage bars drawing close. The light danced on the white wall and Jennet, as she watched it ripple, thought about the sea.

She had turned the key in the lock of this prison gate herself, but she was not the only captive. Through her inaction Lorna, Adam and Vanessa were prisoners as well, not one of them able to find their own way through the gate. All four were as medieval anchorites walled up in whitewashed stone, but only Jennet had the luxury of choice. Now she saw that she had done a harsh thing to those who were dependent on her. Even so she could not simply knock a hole right through the wall and step back into the world. Too much had changed since she had held Jack Owen's head against her breast and thought her happiness eternal. No, she needed to move onwards, as the seasons did, as time did, and, as always when she imagined change, she dreamed about new landscapes. Once again she needed to leave London.

New landscapes. Open spaces. Where? Jennet ached for sea and light and, above all, quiet as refuge from the clatter that was London and the stridency of David's life. Santiago de Las Altas Torres? Not ideal, with her fragile daughter and her mother; beginning to be marred by concrete sprawl and Spain still in thrall to Franco. Cornwall? The landscape of her heart, but lost for ever: she could never see its deep-blue water churning over sharp-toothed rocks without remembering Jack, remembering Lewis. Lewis lying broken with his limbs at nightmare angles while the sea combed through his hair and the gulls screamed high above. She saw that picture often. And its companions: Lewis balanced at the very edge of the cliff on a bright afternoon in summer, looking down at the enticing sea. Jack, skimming stones across the small waves on Porthmeor Beach, turning back to smile at her. No, she would not go there again, except perhaps to scatter flowers for her ghosts. With her son, perhaps. When he was older.

If she could have, Jennet would have chosen the far north. Stillness and infinity: snow and sculpted ice and unbreathed air; clean solitude. She was not yet strong enough for colour, Ionian blue or Naples yellow. In her desire for emptiness she was still yearning towards death. But there was not in her whatever there must have been in Lewis Delafield when he took his decision, if it was a decision, to relinquish his footing on the rocks.

In the end she returned to her beginning. Not to the sea but to the fells, which themselves can be as lonely, where the land sweeps up and plunges like a great mass of windblown water. Not to Litton Kirkdale, where the old house, condemned as uneconomic to restore, had been demolished, but to the high moors above a nearby valley, to Stonesdale. To a square house, Ravens, not beautiful but stalwart, built from stone to withstand wind and rain, planted as firmly on the steep fellside as if the rock beneath had sprouted. An ancient farmhouse, with outbuildings, entirely isolated, nothing to be seen from it but the changing colours of the moorland, summer-green or bracken-brown, heather-marled, laced and threaded by grey walls.

Was Ravens yet another sort of prison, simply more isolated than Bridge House? Yes, in many ways; but it was the one of Jennet's choosing. She was her own warder and she felt safe there, where no one could come near without being seen from miles away and nothing touched her or entangled her in unwanted complications. Its remoteness did not frighten her at all. She had electricity and a telephone, and a Land Rover in which she could negotiate the track leading from the road. In the winter, with the curtains drawn and the doors barred, there was a cave-like feeling to the house: it was warm, impregnable, firelight flickering on the walls.

To Lorna Mallow one prison was much like any other. When she was moved to Ravens, in the spring of 1971, her already frail health was in decline. As rivulets silt up in drought, so did the passages of her blood, leaving empty places in her brain where her thoughts could no longer connect, nor her words join. In Chelsea she had learned to drag herself on crutches about the house but would never go outside for fear of being seen by strangers. Her crippled state caused her great shame, she who had always kept up such a brave front with her gaudy colours and her bright blonde hair. Too soon she subsided into premature old age, un-consoled by much except the cigarettes she chain-smoked and growing quantities of red vermouth with gin. Trying to persuade her that she would be happy going home to Yorkshire, Jennet had murmured promises: fresh air, a garden without threatening steps so that Lorna could sit outside, excursions to familiar places, Harrogate and Richmond; the grandchildren would visit; they would not be so far from Barbara. None of these promises made much difference to

Lorna. The West Riding was just another place that had paled into insignificance in her mind in comparison with Jamaica, which alone stayed vivid. By the start of the new decade Lorna was a drying husk, so thin and light she could be lifted up and carried like a child.

Jennet Mallow turned Ravens into a fortress for herself and those whose lives it was her duty to sustain. Here Vanessa had a latitude she could not have had in London, where she was too dreamy to be let out on her own. On Stonesdale Moor she made herself a small compass around the house where she could wander freely, and explore the world on her own terms at last. Her bedroom soon became a gallery of new findings: sheep's bones, a bird's skull, cracked stones that bore the traces of sea creatures that once swam here millions of years ago. She seemed to flower in the brisk air and the quiet, growing a little taller, more robust, exchanging the blue tinge of her skin for the shyest rose.

At first Jennet did no painting, but she read, all through her solitary evenings and on into the night, when the house was shrouded by deep silence. She read whatever she felt she needed from the books she'd brought with her: nineteenth-century novels, the poetry of T.S. Eliot, the sermons of John Donne and Lancelot Andrewes, the writings of Sir Thomas Browne. These last were from the library of Richard Mallow, bound in calfskin, their pages edged with gold. No one had looked at any of these books for years, but Jennet had kept them and now sometimes, when she opened one, she thought she could sense traces of her father.

And although she did not paint, she drew. Lorna sleeping, Vanessa with her pencil poised, the fells, the purplish feathers of a grass called Yorkshire fog, Adam, her grey-eyed son. In drawing she rediscovered her old rhythms, the rhythm of hand and mind connected and, most crucially, the rhythm of the landscape. In the far west of Cornwall, where she had last experienced that sense of wholeness, of inner vision married to an intense desire to express it, the human spirit measured itself against the vastness of the sea and not the land. Here, in the northern dales, the land itself is inspiration: compelling, austere, remote, indifferent to the transient concerns of anyone who passes through it.

After a year or so of living humbly in this huge embrace of sky and stone, Jennet began to find its implacability soothing. Against it her own ravelled mess of fear and guilt looked small. This landscape unleashed freezing rain to rattle on her windows, howling storms that dug their claws into her walls. As if it were as cold as the ice sheets that once covered it, the land left the core inside her frozen, but gave her space to breathe. And she was grateful. Here, she knew, painting would be possible.

Among the outbuildings was a large, three-sided barn that Jennet saw could be converted into a studio. High-walled and steeply roofed, it took shape in her mind, but she needed someone to turn the idea to reality. As in the past she thought of Roddy MacNamara, her old friend and reliable standby, who always knew by instinct what she wanted and who also had the practical experience of construction that she lacked. He was still married to Dermot's sister and still living in London but, being tired of urban life, was intrigued by the idea of exploring somewhere new. He and his wife had been talking about moving and had by chance already thought of Yorkshire. He would be glad to stay with Jennet and supervise the transformation of her tumbling-down old barn.

Six months it took, in which Roddy became as indispensable as a kindly brother to Jennet and her son. Adam was hardly more than a baby when he came to Ravens, but by the time the studio was finished, in September 1972, he was five. A strange life for a young child, in that house so far from any

212

other. His companions, apart from Jennet, a demented grandmother and the sister he loved, but in whom he saw even then an insecure attachment to the world. He liked playing with Vanessa, but as he grew he wanted more, and Roddy MacNamara gave it. Gentle countervail to the three women, Roddy taught Adam the things he had learned as a boy in County Wexford: how to tell one bird's song from another and discern its egg; how to whistle through a blade of grass and say which way the wind was blowing. In that summer, while Roddy was building Jennet's studio, they were always together, the man and the young child, Adam close at Roddy's heel, clutching a brick or a trowel, intent on being helpful. For Adam's birthday present Roddy found a blithe fox-terrier puppy, which the boy called Skuff. In that quiet household, where no one wasted words and days would sometimes pass when no one spoke, the puppy's was the loudest voice, unafraid of silence.

Jennet Mallow's studio still stands exactly as she left it, her brushes and her paints in place. Solid in ancient stone but with the fourth side, which had been open when the building was a barn, a sheer pane of glass. Oak beams to hold up the roof, pale beech on the floor. Light falling on the wood makes it shine like water. Shelves the width of one wall, neatly stacked with the instruments of Jennet's craft. A long trestle table. And through the window the steep rise of Stonesdale Moor and the endless sky.

Here Jennet began to work again, tentatively, slowly, breathing in the scents of oils and paints to reawaken memory, cautiously stirring one colour with a finger to learn again the feel of it, touching her brushes to her mouth. Here she painted *Cliff Face*, that enigmatic, frightening expanse of what, on careless viewing, looks like pure white but is in fact composed of as many colours as there are in a sheet of ice. Paint, laid thickly and striated, creates the sharpness of a frozen surface on which a man would be torn to tatters if he fell.

And here, at Ravens, Jennet went on painting and Lorna Mallow died and Adam Heaton lived until he was eight years old and Leonard Kaspar claimed him. Adam had been at the village school for a year or so by then and was happy enough, it seemed to Jennet. But, in the summer of 1978, some months after Lorna died suddenly of a cerebral haemorrhage, Kaspar came to rifle through the studio and saw the boy for the first time. A child seldom photographed, whose looks can be recovered now only from his mother's drawings, which show him to be beautiful. Let me have him, Kaspar said, he can come back in the holidays. I will keep him in London during term-time and pay for his education. Listen to him now, he sounds like a yokel. I will give him all the things I never had when I was a child. All the things he needs and wants. I will treat him as my own and he will be my heir.

Did Jennet cry for Adam when he went away to London; did she try to draw from memory the shadows his eyelashes threw across his cheekbones? Maybe. And maybe she re-membered the poet's words on the death of his small son. 'Rest in soft peace and ask'd, say here doth lye Ben Jonson his best piece of poetrie.' Leonard Kaspar had others of her masterworks: should he now have this? And yet she knew that this remote place was no place for a growing child unless he were to be a stone-waller or a farmer. And how could he do that, this boy who had no claim to these ancestral fields? Better then that he should have the sort of education she had had, which she had supposed she would bequeath him in due course. Somehow her plans to supplement the local school

214

with fragments of remembered Latin got lost in the slow drift of days, and she had let Adam loose in his time at home. That he was capable of learning Jennet had no doubt: he had a quick mind and a fine, inventive way with words. He also had a gift for music, and it was this that made up Jennet's mind. She began to think he needed more than she could give. When Kaspar whispered words like chorister and Stradivarius, she saw the promise of her son fulfilled. After all, Adam had reached the same age as hundreds of other little boys who were sent away to school.

And besides, with Lorna gone and Vanessa more self-sufficient, leading her own impenetrable life, there was for the first time in so many years the prospect of unclutter-ed time. Long empty hours of silence, filled with nothing, hours in which she might embalm herself in the fine stuff of dreams. No need to take responsibility for any other beating soul. She wanted no interruption, not even her own son's. Kaspar was used to brushing aside all that he saw as impedi-ment to Jennet's painting. He had always taken what he wanted from her. It did not seem improbable that he should have her child.

So. A decision made, if not taken lightly. Which explains, if I might interrupt just for a brief moment, why I grew up in the sepulchral calm of Leonard Kaspar's house in Mount Street, with my mother's glowing frescoes on the walls and her paintings hung in every room. Leonard was true to his promise, and paid my fees at the best of London's day schools. I learned the violin and he did indeed buy me a Stradivarius. I spent my holidays at Ravens with my mother. I spent my evenings during term-time in the company of Leonard Kaspar. But that is another story, and one that has no place here. What I chiefly remember of the separation is how much I missed that small dog Skuff.

After *Cliff Face* came the series of white paintings. It is for these that Jennet Mallow is best known. Although all of them were bought by Leonard Kaspar, they now hang together in Tate Britain, on long loan. Thirteen enormous paintings on white linen, glued to wooden boards. Terrifying paintings in their cold austerity, layer upon layer of white on an already whitened background, luminous but in no way optimistic, light as it might strike one on the brink of death. Terrifying too in the threats that they embody, literally. In one, the surface has been slashed so deep the wood beneath is bare and splintered. In the fourth a saw-toothed strip of metal is embedded; in the eleventh a ladder of sharp blades. There are coils of barbed wire, jagged tears, lengths of wire pulled so taut against the boards that they seem to slice them, razor edges which would surely scissor through encroaching fingers.

These paintings have no formal titles, only numbers, but in her notebooks Jennet referred to them as the Stations of the Cross. And there is the outline of a cross in another painting, which belongs with this white series, although it is sombre black. Lampblack, also on white canvas, the black paint roughly dragged with a thick brush soaked in stripper to expose a ghostly vertical and its crossbar, like a bare cross struck by lightning when the darkness fell over the whole land.

Jennet Mallow lived and worked at Ravens for almost thirty years. Awards and honours were rained upon her: she was elected a trustee of the Tate in 1982, and created DBE; honorary doctorates were conferred on her by the universities of London, Oxford, Exeter and Leeds. There were major

216

exhibitions of her work in New York, Stockholm, Canberra and Paris, and following the commission of two large murals by the World Bank in Washington, DC, she was made an honorary member of the American Academy of Arts and Letters.

Once these tributes would have pleased her, but now, as she grew old, Jennet grew indifferent to fame. Her responsibility to truth, which she upheld as best she could, was a solitary business. She spent hours and hours alone, working in her studio, and was resentful of the inroads public duties made on her precious time. Until the mid 1980s she still gave interviews and travelled to the openings of exhibitions, but later she became reclusive until, towards the end of her life, she scarcely went out at all.

She did not live alone. There was Vanessa always, and I came when I could. Ben bought a weekend cottage close to Ravens and saw our mother often. Sarah visited in summer. Her children, Luca, Sergio and Gabriella, would only speak Italian and were linguistically sundered from their grandmother, but much loved by Vanessa, who did not care if they spoke or not. Even in her thirties and forties, Vanessa still looked like a child herself. Thin and small and clearskinned, her pale eyes set wide apart and the expression in them unclouded, as if their depths were never stirred by the awarenesses of adulthood.

David Heaton also came to Ravens a few times. He was not wearing well, and each time was a shock to Jennet. In the intervals between his visits he seemed to shed so much – hair and teeth and substance – until by the late 1980s he was a Giacometti stick man, except for a potbelly, with broken veins purpling his nose. Once when he was staying at Ravens, he said, shall we go to bed together, Bird, for old time's sake? Jennet thought that she might like that, but when they got there he was flaccid and soon he fell asleep. Then Jennet lay

217

awake beside him, remembering other nights when she had listened to him grunt and snore, wondering if she would ever make love with anyone again and if she cared at all.

Sheer, glad pleasure was just a memory to her then. If she tried, she could summon up the ghost of it, pale as the scent of faded flowers, but nothing would breathe life into its lungs again. She knew it had existed, in the sway and clarity of water, in the sweetness and warmth of babies, held against her face like loaves of new-baked bread. She remembered having felt it in the night hours in Santiago when her body answered David's and their skin still cold and salt from the moonlit sea. She remembered it most vividly in Jack Owen's kisses, in the galloping horse he had drawn for her, in the perfect meeting of his urgent seeking and her deep acceptance, in the sounds he made, his surrendering, joyful sobs.

This is how it must be, she supposed, now that she was becoming an old woman. The old must be content with memories of pleasure: its keen edge is for the young. But there were sources still of happiness: painting mainly, the satisfaction and challenges of her craft. And also pure water to quench thirst on a hot day, the fragrance of a lime, or nutmeg, a blackbird's song, the sight of two swans flying, purposeful as angels, across the evening sky. The shape and rhythm of a poem.

These are quiet pleasures, not springs of ecstasy, not the glitter of the hummingbird nor the sharp tooth of the dog. It was sad that David Heaton never knew them. For fifty years he hunted busy pleasures as if they could buy off his extinction. Because he was afraid of the blank canvas he flung wine and pills and bright acrylic colours at it, mistaking oblivion for tranquillity, unable to confront the white expanse of death. When he died, in 1988, found after two days in his flat off Beaufort Street, lying in a bathtub of chilled water, covered by a raft of vomit, Jennet could only pray he was at peace.

Jennet loved her husband, she liked and she disliked him, and she hated him as well. Her feelings about David, about most things, were as changeable as water, and flowed into one another constantly, like a tidal estuary where no barrier divides the fresh from salt.

Water running over stone in the stream below her house. Water changing colour with the stones that it caresses: sage-green, weed-green, silver, lichen-yellow, grey, fresh-water mussel shell. Water borrowing blue and pewter from the sky. As the tide alters the shoreline, so these colours seeped into Jennet's paintings, slowly, down the years. Iciness gave way to colour in the gentlest of gradations, like a sunrise, like the slow warming of someone who at the eleventh hour is rescued from a cold night on a mountainside.

For a long time after she moved to Stonesdale it seemed to Jennet that this incomprehensibly perfect landscape intimated death. When she arrived there, she was almost dead herself. The gradual process of renaissance began when she could paint again, and then the sublime indifference of stone and sky echoed in her work. In the first years there was so much pain still to express, which, once poured out into the torn and pierced canvases of the Stations of the Cross, ceased to be so acute. Then she reached a sort of calm. Stonesdale conceded it to her, this calm after the time of guilt and passion, and it gave her an understanding of the finite. This understanding fills the paintings of the years that followed *Cliff Face*, which is not to say that they are morbid or even melancholy. On the contrary they are as meditative as icons, and peaceful with the recognition that it is death which brings to life the beauty of the edge.

How else to paint this recognition except in light and whiteness? That white which is deadly, icy, in the painting *Cliff Face*, changes over time to whites that are life-enhancing, luminous. Remember the four paintings Jennet made in the late 1980s, to which she gave the names of angels: *Gabriel*, *Michael*, *Metatron*, *Raphael*. Harsh angels, not the comforters of children's prayers, nor pinkly dimpled cherubs; these angels, when they came, brought stern commands and were terrifying to look on. And yet they also shone. Each herl of their great feathered wings must have been a filament of bright white. The white light of angels. The light the dying are said to see when they come out of blackness.

But sometimes the dying are pulled back to life from that edge of whiteness. And having been brought back, they must remember how to live. Or learn to live again. A lesson Jennet learned from serious illness.

There are three windows in Jennet Mallow's bedroom, or rather, one large window aperture, divided into three. Each third, a tall sash-window edged by beading, the centre set between two panels, the whole framed in white-glossed moulding with a narrow sill. They are unusually generous, even frivolous, in a house designed as a sanctuary from weather. Jennet used to say the original owner must have hungered for the light and set his heart on having it in this land of rain and winter. Jennet had always admired these windows for their symmetrical effect, and kept them uncurtained, but it was during the first real illness of her life that they became important. Her bed faced them, and as she was confined to it for days on end they were her only opening to the outside world. Until then Jennet had been lucky with her health, her light build and her slenderness belying wiry strength. When, over a period of time that began in the winter of 1993, she found she was becoming inexplicably tired, she put her symptoms down to age and lack of sunshine. It was only when she got so weak that she could hardly climb the stairs, let alone the hill above the house, that she thought she ought to see a doctor.

Chronic lymphocytic leukaemia was diagnosed in June the following year. From the first consultation Jennet knew that the disease was lethal but did not necessarily spell immediate death. She was told its progression could be slow. Nevertheless she should have a blood transfusion, immunoglobulin injections and anti-cancer drugs. Treatment to begin in hospital, convalescence later in her home.

It came as a surprise to Jennet, her unreadiness to die. She would have said, if anyone had asked her, that she was indifferent to death. She had felt for so long like a patient waiting for her turn in some endless corridor, shuffling from chair to chair under neon lights ungentled by a window. If it were not for Vanessa, who was, had always been, her main concern, it would have come as some relief, she thought, to find the waiting ended.

But that was before she knew that she was really dying. An abstraction had become a fact. And the knowledge blurred the boundaries of which before she had been certain, and brought intensity back into her life.

She found that intensity first by accident, staring at her windows. All through the summer and on into the autumn she was bed-ridden; knocked back each time she began to regather a little strength by the successive doses of drugs. It was hard for her, who had never been indolent. Enduring the long days and the interminable nights, Jennet was very glad of Roddy and his wife Louella, who had moved to Stonesdale in the year that David died. Without them she could not have survived at Ravens on her own. They took care of all the necessary arrangements, and of Vanessa, who did not really understand and could not come to terms with Jennet's illness. Louella had been a nurse in London and all through the time that Jennet was ill, she looked after her with great skill and compassion.

It was a new experience for Jennet, to be as undefended as a child and at another's mercy. Louella had the gift of seeing with her fingers. She and Jennet had met before, occasionally, in London, but were never friends. They did not really become friends later, even after Louella and Roddy came to live permanently in a cottage attached to Ravens. The two women shared few interests. But Louella MacNamara was in ways much closer than a friend. No one, not her mother, not David, nor a lover, had ever touched Jennet with such instinctive understanding. Louella would know, without being told, how Jennet was by laying a hand upon her forehead, and her touch would lift with it some of Jennet's pain.

Some of her pain. There was a lot of pain, from bruising and from aching joints, from an ulcerated mouth, and there were days when Jennet felt so sick she could hardly even face a sip of water. For the first time in fifty years she did not want to smoke. She could not read. She could only lie back on her pillows, floating in and out of sleep, often strangely disembodied, unsure whether she was dreaming or where her thoughts came from when she was awake.

And for hour on hour she looked out of the windows. From where she lay she could see nothing through them but the sky. She watched as it changed from moment to moment, as clouds drifted across it, or birds flew, darkly silhouetted, made emblematic through the loss of detail. In the mornings and the evenings, a skein of clacking geese.

All her life Jennet Mallow had thought about the sky. Thought about the colours in it and the shapes of clouds, about the words that might describe the colours, and the paints to show them. But this long, unbroken contemplation of the sky was different. On her sickbed she still wondered at the range and richness of sky colours, from the first flicker-ings of sunrise to the sunset, from palest rose to violet through scarlet, turquoise, cobalt and vermilion, from the cold black of a moonless night to the streaked charcoal of an overcast one, or the ghostly greys of the hour before dawn. When it was full, the moon would wake her with its harsh light, and she envisaged frightened animals caught in its uncompromising glare. She watched the stars, unobscured by city lights; she noticed how they seemed to dance and fall. She watched the rain slide over glass like beads of melting silver, she saw how the air shimmered after rain, how clouds drooped with the freight of water, how hazy light outlined them with gold.

These were old observations, although she saw them now with a new eye. An eye whose focus was adjusted by a new sense of the finite, and with that new sense came new perception of the converse, of the sky's boundlessness. There were whole days towards the end of Jennet's convalescence in a prematurely wintry October when the sky stayed stub-bornly unchanging, as if tired of putting on a perpetual show. Whole days of no colour, of a curious static whiteness without variegation, as if the sky were dead.

Staring out at an unchanging sky alone for hours in a quiet house brought Jennet an epiphany. Long ago she'd under-stood the beauty of finitude. She had steadied herself to face it by renouncing pleasure, love, by filling the expanses of her pictures with pure whiteness. She had chosen loneliness and told herself she must endure it as a condition of her art. Like a hermit in a desert she had renounced distraction, closed her eyes to the seduction of a shifting surface with its play of movement and colour. Now she wanted movement back.

The sky's unending blankness was oppressive. When Jen-net closed her eyes against it, exchanging the view out of her windows for the thin screen of her eyelids, she watched the shapes and colours that danced there with relief. She found that if she stared unblinking at the windows and then closed her eyes, their after-image would form almost at once. Three rectangles with gentle edges, dark against a lesser darkness; a darkness which she could change at will by screwing her eyes tighter, or which was changed beyond her own control by the different intensities of light. At the brightest times the rectangles were not dark at all but began as blocks of light divided by a central bar. She would watch as they developed: from fiery orange first with the horizontal green, to a maroon, to darkest red, until eventually the edges blurred and the blocks turned black before they vanished.

Jennet knew that these were tricks of eye and light, not insight. But at the same time, these colours were consoling. They had inevitability, rightness, and a profoundness that she could recognise but not explain. Something about the proportions of the image and the depth of colour. In Jennet's extreme lassitude they were like messages from God.

Much later, when she was better, Jennet painted them. A series of single blocks at first, relatively small scale, oil on paper mounted on linen. Again she experimented with her paint, thinning it, streaking it, using varnishes, to achieve the effect she wanted. After the single blocks she painted trinities, in exact recall of her three windows. Every rectangle of colour bisected by a horizontal but none with ruled edges; instead one colour yearns towards another, making each more vivid and more significant. Dark blue over dark grey, orange on maroon, two blues divided, sunlight yellow.

*

The final years of Jennet Mallow's life were fruitful. After the colour blocks she returned to the more nearly monochrome, making seven large pictures which are untitled, but again evocative of air and water. She began work on this series after a visit to the west coast of Ireland, to County Mayo, which she made with Ben and his wife Joanna. Her notes record that she spent much time on a still day looking at the play of light on the horizon, and the subsequent paintings reflect that vision of two vast unbroken planes, of sky and sea. Each of the seven images is the same, each one bisected equally by a faint horizontal line; only the shades and tones change, so that in seeing them together one is sharing Jennet's contemplation of the ocean on one particular day. It is not by chance that there are seven paintings just as there are seven canonical hours: this series is a kind of prayer, or meditation, a glimpse of what infinity might look like if it could be painted. The shades of milky-white and grey, mothwing, oyster shell, sand, pale lilac, midnight-blue and inky black, are so subtle that their gradations can hardly be discerned, and yet it is clear from their slight stirrings and their iridescence where the air begins and where the water ends.

In Jennet's work, seen as a whole, and now with hindsight, there was always a debate, or perhaps a conversation, about stillness against movement, whiteness against colour, realism against abstraction. It echoed the arguments she faced in life: the extent of an artist's duty to engage with the questions of the age, or indeed with other people, solitude versus commitment, where she belonged, whether the luxury of self-expression or even of belief could be sustained in tragic and contingent times. To such questions there can be no final answers. But in her three last paintings, which are also

225

perhaps her finest, Jennet Mallow did achieve a kind of resolution.

All three came again from observation. In the first, *Flight*, Jennet remembered the chance sighting of a flock of plover on a flooded meadow. Not especially distinctive on the ground, these birds, with folded wings and mottled plumage, but, once startled by the plunging of a dog, they filled the air with whirling turning flickering gold, possessing the sunlight with pale feathers. On the canvas Jennet caught that movement into light so well you can almost hear the birds' thin cry: a storm of gold across green water, wing-beats, the astonishing precision of their swooping as the whole flock turns.

Flight is one of Jennet's largest paintings. So that she could make it, Roddy MacNamara re-erected the scaffolding in her studio that she had last used almost twenty years before, for the World Bank murals. There is film footage of Jennet working on the painting, a small, indomitable figure with short, untidy hair, in white workman's overalls, the trouser cuffs and sleeves rolled up, perching on a ladder. She is almost lost against the dancing surface of her picture, like a stray swirl of paint herself, waiting for a brush to put her back.

Jennet used that scaffolding again for her final work. But then she needed someone to hold her in position on the ladders. In December 1999 the leukaemia recurred, as she had been warned it would. This time there was less likelihood of remission. She was older now, and weaker. She decided to tell no one. The following spring she set out to keep a promise she had made some time ago to me. I was working in Cambridge then, as an art historian, and had published a first book of poems that year. A few lines of one of these had been chosen as an inscription to a sculpture which was to be installed in the garden of the manor house by the church of Little Gidding, near the Huntingdonshire border with Northamptonshire. There was a pleasing link between the sculpture and Jennet's past in that it was made by Elizabeth Foy, whom she had known in Cornwall. Elizabeth, once deeply in love with Lewis Delafield, had long before stopped being a nun and was now a celebrated artist. She and Jennet had come across each other from time to time in later years, and Jennet had always liked her. It was a cause of some regret to her that they had not been closer. Reluctant though she was to leave safe harbour, Jennet had agreed to go to Little Gidding partly out of affection for Elizabeth.

Little Gidding church is in no sense spectacular. It's more like a small chapel, with two single rows of stalls facing each other across a narrow aisle. But it does have an exceptionally beautiful east window of clear Venetian glass, and in stepping through its heavy door you exchange the ordinary air outside for something almost tangibly different, a deeper, stiller air. This is a place in which years of quiet worship have left their gentle trace, like faint breath misted on the wooden panels, on the plaster, on the blue and white tiling of the floor.

When Jennet Mallow was there, she felt very ill. There was a large party: it was a perfect afternoon, bright with the new greens of young leaves, the hedges frothing with white blossom. Jennet had watched as the widow of T. S. Eliot unveiled Elizabeth's sculpture, *Dual Form*, in bronze. She had heard me read my words. But the other speeches were too much for her; she knew that she could not stand unsupported through them, and she did not want her frailness to be seen. Unobserved, she slipped away and let herself into the coolness of the empty church, where she could rest a while and recruit a little strength.

Jennet Mallow had no conscious habit of prayer. She did

not pray in Little Gidding. She only sat and looked at the light that shone in on her through the east window and the variegated, greenish glass of the large windows on both the north and the south walls. A green thought in a green shade, she found herself remembering vaguely, and some lines of Eliot's poem. Behind the church is a large sycamore whose branches fill the great east window. She thought about the triptych formed by this window's central arch and the rectangles on either side. These shapes are echoed in the panels above the simple table that serves as an altar, the crucifix upon it, and the two candlesticks. The whole frame was alive with the exuberance of a tree on a spring afternoon.

In the end which was the greater consolation? Jennet wondered. The window full of the tree's stirrings or the uninterrupted light from north and south? She recollected other windows, views seen through them, whole and clear or fragmented by lattices and grids. Some time later she felt strong enough to get up and rejoin the party. When she pulled the church door open, light flowed in from east and west. She saw the countryside beyond, the long lane leading from the church.

Jennet Mallow's last two paintings. The first in ink and watercolour, six small panels, like a screen. A wash of paleness, no colour, like rain, and beyond it the suggestion of tall trees. Bare branches. Trees as they might seem in the forest of a dream, or in the thick mists that fall on moorland – elusive and ghostly but still present. The other, *Clear Glass*. Diluted oil and tempera on wood. A tall painting, as high and wide as a church window. Impossible to describe in words. Sheer luminescence. Whiteness like the whiteness of a perfectly cut diamond from which bright, fiery colours dart. Whiteness thick as the petals of magnolia, thin as a mayfly's wing. White with blues in it and golds, the promises of light.

This painting is not quite finished. Its execution in the end surpassed Jennet Mallow's strength. Roddy and I helped her with it, and Vanessa a little bit: all of us taking turns under her direction to paint in the highest corners of the wooden board, which she could not reach. Vanessa mixed iridescent paint like powdered pearl with egg yolk, as Jennet had done so many years ago, before her eldest child was born. Roddy held Jennet firm on the lower rungs of the ladder. I stayed at Ravens for the whole summer, before the new academic year began, but I was not there when Jennet died.

Is there anyone more lonely than a woman in childbirth? Yes, perhaps: a person lying alone on the edge of death. Jennet Mallow died during the night of 27 December 2000. Vanessa came into her bedroom early the next morning, but did not understand that Jennet was dead. Roddy MacNamara found her some time later: he and Louella had been saying to each other just a while before how good it was that Jennet could have such a long and peaceful sleep. The cause of death was ascribed to the leukaemia; there was no need for a post-mortem. The doctor who signed the death certificate did not think she would have suffered any pain. In the last stages of a serious illness, he told us, there is not much difference between the end of life and the start of death. Life and death. For that one moment, time suspended, the length of a single held breath, like the spaces between brush strokes, like the sea and land in balance at slack water, in an equal stillness, life and death.

Acknowledgements

I should like to thank Arabella Currie, Antonia Logue, Pascale Lafeber, Jane Jelley, Greg Spiro, Kirsty Dunseath and, especially, Derek Johns.